AUSTIN WELCH-BROWN

The Crown's Agent

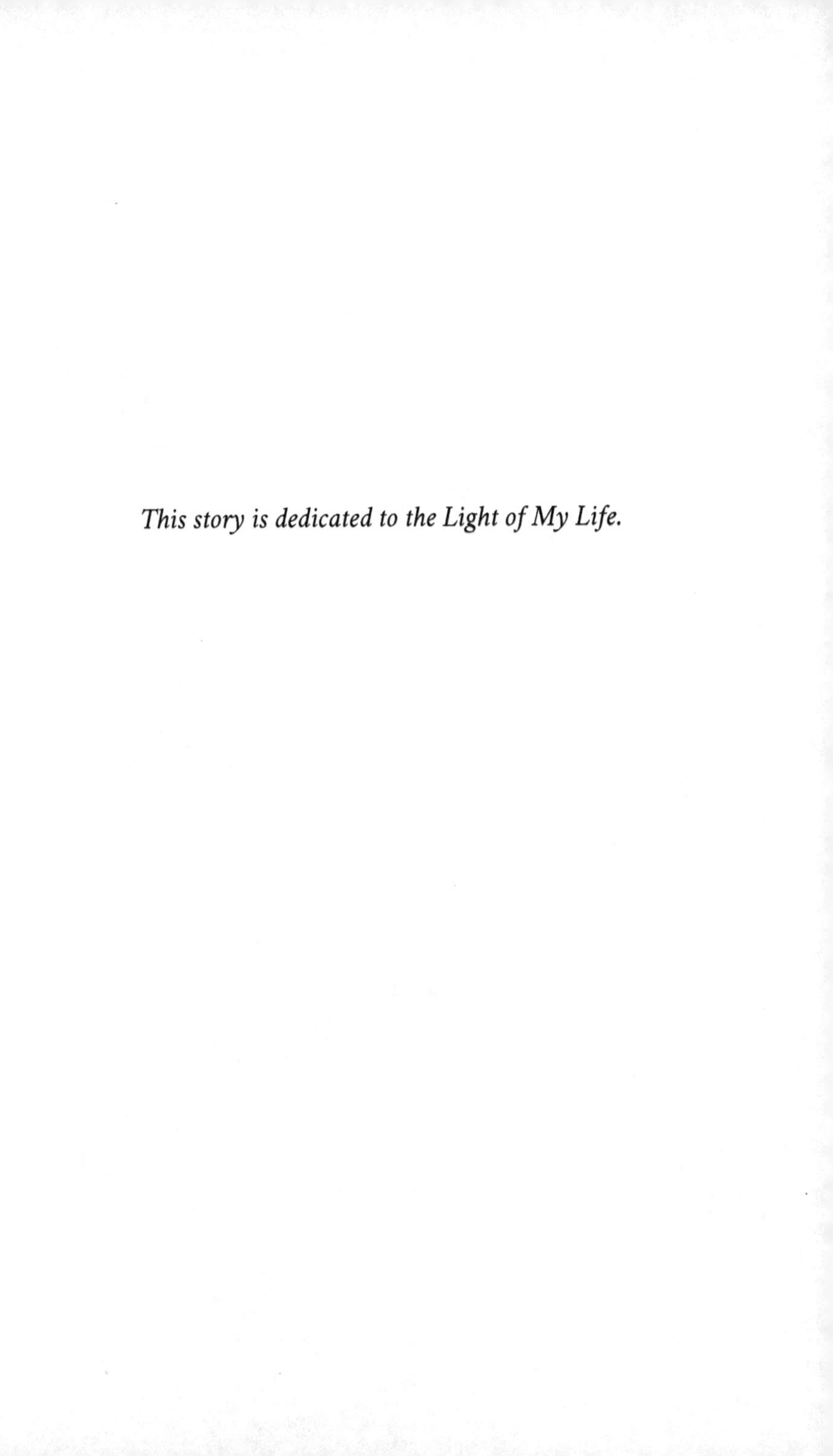

This story is dedicated to the Light of My Life.

Acknowledgement

I would like to thank my wonderful beta readers Jessica, Lisa (MIMI) Edwards, Without them the book would not be complete.

I would also like to thank Elisa 'Pyrospirit' Bacoba for the amazing cover art.

Special thanks again to Lisa (MIMI) Edwards for assisting in editing the book.

Without all of you this dream would never have been a reality.

One

Humbling Truth

The sunset and the moon shone through Leonardo's bedroom window. It was his favorite part of the day, the only time he had to himself. He got into his bed and pulled out his journal. He wrote about his day as always before laying down and rolling to face outside. The entries always started with how his day went but then changed to his desire to be free. Free from the weight of being a Prince, and free to make his own decisions.

* * *

"Master Leonardo, it is time for you to get up, school will be in the study today, the tutor is already waiting," Sebastian spoke from behind his closed door while knocking on it. "She expects you to be there within the hour." Sebastian has been Leo's butler for as long as he can remember. They were not close enough to be called friends but had mutual understanding and respect for one another. Sebastian felt bad for him not knowing the outside of the palace.

Leonardo rolled out of bed and made his way to the closet. He grabbed the clothing that was already picked out for him.

"Another navy blue suit for the day," he thought while tossing it onto the bed. He walked over to the bathroom and let the shower run for a bit. He looked into the mirror and dreaded the thought that he would have to go out of the comfort of his room and bear the boredom of school.

The tutor, Mrs. Jenkins, had the most melancholy approach to life, and her voice was worse than nails on a chalkboard. She was also the reason he always got in trouble with his father. If he should even sneeze wrong she runs a letter to the king immediately. She lived for drama, and even if she had to start it herself it would be there.

Leonardo showered before stepping out he grabbed his towel, the marble flooring was wet from the steam. As he stepped out of the shower his foot slipped and he managed to fall back into it. Since his head was stuck in the clouds, he didn't think too much of it. Leonardo was dreaming again of a day when he could attend a real school, or even just go out shopping on his own.

He went back to his bed and grabbed his suit. It was the same outfit day in and day out. A navy blue suit with a white button-up under it. He may not have known what good fashion was, but to him, it had to be more than this same suit for every day.

A stand-up mirror next to his bed showed his reflection. His blond hair was kept short and tight. He had to look the part of a prince after all. His face was clean-shaven, and his eyes were as blue as the clearest ocean. His haircut was not even an option for him. It was chosen for him by his father even at the age of 18.

Leonardo made his way down the long halls escorted by his 'handy guard'. He never bothered to ask them their name or get to know them since a new guard was escorting him around every day. A military suit is all he ever saw. The walls were stone and colorless, and pictures of his deceased family were hung on the walls. As they passed the kitchen he heard the radio the maids had playing.

"Another threat has been made against the crown. This is getting more intense as we draw closer to the signing of a new legislation that would increase taxes for many of the working class."

He made his way to the study, a ten-foot-tall room with bookshelves covering every wall. Leo was not a fan of reading much. Sure he found himself reading the occasional romance novel and dreaming that one day it could happen to him, but each book in here was only on parliament and history. The tutor stood against the bookshelf staring at her watch.

"Late again your Highness, we will need to start right away!" She spoke in a stern sharp voice. Leonardo sighed and took a seat at the desk that looked away from the only window. It used to face looking out, but Leonardo would stare out the window and daydream. The tutor made his father aware of this and he ordered it be turned to face the door. It was his father's way of making sure he stayed focused on his studies.

Except for a few bathroom breaks, and meals Leonardo sat in the study from sunrise to sunset learning about parliament and proper virtue, and how to balance people and peers. As if he even knew his peers. He wanted to make his parents proud, but never truly felt the crown was his path.

The moon was starting to shine through the window, and he felt his eyes starting to get heavy. Leonardo went back to his room, sat on his bed, pulled out his journal, and began to write in it.

"Well, today was another boring day lined up for me by the King. I want to be able to go for long walks and draw all the things I see. My father will never understand my dreams, or what makes me happy. All he cares about is the crown." As he proceeded his frustration began to turn to anger. To calm himself he began to doodle a bit. He drew a large tree with a squirrel poking its head out of it.

Leonardo cracked his window open and the smell of fresh air allowed him to feel a little freedom. The moonlight shining down made the water around the castle glow. He wanted so badly to swim without being stared at by guards or having his photo taken by the press for just enjoying himself. He noticed the owls flying over the castle and stared at the stars for a bit.

The thoughts of sneaking out were always there, but the castle was so guarded he would be found before he even took two steps. A strong knock was heard from the door.

"Leonardo," He knew the voice behind the door but did not get to see the man much. He opened the door and the king walked through. "Mrs. Jenkins tells me that you were late again for your studies. You know Leonardo, a king is never late." He spoke softly, trying to encourage his son. "You need to buck up, for one day the crown will fall to you. Our family didn't work their lives away to get us here for nothing. You will show some gratitude, and follow in their footsteps. You will see it is what's best."

"I know your majesty." Yes, that is right even Leonardo his son was forced to call his father Your Highness. Leonardo took a breath in and thought his next choice of words carefully. Before he could even bother to speak, the king walked out of the room. Before fully out the door, he turned back to Leonardo. " I expect more from you, you are due to be in parliament tomorrow at dawn." He closed the door. Leonardo could hear the scuffle of boots as the king and the guards walked off.

Leonardo changed and lay back in his bed. His silk sheets wrapped around him, as he looked out the window at the moon once more.

* * *

A buzz could be heard across the small apartment. Alex rolled over and slammed his hand on it. He stretched before sitting up in his bed. He looked around his studio apartment, sighed, and checked the calendar for the date. He punched the wall. It's been over a year and the CIA still has not given him a single assignment. He walked to the front door and grabbed the mail. *The final notice* was written in the mail. He didn't bother to open it and just tossed it on the table.

He walked to his bathroom and turned the wrench attached to what used to be the knob to start the water. The tiles on the wall were falling and held up by what could have been gum. Each shower another fell off the wall. Steam quickly covered the mirror while he was away from the bathroom looking for something clean to wear.

He cleaned the mirror with his hand and looking back was the man he was becoming. His shaggy hair was curly and shoulder length, his eyes a deep brown, he felt that nothing about him stood out, and he liked that it made his job easier.

He showered and dressed in his ripped-up jeans, and tossed a t-shirt on.

He walked out the door to his 2026 Chevy Equinox and headed to the office. He pulled up to a large building with no name on it. At the front desk sat a little old lady. She looked frail, her white hair looked to be rolled with rollers that were three sizes too small. Her glasses were held on by a blue beaded chain.

"Morning Agent Twist." She spoke in a bland voice. She then turned back to doing her busy work. Alex just walked on and waved to her. He made it to his cubicle where he sat and stared at the black computer screen. The television behind him was on.

" Breaking news. King Richard and Prince Leonardo are set to sign…" Alex leaned back in his chair and switched it off.

"What a joke. Must be nice to always be on the news, and never have to work for anything and get it all handed to you," he muttered as he proceeded to boot up his computer. Jannett walked over to him.

"Alex, we need you to finish the training seminar for undercover work." Alex just waved his hand.

A memory of the day Alex fucked up flashed through his mind.

* * *

"Agent Twist, move in," Janet spoke to him from the earpiece. Alex kicked the door down and raced in. His gun at the ready he checked room by room while his team followed him. "Agent Twist, have you located the bomb?" Alex ignored the voice in his ear. "Agent Twist, Respond." Alex continued his search. "Agent Twist, Come in" Alex

did not notice or hear the voice anymore.

"Anyone in here? Hello?" Alex started to shout. "Agent Chleo?" He could not find anything. The only place left to look was a basement. He turned and made his way down the stairs. Chleo was there sitting in a chair. Not tied down, not held hostage. "I knew you would show up," Chloe spoke. She stood with her gun pointed at him. She fired two shots. One into his chest the other into his leg. He fell to the floor having trouble breathing. Chleo escaped through the trapdoor, and before he knew it the building was on fire all around him.

* * *

"Agent Twist, report downstairs for the final test," Janet spoke again trying to get some kind of reaction from him. "If you do not pass this, we will need to think of other options." Janet sighed hoping he would at least attempt to show some care. Alex rolled his eyes and leaned back in his chair.

"Come on Janet I passed this thing a hundred times," Alex said cockily.

"You know the rules, Alex." Janet sighed and shook her head.

Alex took a deep breath before letting out a long sigh. Alex walked to the elevator. He hit the B and waited for the elevator to arrive. He walked inside the elevator and waited. "Breaking news from Parliament. King Richard and Prince Leonardo are…" The elevator opened and Alex stepped out.

Alex made his way to the target setup. He loaded his gun and the extra clips before stepping in. He proceeded through the course.

"Agent Twist ready." The lights turned down and the timer began. Alex began to race through the course, hugging the corners and checking his surroundings before proceeding, executing any threats, and saving any hostages. Alex finished the course and proceeded back to his desk.

Janet was there waiting for him with a box of his belongings from the desk.

" We will be in touch, Agent Twist." She handed him his box, "You need to show you care more, Agent Twist."

Alex grabbed the box and walked to his car. He tossed the belongings into the trunk and went back to his home. He turned on the radio while waiting at a red light to change.

"King Richard and Prince Leonardo…" Alex huffed and turned it off. I'm so tired of hearing about the prince and king…

* * *

Alex slammed the door shut to his house and plopped down onto his couch. He put his gun on the table and looked around. "What has my life become?" His phone began to vibrate on the table. He picked it up and read the message from an old friend Ryan.

Hey Alex it's been a while we should catch up!

He just swiped right and put the phone back down. He grabbed his pipe off the table and took a drag. He felt his issues leave him as he sank into the couch further.

Alex dozed off in his high, and before he knew it, it was midnight. He stood and grabbed a half-eaten sandwich from the fridge. He kicked back and turned on the television.

"Breaking news…. King Richard and Prince Leonardo…." Alex went to change the channel but didn't this time. " Have been attacked today at Parliament. Prince Leonardo barely escaped as the guards rushed the king out of the building." Alex sat up as it actually intrigued him. It was his first time seeing what the King and Prince looked like.

Alex sighed, "I would give anything for some action like that". Alex turned off the television and went to bed. Alex's eyes began to feel heavy and before he knew it he was fast asleep.

Alex's phone began to ring. He looked over at the clock on the end table that read 3:30 AM. He rolled and grabbed his phone. Before he could say anything the voice on the phone spoke.

"Agent Twist you are to report to 12454 Ariel Lake Road at 0500." He knew the voice, it was Janet. He sprung to life, he finally had a mission. He grabbed his black suit from the closet. He dusted off some dust that was sitting on it.

For the first time in a year, he was glad to rush to the shower and get dressed. He opened his safe and pulled out two handguns, and slipped them into the holsters on his belt, and another into the holster on his right leg. He then packed a bag and headed out. It took only 20 minutes to arrive. He was greeted by Janet and a couple of other agents. Looking around Alex saw that there were 20 agents including himself. He knew this was going to be a big mission. Maybe the president of the United States was going to arrive and needed protection, he, thought to himself before getting out of the car. He took his spot next to Janet and waited.

A limo pulled up to the house, and out stepped guards in red. Janet walked up to the guards and they talked a bit. After a bit of talking the guards opened the door and circled the figure getting out of the car. They escorted him into the house and Janet walked over to Alex.

"So are you going to explain?" Alex spoke through his teeth

and looked at Janet.

" King Richard has called in a favor." Alex shook his head and grabbed his bag.

"No… No. I will not babysit for a stuck-up prince."

"Agent Twist, you do this or you're done at the agency I will consider it your resignation," Janet called out to him. Alex stopped and turned around looking at the house. The house was three floors from what he could tell from the outside. He knew he would have to swallow his pride and take the mission.

All he ever wanted was to be part of the CIA. He knew he had no choice left. He walked to the house and smirked as he passed Janet. He took a deep breath and put his hand on the knob.

Two

The Mission

Alex pushed the door open and stepped inside. He was greeted by a foyer that had a mahogany wood finish. The woods smell filled the home. He smiled slightly since it reminded him of his old hobby of wood carving. The wood flooring shined and matched the finish of the walls. Alex knew how long it took to get that kind of shine on mahogany. He took off his shoes to not scuff the finish and walked into the sitting room. The guards were there still circling the prince.

"At ease boys. I can take it from here." Alex spoke, but the guards did not move. The guards knew the orders were to escort the prince into the house and await Janet and report back.

Janet walked in and the guards left. Janet headed to the Prince and bowed. Alex followed her to the room and stood there. Janet looked up at him and pointed at the ground, hinting for him to bow. Alex stood straight up. Janet elbowed

Alex in the stomach and he bent over a bit.

"Your Highness, this is Agent Twist, He will be your personal guard until things slow down at the castle." She stood back up and started to show Leonardo and Alex around the house. Alex's arms remained folded as they went around the main floor.

"Well, at least the kitchen is nice," Alex muttered to himself. He loved to cook but wouldn't ever tell someone that. She took them to the second floor where they were shown their rooms. Leonardo's room was the biggest room Alex had ever seen. To one side was a study with some books behind an oak desk, and to the other a couch and sitting area. Alex walked over to the desk and hopped up on it. He felt the wood and could tell the amount of care that went into making it. Two closed doors would lead to the bathroom and a closet. Windows let in light from every direction.

Janet waved her hand for the Alex to follow her. Leo walked around his new room and looked out of the windows. He smiled seeing the backyard. A modest size that was fenced in. He closed his eyes and pictured himself out there. He reached into his blazer and pulled out a notebook and a pencil. He sat at his new desk and started to draw the image in his head.

Janet showed Alex to his room next to the prince's room. The room was not as big; it had a bed and some windows. The windows overlooked the front and back of the house. Alex tossed his bag on the bed and closed the door.

Of course, I get stuck with the basics. I'm only here putting my life on the line to protect some spoiled brat. Alex thought to himself before turning back to Janet. "You hate me don't you, Janet!" Alex started talking to his boss, but did not relize how loud he was talking." Leo heard them and walked over to the closed door and tried to listen.

"Listen, you wanted a mission, and who knows maybe you can learn something from him."

"Learn what, how to do nothing all day?"

"Agent Twist, You will guard the prince day and night. If anything happens to him it is you that will have to explain it to the king."

"Oh, and let me guess" Alex takes a breath "His royal highness," he says in a mocking tone, "will he need me to cook for him and clean after him as well? So I am nothing more than a glorified babysitter, right? Geez well let me just put on my biggest smile and hug you Janet for this mission."

Janet sighed and rolled her eyes.

"Like it or not you will do this Alex." She turned and opened the door where the prince fell in the room. Leonardo was trying to listen from the door and was not ready for the conversation to end so abruptly. Janet helped the prince to his feet and Alex just shook his head and sighed.

"This will be harder than it should be I guess with an accident-prone prince around" Janet shot him a look that he knew meant shut up or else. Alex joined the two on the way downstairs. Janet walked to the front door and told them if they needed anything there were numbers on the fridge for food delivery and maintenance.

"You two are to stay here and not leave, understand?" She looks right through Alex. "That means you, Agent Twist." Janet closed the door and went off. The hunter moon shone through the skylight and Leonardo muttered,

"Great another prison."

Alex walked over to the prince and chuckled at the navy blue suit before making his way into the kitchen. The prince followed him and took a seat at the table. Leonardo tapped the table not knowing what to say, he looked around the room.

"So your Agent Twist?" Alex turned around and walked to the table, he bowed again in a mocking voice

"At your service your royal highness"

He pulled out a chair and took a seat eating a sandwich that was pre-made in the fridge. He pushed another plate to Leonard who made a face looking at it. "Not up to your royal standards." Alex kicked back in the chair balancing. "Welcome to America where everything is shit?" Leonardo stood up

"Listen, I don't like this any more than you Agent Twist."

Alex walked over to the prince. "You can call me Alex. We are gonna be stuck with each other for who knows how long, and I don't wanna hear Agent Twist every time you need something." Alex goes to leave the room. "Should we see what the house has to offer at least?" Leonardo shrugs and gets up eating the sandwich as he follows Alex. They walk through the living room and past the foyer to a game room where they see a PS5 and a wall of games, a pool table, and an air hockey table. At the corner of the room is a small bowling alley complete with different weight balls.

"Maybe it won't be all bad Princy," Alex says hopping up on the pool table for a seat. Leonardo rolls his eyes before walking over to Alex extending his hand.

" You can call me Leonardo."

Alex takes his hand and comments sarcastically. " I'll stick with Princy." Leonardo shakes his head, and heads to the stairs. "What? Going to bed already?" Alex calls after him. Leonardo stops and turns to him.

"Why not nothing here but an asshole." Alex holds his hand over his chest. "Oh, my heart" He falls back onto the pool table

Leonardo smirks and walks back to him.

" You really are a smart ass aren't you?"

Alex sits back up and nods "You'll learn to love it."

Alex gets up from the table and turns to Leonardo. "So what do you wanna do? Do you really wanna go to bed?" Leonardo doesn't answer, he just looks around for a bit. "Hello, Earth to Princy?". Leonardo smirks.

"I'm not sure, my whole life is always scheduled for me." Leonardo was embarrassed to admit it.

Alex walks to Leonardo, "Well that sucks, but now you're here, and I'm not making you a schedule." Leonardo laughs. "It is still early though, but if you're tired I won't judge," Alex spoke in a condescending voice.

Leonardo looks down the hall, " I think I might just hop in the pool."

"There you go Princy, there's an idea, thinking for yourself." Leonardo went to his room to change and hopped in the pool. Alex took a seat on the couch and started to watch television.

* * *

Leonardo swam laps around the pool, stopping now and again thinking about his family. Wondering if he would ever see them again. Every time he wanted to cry he swam another lap. He could hear the television and Alex laughing every now and again. He thought Alex's laugh was cute. He always found himself looking at the men in magazines and fantasizing about being with them. At first glance, Alex kind of reminded him of them.

Some time passed and Leonardo got out of the pool. He wrapped himself in a towel after drying off and went up to his room, he brushed his hair and reapplied his cologne then walked into the living room where Alex was still sitting. He took a seat on the leather couch next to Alex. " Anything good?"

Alex is still glued to the television "Nah never is". Alex gets up and walks to the kitchen to get a soda. When he turned back around he noticed that the prince was still a little wet from the pool. He paused, as he looked at the prince from around the corner. He watched as a bead of water traveled from his wet hair down his neck over his pecks, and down his six-pack. Who knew the prince worked out? He thought to himself and licked his lips as his mouth began to dry out. He had to look away before his pants became too tight. He walked back to the room and handed a soda to Leonardo.

"I saw there is a workout room on the second floor," Alex mentioned to him trying to start up a conversation.

"You calling me fat?" Leonardo joked, tookking the soda from him and cracked it open. He took a sip before settling back into the couch. They both watched television for a bit.

Soon after Alex's phone started to go off. It was Janet. Alex stood up and stretched. He noticed that Leonardo was passed out on the couch. His hair completely dry now. Alex reached behind him and grabbed a blanket. Alex was intoxicated by the cologne the prince had on, and couldn't help but take a little longer to enjoy the smell. He covered Leonardo after enjoying being so close to his neck.

* * *

It's been six long days since the two were placed together in the house. Leo felt caged more and more as time went by.

The little amount of freedom is not what he had imagined when he thought of America. However, he could not deny that although Alex was always a smart ass he was enjoying the time with him. He found himself wondering if this was what it was like to have a friend. Leo spent most of the days trying to get to know Alex and tell him a little about himself as well. The more time he spent with him the more he had feelings growing for him, but he decided to hide them not knowing how Alex would react.

"Princy, get in here". Alex called out to Leo who was sitting in the kitchen. Leo came running in. "Wanna game?" Alex asked, holding a spare controller up for Leo. Leo took the foreign object from Alex and sat next to him on the loveseat. The loveseat must have been old because when he sat down it creaked.

"I never played before, I might not be great."Leo looked at Alex's hands and copied how he was holding the controller.

"It's not that hard just use this" He pointed at the joy con "To move your character. You press the X to jump." He went to press the back L2 and brushed his hand. Every time he touched Leo his heart skipped a beat. "You use this button to aim, and this other one to fire."

Leo nodded, "so are we a team or enemies"

"We can do either one you want. But let's start as a team till you learn how to play a little more." Alex suggested to him. Leo nodded in agreement. Alex glanced over and saw Leonardo smiling and having fun. He smiled seeing him happy. After about ten games of being on a team, they decided to verse each other. They both had one life left.

Leo found himself to be more competitive than he thought he would be. He nudged Alex with his shoulder trying to throw off his game. Alex returned the gesture. This continued for three minutes before Alex nudged Leo a bit too hard, and the cheap sofa flipped onto its side. Alex landed on top of Leo and found himself drawn in again. He felt his heart start to race. They both laughed but neither moved.

Leo enjoyed having Alex lay over him. It made him feel safe but also reminded him that he finally had a friend. He never got a chance at love, and maybe this was it he found himself thinking.

Alex was engulfed in the aroma again from his cologne. It was warm and inviting. He liked his lips looking at Leo's neck. He took one last breath and sat up, sitting on Leo's lap.

"Game over. " The game spoke out "Winner, PlayerTwo" Alex stood up and extended his hand to help up Leonardo. Leo took it and he pulled him to his feet."Well looks like you have some beginner's luck on your side."

"Do you wanna play again?" Leo asked, hoping that Alex would agree. Alex looked at the time.

"Maybe later, we have to eat something," Alex suggested, and Leo shook his head, and followed Alex to the kitchen. Alex tossed a pizza in the oven for the two to share. "Would you wanna watch a movie tonight? We can break Mom's rules and eat in the living room." Alex joked, Over the past six days Leo noticed that even though they were stuck in the house, Alex tried to give him a taste of what freedom was. Leo was thankful and played along.

"But what if she finds out? Seems she has eyes everywhere."

"Go pick out what movie we watch tonight."

Leo went to the living room and put 50 First Dates into the DVD player. Alex joined him on the couch with two cups of soda. "A rom-com." He looked at Leo. He laid his head on

Leo's shoulder. "Are you a romantic?" He said smugly. Leo lightly pushed him but didn't mind him laying there. They started the movie and sat close on the couch., Alex grabbed the Pizza out of the oven and brought it in for them. The two ate and watched the movie.

The movie was almost over and Leo had fallen asleep. He ended up falling over into Alex's lap. Alex looked down at him and smiled.

"Must be past your bedtime Princy." Alex chuckled looking over the prince. He still chose to wear the blue suits he brought with him, and it confused Alex. He knew that the CIA would have given him new clothing to wear.

Alex's phone started to vibrate. He looked down at the phone and saw he had 5 missed calls from Janet. "Shit" He whispered, lifted the blanket from behind the couch, and covered the prince up before sneaking out the front door.

"Yes," Alex answered the phone.

"The king's men called."

Alex cut her off "Oh no they couldn't put Humpty Dumpty together again?" He questioned sarcastically.

"Now is not the time. Whoever tried to take out the King knows where Pince Leonardo is. They fear they are going to try and use him to draw out the king. Alex looked into the window and looked at the Prince, who was still asleep. He felt his heart skip a beat.

"On it," Alex replied, hung up the phone, and walked back inside. He picked up the prince and brought him back to his room. He laid him on his bed and closed the door. "Well, time to work." Alex went around the building looking for any blind spots, checking each room from top to bottom making sure they were still secure.

He parked his car in the garage so no one could tinker with it. Then went back inside. He laid out some paper on the table and began to draw maps, and plans of attack and escape in case it came to this. The day was almost out of light by the time he finished. Leonardo came down the stairs, rubbing his eyes.

"Alex Did you ca…" He stopped talking mid-sentence when he saw Alex out cold on the couch. He looked down at all the papers on the table. There was a file with some notes Alex wrote up. Leonardo took them and went into the kitchen. He turned on the light and began to read them.

Location known… That is all he was able to read before Alex walked in. "My… My.. the prince is nosey too?" Alex teased, taking the files.

"What does your location known mean ?"Leo asked, reading the files. Alex tousled the prince's hair.

"Nothing you need to worry your little royal head about. You're in good hands." Leonardo grabs Alex's hand. Alex felt his heart skip a beat as Leo pulled him back to face him

"I think I am starting to understand you more. When you are nervous, or scared you act like an arrogant fuck, yet it's not who you really are. That same person would not have carried me up to my bed, or covered me up would they?"

Alex looked at him coldly, "You don't know me and we are not friends. I am here to protect you and that is it." Leonardo felt like a bullet was shot right into his chest. It reminded him of being back home, not having anyone, just some guards. He got up and went back to his room. He lay in his bed and stared up at the ceiling. Just here to protect me. I should've known this wouldn't be any different.

As Alex watched Leonardo walk upstairs he sighed. He was

a little surprised and confused as he realized his comment to the prince seemed to hurt him as much as the prince! He couldn't shake the feeling, but it was the truth, wasn't it, he thought to himself. He turned off the television and went up the grand stairs to Leonardo's room. "Leo.. Look." Leonardo sat up,

"What did you call me?" Alex walked into the room,

"Do you prefer Princy?" He walked over and sat on the bed next to Leonardo. " They know where we are keeping you, I try to keep my personal life and work separate. It's nothing against you, but right now my mission is to keep you safe by any means." Leonardo brushed some hair out of Alex's face and smiled. Alex felt his heart skip a beat and as Leo's hand brushed his ear his heart skipped a beat. He sucked in his lips and part of him wanted Leo to lean in and kiss him. But he was on a mission.

"It's okay Alex. Thank you for explaining."

* * *

It's been a month and Alex's feelings for him started to become stronger. He was done questioning his sexuality, and the attraction he felt for Leo. Leo on the other hand was fighting to find ways to conceal his feelings for Alex. He did not want to press the issue, and constantly was reminded that Alex keeps his personal and work life separate. He wanted to respect that, but it hurt him to deny how he felt.

The two spent the night previously talking on the couch. Alex woke before Leo that morning, and when opened his eyes he found Leo lying on his chest. He found himself smiling and ran his hand through Leo's hair. He loved the feeling he got when they touched. He tried to find reasons to make their hands meet or a reason to get close enough to smell his cologne. Leo opened his eyes shortly after and looked up to Alex.

"Good morning," He spoke with a raspy morning voice. "Did you sleep okay"

Alex looked down at him, "I did, and how about you Princy?"

It was the best night of sleep he had since the attack on his life. He looked up to Alex and did not want to cross the line though. "I slept okay," Leo spoke as he got off him. "Sorry, I fell asleep on you."

"It's okay," Alex said, suppressing his excitement that he got to sleep the night holding Leo.

Leo took off his blazer and shirt as he walked towards the pool. He slipped his pants off once he was closer to it. Alex followed him and took off his clothing as well. "Maybe I'll join you today." He shouted running past Leo and jumping into the pool.

The two swam around for a bit before Leo swam up to Alex. He splashed water at him, and Alex returned the gesture. The two splashed as they tried to move closer to each other. Leo found himself backed against the wall, and with Alex in front of him, He swallowed hard as Alex grabbed his hands. He held them down by his waist, and Leo found himself becoming aroused. He closed his eyes and waited for Alex to kiss him. Alex moved in closer hypnotized.

He closed his eyes and a flash of a burning building crossed his mind. He pulled back from Leo. Leo walked back to him and grabbed his hands.

"Are you okay?"

"It's nothing."

Every time he got close to his first kiss something happened. It was starting to upset Leo the more it happened. The rest of the day the two spent time together playing more games on the PlayStation and talking on the couch. Leo pretends to fall asleep on the couch as they watch another movie. He let his head rest on Alex's shoulder. Alex picked him up and carried him to his room. He put the blanket over him and leaned down.

He closed his eyes. "I want to kiss you. I want to cross that line, Leonardo." He whispered and kissed Leo's forehead.

Alex got up and walked out of the room and shut the door a bit. He grabbed a chair and plopped it down in front of Leo's room. He sat there with his gun in hand ready in case whoever knew their location was going to show up today, and fell asleep.

* * *

The building was already on fire. Alex made his way to the basement. "I knew you would show up," Chloe spoke. Two gunshots fired off at Alex. " I thought you loved me.... Was all of it a lie?" Chloe walked to Alex and kissed his head. "Duh?" She pointed the gun directly at his head. "Alex pulled out his gun from his right side. He shot three shots.

* * *

Alex had the same dream again and sprung to his feet. This dream again he thought to himself. His biggest mistake was always playing on repeat every time he closed his eyes. Alex cracked his neck and pushed the door to Leonardo's room open. Why couldn't he stop dreaming of this memory? Why was it that when during the whole day all he could think about was the prince? He walked closer to the bed again. He sat against it to not wake him. He looked up to Leo. He was still asleep and looked peaceful, even with everything going on. Alex noticed himself getting close to him faster than anyone before. "What is it about you, I have never wanted anything more than to protect you. What makes you so special to me?"

Leonardo woke during the night and saw Alex sleeping against his bed, he knelt next to him. "Alex," he whispered. Alex doesn't stir. Leo slid his arms under Alex and picked him up, placed him in his bed, and got in next to him. He covered them both up. He rolled away from Alex and fell asleep.

A Day To Remember

Alex woke the next morning before Leonardo. He sat up and stretched and cracked his neck. He didn't remember getting into bed last night. He looked over and Leonardo was sleeping next to him. His eyes went wide, and he quickly got out of the bed. Leonardo was not under the blanket. Alex could see the muscles in his back, which he followed with his eyes to Leonardo's hips. Then he realized that Leonardo was only wearing his boxers. He felt his face flush but didn't know why.

He quickly left the room and prepared for the day. He showered, tossed on some new clothing, and went downstairs.

Leonardo awoke shortly after Alex finished getting ready. The smell of sausage and coffee was enough motivation to have the Prince roll out of bed. He walked down the stairs and into the kitchen.

"What smells so good?" Leo questioned walking in and

stopping in the doorway.. Alex turned to Leonardo and nearly dropped the plate of food. He saw the Prince leaning in the doorway still only in his pajamas. Alex walked to the table and placed some food down.

"I uh, made breakfast." Alex managed to get out while stumbling on his words. Leonardo took his seat and started eating. Alex was doing everything he could to not look at the prince.

"I read into the case a little more," Alex spoke, trying to take his mind off the chiseled body that stood in front of him.

"Find anything interesting?" Leonardo asked between bites of food.

"No not really, just that the people after you and your father are part of some mafia," Alex spoke looking anywhere else in the kitchen except at Leonardo, who just finished his food.

" I'm going to go and take a shower. I'll be back in a few." Alex just shook his head.

Leonardo vanished from the kitchen and started the shower. Alex heard the water as it echoed in the big empty house. He felt himself swallow as we drank his morning coffee. He could not stop thinking of Leonardo in the shower just upstairs, right above him. He could hear the water as it changed. He knew exactly when Leonardo stepped in. He tried to think of anything else, but the thought just wouldn't leave his mind no matter how hard he tried.

Leonardo walked into the closet for the first time and realized that it was big enough to be a bedroom, he saw it was filled with clothes he would never be allowed to wear at home. He looked through the shirts, and the pants trying to decide what his style would be. He tried on about four outfits and smiled looking in the mirror. He enjoyed the freedom he had to pick an outfit, that was not just some blue suit. He dressed quickly and went down the stairs.

"Well Alex, how bad does it look?" Alex turned to see the prince standing there in front of him in a pair of slacks that were rolled up showing part of his muscular legs, a t-shirt that was just the right fit that showed off his pecks, and abs, along with a pair of white Converse. Alex swallowed hard again.

"Well, you don't look like a stuffed Prince that's for sure." Leonardo looked at Alex,

"And you don't look too much like a bad ass CIA agent either." Alex stood up,

"Take that back I totally look bad ass."

Before Leonardo could speak the doorbell rang. Leonardo went to walk to the window, and Alex tackled him to the ground. Alex covered Leonardo's mouth and whispered close to his ear.

" Are you mad? Stay down!"

Alex instructed Leo to stay put and walked to the front door. He slid his gun into his pants and took a deep breath before opening the door. A FedEx driver dropped off a package. Alex took out his knife and cut it open. Inside was a small cake that read Happy Birthday. Alex read the side of the box. It was from the Queen. Alex brought the package in.

"Get up Leo." Leo stood up. And took the package Alex was holding out for him. "You didn't tell me it was your birthday," Alex spoke softly, feeling hurt for some reason.

"Sorry, it was never a big event for me. Growing up in the castle I never really had a friend, and my parents were always busy. I mean Sebastian, my butler tried his best to remember but he was old." Alex sat next to Leo on the couch and cut the cake. He dished it out onto plates and looked at Leonardo.

"Well, today it is special." Alex took some icing on his finger and put it on Leonardo's nose. "It will be a birthday to remember."

Alex and Leo ate their cake and talked for a bit before Alex stood up. " Go get a coat, I'm taking you out." Leo didn't get up,

"Won't you lose your job though? There are cameras outside." Alex laughed.

"I know every blind spot in this place. And if we get caught, oh well, it's the thrill we need." Leo jumped to life and grabbed his coat. Alex guided him through the yard like a mother duck leading her young. Once they made it to the corner they were safe. "Listen closely Leo you need to stay close okay? "

Leo nodded and grabbed Alex's hand. Alex felt his face flush red again, he pulled up his scarf to hide his face. Leo rested his head against Alex's shoulder.

" Now people will think we are together. Completely undercover right Alex?" Alex took off his scarf and covered Leo's face.

"Now you're undercover." Alex led Leo through town showing him all the different statues, and monuments. They went to the boardwalk. Even though it was closed down for the season they went through it.

"I never got to go on any rides, my guards always said it wasn't safe," Leo spoke with a little undertone of sadness.

"Come on" Alex, still holding Leo's hand, led him to the Ferris wheel. He opened the door of the carriage and bowed. "After you, Your Royal Highness" The prince bowed back and went in.

A man walked up in a black and white suit and started the ride for them. The lights kicked on and the wheel slowly began to move.

"Thanks, Agent Wilson, don't forget the deal," Alex shouted to the man. The man stood there counting the money Alex left on the station for him. Leonardo was in awe as the higher they went up he could see further out in the ocean. He even got to see fishing boats traveling back to port heavy on the water with tons of fish. The ride stopped when they were on the top. The moon shone down on them both. Leo moved over next to Alex and laid his head on his shoulder.

"Thank you," he whispered. Alex turned to answer him. He looked into his eyes for the first time in days. They were the bluest eyes he had ever seen. The lights sparkled like dancing fireflies through them. Alex felt hypnotized and surprisingly safe for the first time in a year.

The ride started to move again and it jerked him back to reality. They sat in silence, Leo so impressed by his surroundings, and Alex just in shock not knowing what to say for once. They got off the ride and went down to the ocean. The two ran around the beach and tried to push each other in. They sat in the sand and talked about anything that came to mind. Leo was enjoying his day out with Alex and wanted to remember it. He put his arm around Alex, who felt his heart skip a beat when his hand rested on his arm. Leo took a photo of the two. Alex pushed him jokingly, and he fell back into the sand. He grabbed Alex's arm and pulled him with him. Alex landed on top of him again. He looked down and smiled, but quickly got back to his feet and extended his hand.

"Let's head back, Princy," Alex suggested. The cool salt air was starting to pick up with the wind. Leo agreed and took his hand to get up.

Leo did not take Alex's hand again on the way back. He still walked close to him, he could tell that something was going on with Alex. They were just about back to the corner of the street they were staying at when Leo stopped walking.

"Alex…" Alex stopped and turned to him. "Thank you again, it was a great birthday. The best I have had in a very long time.." Alex walked back and put his arm around Leo.

"Come on Princy before you get a cold, and Janet kills me. Leo put his arm around Alex and they walked back to the house. Not thinking of anything other than the fun they had together they walked right through the front door. Right as they walked in, his phone started to ring over and over again. They both knew who it was. Alex tossed his phone on the couch ignoring every call that came in. They hung up their coats and made their way into the game room.

Leonardo grabbed a pool stick,

"Wanna play?" Alex chuckled,

"That depends on how bad you wanna lose." Alex grabbed a pool stick and racked the balls. "I'll let you break." He said sliding Leonardo into the queue. Leonardo took his stance and went to strike the ball. He missed three times before Alex walked behind him. "Do you need me to show you how it's done?" He whispered in his ear. Leonardo turned around and looked him dead in the eyes.

"Think you're so good, let's make a bet." Leonardo knew Alex would not turn down a bet.

"And what do I have that a prince would want?" Alex mocked him.

Leo shrugged, "What would you want?" Leonardo questioned Alex.

"If I win you have to give me that gold ring you always wear."

"Deal." Leo turned and hit the cue ball, he pocketed three

balls off the bat. He proceeded to pocket every ball leading up to the eighth ball. He called the corner pocket and sank that too. He turned back to Alex.

"Did you just swindle me?" Alex said in shock that he got defeated in one turn.

"Come on Mr. CIA I thought you were trained to find liars," Leo spoke smugly.

"Okay Princy Okay, what do I owe you?" Alex asked as Leonardo walked over to Alex who was sitting on the corner of the pool table. Leonardo walked between Alex's legs and put his arms around his neck. He leaned in close. Alex could feel his breath on his neck. He was intoxicated again by the prince's cologne.

Leonardo undid the clasp of the necklace Alex had on. A simple chain with a wolf head on it. Leonardo backed away.

"We'll call this even for now." Alex hopped off the table to cover up the unexpected result of their little encounter.

"If you wanted a three-dollar necklace we could have gotten you the same one," Alex spoke walking to the living room.

"It's not the price that matters. Once this mission is over I'll be going to London. Maybe I just wanted something to remember you by." Alex felt hurt at the thought that Leonardo was right, he would be going back. He didn't want to think about it anymore. His phone was still ringing nonstop. Leonardo got tired of hearing the phone vibrate and picked it up.

"Agent Twist, so help me god you better have a…", Janet was cut off by the prince.

"Hello, Janet." Janet's voice changed. "Why hello Prince Leonardo, I hope you had a nice birthday."

"I did thank you for remembering Janet."

"Of course, is Agent Twist available? "

"I'm sorry he is not, I currently have him making me some food. But I do want to apologize if I caused any issues, you see I was so terribly bored here at the house, and I saw that there was a nightclub nearby, and thought I would go check it out. Agent Twist shortly caught up with me and brought me back to the safe house." Alex stood there eyes wide as he tried to listen to the conversation.

"Your Highness, your food is ready," Alex called out trying not to laugh, and barf at the same time.

" I'm sorry Janet but I do like to eat my food hot. So I have to go."

"Prince…" Janet was cut off by Leonardo hanging up. Alex sat on the couch and looked at Leonardo.

"I'm so fired," He said, laughing slightly.

"Would that be all bad though Alex, we could be friends then.." Leo spoke before thinking, and Alex was just reminded of what he said the other night to him.

"Leo.. I'm sorry about that. It's just."

"It's okay I get it." He paused for a moment looking at Alex. "I think I am going to call it for the night. Thank you again for today. It was something to remember for sure." Leo started to walk up the stairs and Alex got up and ran to him.

"Leo, wait." Alex caught up with him and Leo turned to face him.

"Happy birthday," Alex whispered and kissed Leo's cheek. Leo didn't know how to react, he didn't want to just walk away. He took off his ring. "I have something to remember you by. It's only fair," Alex looked at the ring in Leonardo's hand. It had the family crest on it with diamonds around it and was solid gold. Alex closed Leo's hand and shook his head.

"Don't worry I couldn't forget my time with you Princy." Leo smiled and looked at Alex,

"You know the room is really big, and if you don't mind you're welcome to just stay with me in there. I mean it would be easier to guard me from there wouldn't it?"

Alex smiled, "If that is your wish, your highness." He bowed to the young prince. Leonardo went to the room smiling, he cracked open the door and held it open for Alex.

He went to the bathroom and Alex walked around the room some more. He was looking at the bookshelves and saw a book that didn't match the rest. One of those romance novels with Fabio on the cover. He knew Janet and that was plan B in case the prince was in danger it would open a passageway to get the prince out of the house. Leo opened the bathroom door and walked to Alex. Alex turned around and saw him standing there. He was close enough to get lost in his scent again. He swallowed hard and tried to keep his eyes in line with Leo's.

Leo pulled Alex close to him, "I really enjoyed the day with you."

Alex wasn't able to get any words out. He was too distracted by the hard body pressed against his. He could feel Leo's heart racing and each breath he took in. He didn't want the hug to end. The muscles in Leo's arms surrounded Alex. He soon snapped out of it and back to reality.

He broke out of the hug and walked over to the bed. He took off his shirt, and pants before climbing into the bed. He rolled to face the wall and closed his eyes. He felt the bed shift as Leo entered. He rolled over to face Leo who had the blanket down by his waist.

"Tomorrow we are going to teach you to defend yourself, Princy. I won't always be around to help you." Alex felt a pain in his chest again, but he wanted to make sure that Leonardo would be safe.

Leo nodded in agreement and rolled to face Alex. "Okay." He moved closer to Alex inching his way till there was less than a few inches apart. Alex's eyes were starting to get heavy. As he closed them he noticed that Leo had on his necklace. Leo saw Alex fall asleep and moved closer to him so their bodies were touching. He closed his eyes and gently kissed Alex's head.

" Thank you for finally giving me freedom." Alex groaned and nuzzled into Leo's neck. Leo smiled and put his arm around Alex. "I don't think I ever want this mission to end."

Four

Something New Together

Leonardo's eyes shot open and there, still asleep in his arms, was Alex. He let out a sigh of relief, afraid that it was all just a dream. He carefully pulled his arm out from under Alex and made his way to the bathroom. He looked into the mirror. There was a glow around him. He has not been this happy in a very long time. He finally had freedom and a friend he so desperately yearned for. He looked down at the necklace around his neck and smiled, holding the wolf's head in his hands. He looked back at the sleeping brunette in his bed and sighed.

Leonardo went to the workout room and started to do his morning run on the treadmill. Alex rubbed his eyes awake, stretched, and smiled. It was the first night in a year he had not had that same nightmare. He rolled over and noticed that Leo was not in the room. He quickly grabbed the gun from under the bed and went around the house looking for him.

"Leo?" He called out here and there until, finally, he heard a response.

"In here." Alex knew he messed up when he walked into the workout room. Leo was lying down on one of the benches. He put the weights back on the rack and sat up. His breaths were heavy, and his chest glistened with sweat. Leo grabbed the towel that was draped over the bench between his legs and dabbed his forehead before rubbing his neck with it.

Alex, still only in his Calvin Klines, walked back out of the room. Leo stood up and ran after him.

"What, no good morning?" Alex turned to Leo, and instantly regretted it. He could feel his shorts becoming too small. He turned back around and walked into the bathroom.

"I just woke up and needed to use the restroom, but you were gone. I'll be out in a bit!" Alex called out as he slammed the door behind him. Leo smiled when he caught a glimpse of what was going on. He turned and headed down to the kitchen. He opened the fridge and took a look inside it. He grabbed some eggs and started to make breakfast for the two of them.

Alex stepped out of the shower and instantly smelt smoke. He grabbed his towel and tied it around his waist, before racing down the stairs and into the kitchen. The stove was on fire, and Leo was covered in soot, and batter. Alex quickly grabbed the fire extinguisher and put out the flame. He turned to Leo and saw the mess he was in and started to laugh.

"Princy, what in the world are you doing?" Leo put down the bowl he was holding of what should have been pancake batter and smiled.

"I wanted to see my hero sooner?" He spoke, trying not to laugh. He looked at Alex. It was the first time he was able to see what he truly looked like. Alex had a smile on his face but was obviously worried. His eyes screamed it. He saw Alex's chest that had a tattoo of a paw print on it with a date. Leo saw that he had some scars on his chest as well as bullet hole wounds. Alex's biceps are bigger than his own, and his abs glistened with the water that had not been dried off from the fire.

Leo walked over to Alex and put his hand over the scars.

"What happened?" Alex backed up, he was not ready to talk about it. Not to him. Leo looked away, feeling like it was okay. "We all have our secrets." Alex grabbed Leo's hand and led him back up the stairs to the room.

"Why don't you get cleaned up, and we can talk about it." Leo nodded and let Alex get dressed. Alex went downstairs to clean the kitchen and ordered them food. In the bathroom, Leo took a seat on the toilet.

" I can't even make a proper meal, why would I think he would ever fall for me."

* * *

Leo hurried down the stairs and missed one. He started to fall but Alex managed to catch him as he was about to go up and check in on him. Alex stood Leo up against the wall. His arms were on either side of him and his eyes met with Leo's.

"Princy, when will you learn? I won't always be there to protect you." He watched as Leo's Adam's apple moved when he swallowed hard. Alex felt his breath quicken. It's been over a year since he felt this way. His eyes were still locked with Leo's. He leaned in, closed his eyes, and whispered.

"I'm going to kiss a prince." Leo closed his eyes as Alex gently placed his lips on his own. He felt his heart skip beats. Alex pulled away and looked at Leo. "Sorry," Alex spoke quickly and felt his face starting to blush.

Leo shook his head, "It took you long enough." He kissed him back. Alex quickly pulled away though.

"Leo… I.."

Alex walked up the stairs and into his room. He placed his hand under his shirt feeling the scars that still remained. The ones on his chest, but also the ones in his mind. Leo knocked on the door before walking in.

"Alex, what is it?" Leo sat next to him on the bed.

* * *

"A year ago the person I was…. They betrayed us. I let my guard down. I knew something wasn't right. It cost me my team… And nearly my own life. The person I thought was the one, I let see me, the real me. I ran into a trap set by them to save them. I let my guard down and everyone around me paid the price for it" He stood up, and took a breath. "That is why I…" Leo stood up and hugged him.

"So you're afraid that if you let me in, I will get hurt, or you will ?" Leo asked.

"I already said I would put my life on the line for you, but now… Now it's like…" Leo cut him off with another kiss. Alex did not pull away this time.

"If it helps I never felt more safe than being around you Alex." Alex dried his eyes as the doorbell rang.

"Stay here." Alex walked down the stairs and opened the door. A man in a black suit stood there in front of him. His hand is in his pocket. Alex was distracted and forgot to grab his guns. "It's happening again." The man pulled a gun out of his pocket and pointed it at Alex.

Leo heard banging from down the stairs, he knew Alex told him to stay put but he was worried. He could hear the sounds of glass shattering. He looked out the window and saw a black Mercedes with tinted windows. The window started to roll down, and he dodged from view. As he dropped to the ground he saw Alex's gun on the bed. He crawled over and grabbed it. He ran to the stairs, where he saw a man holding his leg that was bleeding and barely walking up to him. The man was bald, with dark glasses on, and was clenching his stomach that, Leo could see was bleeding. Alex was crawling after him already on the banister.

"Leo, run," Alex yelled to him while coughing up blood. Alex tried to stand but couldn't. Alex up the stairs between him and the man crawled, he grabbed the man by the foot and tripped him. The guy fell and turned to Alex. Leo watched as the guy squeezed the life out of him. Leo held the gun at him and fired. The bullet went through the guy and Alex pushed him off. Alex used the banister and stood up. He walked up the stairs and took the gun from Leo. Leo stood there shaking.

"Come on. We have to move." Alex pushed Leo gently up the stairs, and into his room. He locked the door behind them. He grabbed a duffle bag and filled it with clothing before falling over. Alex tried his best to hide how hurt he really was.

He pulled the book off the shelf and the bookshelf moved. They went inside a secret tunnel bunker. Alex lit some of the candles inside. He took Leo's hand and held it up to his lips. He kissed it gently,

"Thank you." Alex's vision was starting to blur but he sat

himself against the wall.

"Give me a minute and we will get out of here Princy," Alex's body leaned over as he spoke, his words becoming more slurred. Alex stood again and pulled out his phone. He pressed 1 on his phone and called Janet.

"Agent Twist, so help me if you two have snuck out again." Janet started to reprimand him.

"We have a code Magenta." His eyes closed and he fell to the floor.

"Hello… Agent Twist Come in…" Janet yelled through the phone. "Agent Twist."

Leo was still very shaken and lost in his mind. He did not hear the voice on the phone. But did notice that Alex had fallen over. He managed to catch him right before he hit the ground. He pushed Alex's blood-covered hair out of his face and felt tears fall down his eyes.

"I am so sorry, I shouldn't have pushed you…." He wiped some of the blood off his face. "This is my fault…" He picked up Alex and started to walk down the hall. At the end of the hall was a bed where he laid Alex down. He noticed that Alex's shoulder was red and took off his shirt. He could see his chest was blue, and his once glistening abs were bruised. He noticed that there was also a bullet wound on his shoulder.

"I shot him…" He took off his shirt and held it down on Alex's shoulder. "Alex hold on please." Alex opened his eyes.

"Welcome to America Princy. Freedom always comes with a cost."

Janet was the first to arrive on the scene. She readied her gun and walked to the house. She swung the corner of the open door and headed in. Looking around she could see various signs of struggle. She saw glass shattered everywhere. A pair of brass knuckles on the floor, and a bloody knife. She bent down and picked it up. It was the knife she gave Alex back when they were partners when he first started at the agency. She looked around the room and noticed there was so much blood, but only one dead. She put it back down looking up at the stairs. She walked over to the man who was lying in a pool of blood on the landing. She checked for a pulse. Once she made sure there was none she moved up to the safe room.

Leo turned back to the doorway they came in from. He was able to hear someone out there.

"Agent Twist, this is Director Janet, the color of the day is teal. We are coming in, do not shoot." Leo turned back to Alex, still holding his hand, and fighting back his tears.

"They are here, Alex, hold on. Please," he whispered into his ear.

"Agent Twist," Jennette yelled from down the hall, as she ran towards the two. She looked at them. "Prince." She was cut off immediately by Leo.

"Help him please," Leo begged, no longer holding back his tears. Janet took off her jacket and tied it into a tourniquet around his arm. She looked at the Prince,

"Can you walk?" She questioned and Leo nodded. "Then help me carry him," Janet spoke calmly. She went to pick up an arm, and she realized Alex's body was cold to the touch. Leo slid his arms under Alex and picked him up. His arms were limp and he could feel the shallow breaths he was taking.

Leo carried him to the car where he got into the back seat with him. He laid him on the seat with his head resting on his lap. Janet rushed them to the hospital.

"We can't call for help, there is a damn school parade and they can't get through. We will have to take the long way. Hold on Prince Leonardo." Leo ignored her, he was not able to take his eyes off Alex. He leaned down and whispered to Alex.

"I don't want it to all end like this. Please hold on."

He kissed his head and tears fell on Alex's face. Janet was looking back in the rearview mirror to make sure they were not being followed. When Leo leaned down and kissed Alex. Alex lifted his hand, touched Leo's cheek, and smiled.

"I like it when you smile better Princy." He whispered before closing his eyes again.

"Prince Leonardo, we are here". Janet swung her door open and Leo picked up Alex and ran into the building. The nurses were waiting with a gurney. Janet had alerted them when Alex called her. Leo placed him on it and held his hand.

"You will have to wait here, Your Highness." A small blond nurse placed her hand on his chest stopping him from moving on. Leo didn't want to let go of Alex's hand, he was scared that this would be the last time he saw him. The last time he could tell him how grateful he was for meeting him. Janet stepped over and grabbed his arm.

"You have to let him go, Your Highness." Hearing those words made it even harder for Leo to let go. Five more agents walked into the hospital and pulled the prince into a secure room. His hand left Alex's, and he could no longer hold back his feelings. He started to punch the agents holding him back. Janet nodded and they left the room and stood outside the door. She pulled up a chair for her and Leo.

"Why don't you take a seat? I'll stay with you."

Leo pulled up a chair and punched the table.

"I pushed him, I made him cross that line." He mumbled to himself.

Five

The Long Wait

Leo took a seat at the table, and couldn't stop his leg from bouncing around. A knock came from the door before it opened.

"Prince Leonardo, I'm Doctor Harvey." He spoke as he bowed. "Janet has asked me to check you over for..." Leo stood up

"I am fine, not a scratch on me, Alex did his job and protected me. Go save him." Leo begged the doctor, and Janet walked over to the Prince,

"Alex is in good hands, This is protocol, we have to make sure you're okay. You may not feel anything now, but you can be hurt." Leo looked over at Janet.

"They never even made it to me. Alex made sure of that." She waved and the Doctor left the room.

Janet sighed. "He did it again, didn't he?" Leo sat back down and rested his head in his hands. They were still blood-covered.

"He lost so much blood Janet." She looked up from her phone to Leo.

" Come on Prince Leonardo, we both know Agent Twist…" She paused for a moment, " Alex is a fighter." Janet points to the back of the room, "There is a bathroom back there why don't you try and wash up a little." Leo walked to the back room and washed away the dry blood from his hands and face. He splashed some water on his brow before noticing a navy blue suit behind him. "Welcome to America Princy, freedom comes with a price." Played back in his head. Why did his freedom have to come at such a high cost? He thought to himself and let out a few more tears.

Janet knocked on the door, "Press will be here soon, we want to keep you away from the cameras, but change into the suit in case." Leo took a deep breath and put on the suit. He hated seeing himself back in it. It reminded him that soon he would have to go back home, and be the Prince once more. He opened the door and Janet was there waiting for him with a cup of coffee and some donuts on the table. "I was not sure what kind you liked so I had them get some options." Leo took the coffee but had no appetite. He sat on the couch in the room and took a small sip before putting it on the table.

Leo looked down at his phone and he realized he had about 17 missed calls and 15 texts from his father. He listened to his voicemails and stood up. He redialed a number on his phone and called his mother.

"Leonardo? Are you okay?" He could tell his mother had been crying.

"I'm fine Mom, not a scratch on me," Leo spoke back trying to hold back tears, every time he said that, he could only think of Alex lying in his lap, grasping at life's strings. His voice was so soft when he whispered to him that he liked him better smiling.

"I want you on the next flight back, this would have never happened here."

"Mom, I am not coming back yet. They are still after us, whoever they are. I need to make sure that Al… Agent Twist is okay. He sacrificed everything to protect me."

"You are being ordered by the King.." replied his mother.

"Mom, no. I am staying here, The CIA is trained for stuff like this. I am okay."

"Are you sure?" His mother questioned, the amount of worry in her voice could drown a fish.

"Yes Mom, I am staying here, Janet is here as well, I am fine, I am safe." Leo hung up his phone and looked down at it. He went into his gallery. The first photo there was of him and Alex at the boardwalk. They were sitting in the sand. They had just finished talking about London, and how Alex wanted so badly to see it. Leo felt himself starting to cry again. Janet got up and sat next to him. She looked over his shoulder and saw the photo.

"So you snuck out to go to the club huh?", Leo quickly locked his phone and looked over at her. "It's okay, Agent..Alex has done much worse. When I assigned him to this case I knew he would not let anything happen to you. He is one of my best agents. I remember when he saved my life a year ago." She closed her eyes. " It was so hard for him, I feel he still feels the pain from it all." She looked at the Prince. "May I?" She reached forward and undid the knot in the necklace around his neck. "I was with him when he got this." She smiled. " Corny little thing I thought. You know it's engraved." Leo turned it around. *May the memory of me live on forever within you.* "I had them engrave it for him after he lost...."

Leo looked over at Janet, "What happened a year ago? Why is he so afraid to let his guard down?" Janet looked back at the wall and sighed.

"A year ago we found out there was a traitor among us. Alex was too close to the case, but he insisted we let him work it. Janet paused and was lost in thought. For as long as I remember he had that dog. I swear he loved it more than himself. Chleo his lover, if you can call her that, killed her. Hence the necklace. We discovered she was a trader selling secrets and locations to make a fast buck. Shame, she was the best agent we had. She set a trap that only Alex would have been able to see through. But she was in his head.

He was so sure that she was being held hostage. He led a team of agents into a warehouse. She killed them all. Except for me, she wanted me to watch as she killed him. She knew how close we were. She wasn't expecting him to fire back at her though. He had to kill the person he loved and save me. I owe him everything you see. We had to take him off cases till now. He wasn't ready." She paused and looked at Leonardo. *"How did you end up with it?"*

"I won it in a bet." She smiled and said,

"Ah, you mean he let you win?" Janet spoke sure of herself. Leo smiled for a moment, something he thought he wouldn't be able to do again.

"No, I tricked him with my amazing bluffing skills." She shook her head.

"Trust me he saw right through you. He is my best agent. He knew your location was compromised. He knew what he would have to do. He started to let you in. He gave it to you because he wanted his memory to live on with you. He wanted to make sure that no matter how things turned out you never forgot him."

"So he knew this was going to happen?" Leo looks at Janet asking.

Janet paused for a moment, "He knew it could happen. I guess that is part of the reason he wanted to make sure you had a great birthday." Leo looked at her thinking of the day before. He really did have a blast on what he was considering to be a date with Alex.

"Does everyone know everything about me?" Leo asked with tears in his eyes. Janet looked back at him,

"Hey, it's my job to know these things."

* * *

Leonardo had fallen asleep and was awoken by another knock on the door. He stood up along with Janet. They both fixed their blazers before she spoke,

"Come in," she had her hand on her holster ready just in case. A nurse walked in, her face showed no emotion at all. Leo could not get any words out. "How is he? Janet spoke softly. The nurse looked at us and took a deep breath.

"The doctors have done everything they could. There was a lot of internal bleeding, and he lost a lot of blood. He has four broken ribs, one of which punctured his lung. The bullet grazed the vein. We are keeping him in the ICU."

"May we see him?," Janet spoke up. The nurse nodded.

" He is in bad shape. The doctor said it's up to him at this point." She looked at them both. " Does he have something worth fighting for? If so, it's best to remind him. He can still hear you." Leo felt his heart drop to the floor. It felt like it had been ripped from his ribs. Janet held the door open for him.

The agents formed a line around him and escorted them both to the elevator. Janet hit floor 7. The elevator ride up felt like an eternity to Leo. The elevator doors opened to a poorly lit hallway. Leo grasped the necklace around his neck.

"He wanted you to have it to always remember him."

They made their way to the nurses station. "Agent Twist please," Janet spoke softly to the nurse behind the counter. She looked over the computer screens.

"Room 704." The young nurse spoke. Leonardo felt his heart skipping beats as they inched closer to the room. His door was shut and Janet turned to Leonardo,

"Let me go in first." She spoke softly, holding her hand up to the Prince.

"Alex, you need to get up, once being here is more than enough." She took his hand, and she squeezed it. "You really are the best agent we have. We can't afford to lose you." She pulled a chair up next to the bed. "What happened there, Alex? What made you break every protocol we have? What was the slip-up? Damnit Alex, open your eyes, that's an order." Janet yelled at him as she felt tears fall from her cheek and hit her hand.

"Who am I kidding, you never listen to orders." She leaned back in the chair, "It should have been me in that bed last year, instead it was you, and here you are again." Janet stood up and went back to the door.

Before Leo could walk in she looked at him and patted him on the back.

"Visiting hours end in 5 minutes," A voice spoke over the speaker. Leo walked into the room and turned to shut the door. He took a breath to ready himself before turning to see Alex. He turned and could not believe what he saw.

Alex's eyes had cuts all over them, his cheeks were swollen and his hands were cut all over. It was hard for Leo to see Alex with the breathing tube in. He pulled the chair up next to him and took a seat.

"Alex, I don't even know what to say. You saved me, I owe you everything." He grabbed his hand. Alex's heart monitor started to quicken. "The nurse said you can still hear us, and I hope that is true." He clenched Alex's hand a bit tighter and noticed the bandage wrapped around his shoulder. "Alex, I'm so sorry I never… I didn't mean to." He leaned over the bed. "I spoke with Janet, she said you knew this was going to happen, or a strong possibility it would. You gave me this so I will never forget you no matter what." He held the necklace. "Alex, I don't need a necklace, I need you to open your eyes." Leo felt his words being choked by the emotions he was feeling. "My family wants me to go back home." He turns away, "Maybe it's for the best." He kissed Alex's hand. "If I never came here this would have never happened to you. Alex, please open your eyes, I need you to live. Wake up, insult me, call me Prince, anything please."

"Alex I know that we just met not that long ago, but I already know I can't live if anything happens to you. Especially knowing that it was because of me." He leaned down and kissed Alex's head. His tears fell hard and landed on him. "Alex please."

A loud alarm started to sound from the machines attached to Alex. Janet broke through the door and pushed the prince back away from the bed.

"We have a code blue in room 704", was called over the intercom system. Doctors and nurses raced into the room. The doctor ripped Alex's gown open. They rubbed an ointment on his chest. Leo saw more bandages around him that had been hidden by the gown.

Janet tried to turn the prince away from the scene, but she was unable to budge him an inch.

"Clear!" The nurse called out and pressed the paddles against his chest. Leo watched as Alex's body jumped.

"Clear!" They pressed the pads against him again. Leo buried his face into Janet's shoulder; he couldn't bear the sight.

"Visiting hours are now over." A voice called again from the loudspeaker.

"Clear!" Leo could hear the shock as they pressed the paddles again against his chest.

"He waited to see you one last time, Prince Leonardo." Janet fought back her tears, trying to be strong for Leonardo.

"Clear!" They shocked him again. His chest monitor detected a heart rhythm once again. He had a pulse once more. Leo let out a breath and ran over to him.

"Alex I swear, you must always put on a show," Leo yelled at him. Janet took a breath before walking to Leo.

"Prince Leonardo we need to leave, visiting hours are over." Leo did not move; he stayed holding onto Alex's hand.

"I'm not leaving Janet, you will have to put me in cuffs." She shook her head. I will have agents outside the room if you need anything.

* * *

Leo did not move from Alex's side all night. He fell asleep sitting there with his head on the bed next to his hand. The breathing machine started to beep and the nurses came in again. Leo sat up barely awake.

"What's going on?" Leo blinked trying to adjust to the hospital lights in the room.

"We are taking out the breathing tube. The machine says he is breathing on his own. We don't want to give him too much oxygen." Leo still didn't let go of his hand. The nurses shortly went to leave the room.

"Can we get a blanket for him please," Leo called to them as they left. A few moments later one of the agents came in with a blanket. Leo unfolded it and covered him gently. Once the door was shut again Leo leaned over and kissed Alex every so cautiously on the lips. He brushed his hair out of his face.

"Alex, come on. There has to be something worth living for."

Leo rested his head against the wall and held his hand again. His eyes drifted back shut again.

* * *

The sun was shining through the window of the hospital room bed. Leo was still fast asleep clinging to Alex's hand. Janet walked into the room and placed a cup of coffee on the table next to Leo. She was relieved a bit to see the breathing tube finally removed. A nurse walked into the room and Janet got up from the seat to speak with her.

"Any changes?" She asked, waiting for the nurse's response.

"He is breathing on his own, there is some brain activity, but no signs of change really." She spoke while taking notes and checking the I.V.

"Prince Leonardo, if you would like, I will stay here with Alex and you can go to the shop downstairs. Maybe grab something to eat? One of the agents would go with you." Janet spoke, resting her hand on his back and waking him up. Leo nodded and stood up. He wiped his eyes and leaned down to Alex.

"I'll be right back." He snuck a peck on his cheek as Janet was checking her phone. He stood and walked out of the room going to the cafeteria with an agent. He grabbed a bagel and put it in a bag. He wanted to get back up to Alex as soon as he could.

The agent and Leo walked by the gift shop, and he stepped inside. He looked around a bit and grabbed the biggest bear they had, he went to the front counter.

"Must be someone special." The old lady said as she rang up the bear.

"He is." Leo smiled as he spoke thinking about being at the boardwalk with Alex.

She smiled, "Anything else?" Leo looked around all of them, and he pointed behind her at some roses.

"I would like all of them," Leo spoke softly.

"All?" She asked as if she was being pranked. Leo nodded. "But sir, those are twenty dollars each."

"All of them please, " Leo repeated. The lady shrugged and rang them all up. "That comes to one thousand dollars." She replied rather smugly believing he probably couldn't afford it. Leo reached into his pocket and pulled out his card. "He really is special?" Leo took the receipt from her smiling.

"He saved my life. Can you have them delivered to room 704 please?"

She nodded "Right away, sir."

Leo walked with the agent back to Alex's room. The floor felt so different than every other floor in the hospital. It feels like hope just leaves you when you enter the floor, like there is no happiness. He made it back holding a small brown bag with the bagel and a bear as big as him. He placed the bear against the wall on the shelf so it would be the first thing Alex saw when he woke up. He sat at the table and opened his small brown bag.

"Anything?" Leo asked, hoping for some good news. Janet just shook her head.

"Your Highness, you need a good night's rest. You've been through a lot. Why don't you go to the station? We have some beds there. Sleep a little?" Leo spread some jelly onto the bagel.

"I'm not leaving him," Leo said sternly, not budging on the matter. He yawned and grabbed his coffee to take a sip. His hands were shaking and the coffee splashed about.

He managed to get a couple of sips in when someone knocked on the door. Janet didn't move but her hand on her hip. The agents came in one by one with bundles of roses. Leo stood and took them from the agents placing them around the bear.

"What's all this?" Janet asked.

"I wanted to make sure when he wakes up he knows he has something to live for. The nurse asked if he had something to live for. He does have something right, Janet? "

She looked at Alex, and back at Leo.

"I'm sure he does." Leo took his seat back next to Alex and took his hand. It felt cold, as his lips had a bluish tint.

"Janet, get a nurse, something isn't right." Janet ran out the door.

"Alex, come on. You have something to live for. I know it." He squeezed his hand hoping that he would wake up and squeeze his back. He picked up Alex's hand and gently kissed it.

Six

A Dying Rose Or A Red Hope.

The flowers in the room were dying, petals remained on the counter reminding Leo how many days he had been there. Janet stopped showing up, work was getting very busy for her, and with the King under attack every day, she was trying to convince him to come to America and let her men help protect him. But the king was stubborn and would never leave. She knew this, but she had to try something. Leo on the other hand barely left Alex's side. He learned the name of every nurse in the ICU, and how to change the bandages for Alex. He wanted to help in some way.

It was a sunny afternoon outside as Leo stood at the window looking out. There was a park where couples would walk around, and have picnics. He could see how happy everyone seemed and it just made his chest hurt more. He pictured himself out there with Alex sitting against the oak tree in the middle of a park. Alex packed a little basket with sandwiches for them, and he carried the basket. They posed together while someone painted them. His head in Alex's lap and Alex looking down at him. They both had the biggest smiles.

A loud beep brought him back to the room he was in. He shook his head and ran over to Alex's side and grabbed his hand. He gave it a gentle squeeze waiting for him to squeeze back but nothing still. He looked up at the machines. His heart rate was normal, breathing was a little low, but everything looked okay and no one came running in.

Leo was starting to lose hope. With each dying rose more of his hope faded that Alex would wake up. His mother calling him daily didn't help either. He knew she meant well, but it was a reminder that there was nothing he could do here to help Alex. Back home he would again just become a slave to the same old routine. Leo went to the front desk and asked for some paper and a pencil. Once he returned to the room, he pulled out his phone, set it up on its side with the photo of him and Alex on the screen, and began to draw it out.

He focused on Alex first. He managed to get every detail of him captured and ended with the sparkle in his eyes from the lights. Drawing helped him relax and took his mind off everything. He started shading the parts of his face to give it more texture and detail. Once he was happy with the outcome he moved on to drawing himself and the ocean. He managed to pass the whole day with one drawing, adding every little detail to it. He put it next to Alex on the little table.

"Alex, when I was back home I wanted so much to be free. Free from the king's grasp, free to live my life. But it's only going to hurt those around me… Is it really worth it?" He got up and started to take off the bandages around Alex's shoulder. He grabbed the cleaning pads and started to clean the area.

"Alex, you sacrificed everything. And here I have so much power and money, and yet can do nothing to help you." He started to tape back up Alex's arm. "Maybe I can give you hope." He leaned down and kissed Alex's head. He placed his hand over his cheek and gently brushed his skin with his thumb. "If you really don't have anything to live for… Then live for me." Leo took off his family ring and placed it on his finger. "If I get pulled back home before you wake, know I am always thinking of you."

Leo walked around the room, to get some exercise and give his body a chance to tire itself out before sitting back down next to Alex. His back hurt him more each day from leaning over the bed. His eyes felt like they could never cry again. He had cried so many nights till he fell asleep worried that the minute he closed his eyes it would be the last he saw Alex.

"Leo…" Leo heard a soft whisper and opened his eyes, he looked up to Alex.

"Leo.." It was so faint and Alex's mouth didn't seem to be moving. But he knew he heard something.

"Alex… Can you hear me?" He moved closer to him.

"Le…" Alex's breath fainted before he finished. But Leo knew he heard him. He ran out to the nurses.

"He is talking," he managed to push out between the tears. The nurse got up and came to the room. She opened Alex's eyes and flashed a light into them. There was no reaction. He took Alex's free hand.

"Agent Twist squeeze my hand if you can hear me." She waited but Alex did not squeeze her hand. She looked at Leo. " Prince Leonardo, you have been here a long time, and you're very sleep-deprived. I really recommend you go somewhere to get a good night's rest."

"I'm okay, thank you for checking." The nurse turned to leave.

"Leo…" Alex whispered again. The nurse could not make out what he said but heard it too. She turned back around and listened to his chest.

"Leo," Alex softly repeated. She heard him this time. Her eyes widened. They had all seemed to lose any hope of him waking up.

"I have to go call his handler, and notify the doctor," said the nurse as she left the room. Leo took his hand again, his heart surging with hope.

"I'm here Alex," the prince whispered in his ear.

But there was no response.

Was he dreaming, or sleep talking? Either way, Leo was taking it as a good sign. There was hope again. He leaned down after a bit waiting for him to open his eyes. He kissed his cheek.

"If you have nothing to live for, live for me, Alex. Live so we can have a small chance." The nurse came back in. "

Janet will be here first thing in the morning." Leo nodded and turned back to Alex. He laid his head down by his legs and let his eyes drift closed.

* * *

Images of Leo passed through Alex's mind. He could hear his voice,

"If you have nothing to live for, live for me." Alex blinked his eyes open, it took a few minutes for him to fully adjust to the lights again. He looked around the room, his body stiff, only his eyes moved. He noticed the bear and roses and smiled at the gesture. He looked down and saw Leo. He sat up in the bed the best he could and put his hand on Leo's back.

"Leo…" He whispered it was hard for him to talk. Every breath he took sent him into an agonizing pain. It made him breathe harder and hurt more. He looked at his shoulder and saw the bandages. With his free hand, he lifted the blanket seeing his taped chest and bruised pecks. He could feel how swollen his face was. He mustered all the strength he could and squeezed Leo's hand. Leo slowly opened his eyes and sat up.

"Alex?" He started crying. "Tell me this isn't a dream."

"You're not dreaming, Princy," Alex's voice was raspy and sharp. Leo could hear the pain in his voice.

"I'll go get the nurse." Leo went to get up, and Alex squeezed his hand again.

"No… just sit with me." Leo nodded. Alex pushed himself up in the bed. "Princy, why are you all dressed up expecting me to die? You know one bullet won't get rid of me." Leo smiled,

"Even in this much pain, you're still an ass." He kissed his hand. " I was so worried."

Alex looked back at the flowers and bear. "How long have we been here?" Leo looked over at the bear.

"About two weeks." Alex squinted from the pain. Alex saw the drawing on the table as he looked around the room getting his bearings.

"Did you?…" Leo nodded. "It's amazing," Alex whispered. His eyes started to droop, the pain was a lot for him to handle. He started to fall back asleep, "Thank you for giving me a reason to fight, Leo." He spoke as he drifted back off.

Leo wanted more time, He wanted to tell him how he felt the

past two weeks. He wanted to tell him everything, he wanted to talk to him all night. He stood up and kissed Alex softly. Alex moved to the side of the bed and patted the empty spot next to him inviting Leo to join him. It was a tight fight and Leo dared not hold him with the pain he was in. But for the first night in two weeks, he was lying down. Alex used what strength he had left to put his arm over Leo. The two fell asleep.

* * *

Janet got to the hospital at six in the morning. She made her way up to the room. She relieved the agents at the door and entered. She saw the prince lying in the bed with Alex and shook her head.

"He did it again," she thought to herself. She sat in the chair and cleared her throat. Leo woke right up and got out of bed gently, trying not to disturb the patient. Alex let out a groan from the pain and slowly rolled over before opening his eyes.

" Welcome back Agent Twist," Janet spoke glad to see him awake.

"Oh stuff it with your Agent Twist bullshit. I am in far too much pain to deal with it" Alex griped. She shook her head.

"Already feeling back to normal I see." She looked to Leo, "And how are you feeling, well rested?" The bags under Leo's eyes were finally gone. Leo rubbed the back of his head, not sure how to respond.

She looked around the room and saw the drawing of the two. She picked it up.

"You know Leo, this is very good. I see a lot of talent here." She put the picture back down. "So do either of you wanna tell me the extent of the relationship here?" She looked at Alex, and down at his hand where the prince's ring now was. They both looked at each other. "Never mind, the less I know the better." She looked at Leo, "The king called, he wants us to either move you or send you back. The call is yours." Leo looked down at Alex.

"What about him?"

"He is in no condition to travel," Janet spoke quickly, not giving time for anyone to question her. Alex sat up in the bed biting his tongue.

"I'm fine, I can still protect him." She looked at him.

"And who is going to protect you, Alex, you can't even sit up. Remember, I taught you everything you know. I know how much pain you're in, and if you bite your tongue any harder you're going to bite right through it."

Alex could feel his face on fire, he was getting emotional again, and if he could he would have gone off on her, but the pain held him back. Leo looked at him and squeezed his hand.

"I will, Janet. I'll protect him, but I'll need you to teach me." Leo looked at her and waited for her response.

"You aren't going to accept any other agent?" asked Janet. Leo shook his head with a hard look in his eyes. "We only have a week." She took off her blazer and stood up. " It won't be easy, and it will hurt, you're no longer a prince to me during training."

"Janet, no," Alex spoke out. "I couldn't walk for a week." Janet walked to Leonardo, her hand clenched into fists. Leo let go of Alex and met her halfway.

"Then I guess it's a good thing we are already at a hospital," Janet said smirking, it had been a long time since she got to spar. Leo went to punch her. She grabbed his arm and tossed him over her shoulder. Alex winced at the sight. Leo felt a pain that went from his tailbone up his back. He was slow to get to his feet.

Leo got back up and turned to Janet. She cracked her neck and flagged him back. Alex sat up looking around the room quickly. He spotted the tray from Leo's last meal. He grabbed it and tossed it under Janet's foot as she went to grab Leo's arm again. Janet's foot landed on the tray and her foot slipped out from under her.

"I can protect him, and myself Janet, that's enough of this," sniped Alex. Janet got back to her feet and grabbed her blazer. She walked towards Leo and whispered in his ear.

"He is right, he can protect you even in the state he is in." She went to the door, "I'm going to get food. Do you two want anything?" Alex sat up again.

"Some clothing would be great, maybe a shot of whisky, and some damn pain meds." Janet rolled her eyes and walked out the door. Leo walked over to the bed and looked down at Alex.

"I only want you to protect me," Leo spoke softly to Alex who laid back in the bed and closed his eyes.

"If that is your wish Princy," Alex spoke softly.

* * *

Janet came back to the room and looked at Leo.

"I spoke with the King and Queen," she reported.

Leo sighed, "How did that go?" She tilted her head to the side.

"They are not happy you are staying here," She looked over at Alex, "And even less happy he is still the one assigned to you." Leo stood up.

61

" I don't care what they think, it's my life, I'm staying." Janet raised her hand,

"I know I fought for you. You're staying." She nodded in the direction of Alex. "Is he asleep?" Leo nodded and she took off her blazer. "You promise to protect him and stay safe yourself?" She held up her hands for Leo to punch. Leo nodded and started matching her left and right.

* * *

"Okay now let's start with defense, block ready?" Janet waited for Leo to nod and started swinging at him with her palms. Leo managed to keep up with her. He grabbed her arm and went to toss her over his shoulder, but Janet didn't budge. They were so focused on sparring that they did not notice Alex get out of bed. Janet pulled her arm back and before she could swing, Alex flipped her over his shoulder. He stayed hunched over and Leo ran to him. He put his arm over his shoulders.

"I said enough Janet, I do not need protection." Alex panted, hunched over. He looked at Leo while holding his stomach. "Widen your stance, and tighten your back. Flipping someone is not all strength." Leo helped Alex back to the bed and covered him back up. Alex wiped a little blood off Leo's nose as he had a small cut. "Go wash that before it gets infected."

that before it gets infected."

Seven

Deep Cover

Janet reached down into her bag and pulled out a file. "Alex if you take this mission . . ." He looked at her,

"Not if, I am," Alex replied as she slid the file on the table.

"You are on your own, you are in deep cover. The agency will continue to send you checks, but that's it. You can not contact us, you must use burners." Alex groaned as he sat up and grabbed the file.

"I know the drill mom." She looked at him concerned.

" Please Alex take this seriously," Alex could hear the worry in her voice, he looked up at her and smiled.

"Yes, director." He opened the file and took a look through it. There was not much to go off on.

The mission was titled Crowns Agent, and had the prince's information in it, and an address, 200 Lake Underhill Blvd. PA

63

"I'll come up every so often to check on you guys of course, but no contact by any means, only if.." She paused when she heard the bathroom door handle. She sat back down and smiled.

"Not too bad Prince Leonardo for your first time sparring. Careful Alex he might just give you a run for your money," said Janet as she stood up when her phone rang. She went to leave and stopped. "Your flight leaves tomorrow, tickets are in the file, make sure you can walk by then Alex." She walked to the bed and hugged him. "Be safe out there Alex." Janet dried her tearful eyes and went to the door. "Your mission starts now. Agent Twist."

As Janet walked out of the room they saw the other agents leave the room. A nurse walked into the room and placed a sweatshirt and sweatpants on the bed then closed the door without a word. Alex stood up and removed the gown. He tried to bend over to put on the pants. He could not even bend halfway over. He sucked his lips in and bit his tongue trying to hide the amount of pain he was in. Leo walked over to help him.

Alex looked at the clothing with disgust, but it would have to do for now. They did not bring him any underwear, and Alex just nodded. Leo went down onto his knees to help get the pants on Alex. He kept his eyes down to the floor to respect Alex's space. He grabbed the shirt and slid it over his head. Alex was not able to even lift his arms above his head.

Alex sat down on the bed and reached for the coffee Janet got for him hoping it would do something to help his mood if not his healing. The doctor came into the room and grabbed his chart from the foot of the bed. Flipping through the papers.

"I was told you're looking to leave Mr. Twist." The doctor

spoke without looking at either of them. "I would have to strongly suggest against that course of action. You're in no condition to leave any time soon. It will take more time for your ribs to heal not to mention that wound on your shoulder."

"I'll manage," Alex spoke with a heavy breath.

"I will have the nurse bring in some supplies and medication for you." He put the chart back and walked out of the room.

"We can stay here one more night Alex." He shook his head in response,

"We have to grab some supplies." He felt his hair, "And I need a shower." Alex picked at the suit Leo was in. "Maybe get you into some real clothing." Leo laughed and fixed his blazer.

"What's wrong with my suit?" he asked haughtily.

"Nothing if you wanna be a stick in the mud. I mean you pull it off, but come on." The nurse came in with a bag.

"Here are some painkillers, bandages, and alcohol pads. You can go whenever you are ready," and with that, she turned and walked out the door. Alex sat up in the bed and scooted his way to the edge. He grabbed the photo Leo drew for him, folded it up, and put it into his pocket. Leo grabbed the bag of medicines and put Alex's arm over his shoulder.

As they went to walk out of the room an orderly showed up with a wheelchair to escort them out and Alex groused. Leo ordered him to sit in the wheelchair and pushed him out of the hospital.

"See, I can be helpful too." Leo joked, enjoying the feeling of being needed.

"Just wait Princy," Alex threatened.

By the time they made it out of the hospital, their Uber was waiting for them. They proceeded through the city til they ended up at Alex's apartment.

"Can you get the spare key?" He asked Leo, pointing to his doormat. Leo bent down and grabbed it before unlocking it. "Don't mind the…" The door swung open. His studio was cleaned up. His clothing was all folded, paper wrappers he had on the table in the garbage. Alex mumbled under his breath. "Janet." She knew they were going to stop there.

Leo closed the door while Alex leaned against the wall.

"So the top agent at the CIA keeps his spare key under the doormat?" Leo asked with a sly grin. Alex looked around his house,

"When you don't have much there isn't a reason for secrets." Alex put his arm over Leo again and walked to the closet. He grabbed a long sky-blue t-shirt and some jeans that were too big for him and handed them to Leo. "These should fit you." Alex pointed to the bathroom and sat on a chair in the kitchen. "I'll be okay, go."

Leo walked into the bathroom but didn't close the door, he wanted to keep an ear out for Alex in case he needed anything. Once Alex heard the water hitting Leo's body he pulled out his phone and called Janet.

"Alex, I told you . . ."

"Janet do me a favor, call whoever you have to, I want a room in the house to have…"

Leo turned off the water and dressed quickly. Though the shower was small and falling apart it felt nice to him. He enjoyed the small space, it felt more like a home to him in the minutes he had been there than his own. He walked out of the bathroom and back to Alex who stood up and held onto the wall walking to the bathroom himself.

"I'm gonna shower." Leo walked with him and took off Alex's shirt and undid the bandages.

"I'll be on the couch if you need me," Leo said as he turned toward the small living room. Alex closed the door and stepped into the shower. He let out a scream, each drop of water felt like a bullet going through him. Leo was pounding on the door but Alex locked it. After a few minutes, he became numb to the pain.

He turned off the water and dried off the best he could. He wrapped the towel around himself and opened the door. Leo was there waiting for him. Alex fell for a moment into his arms. Leo picked him up and laid him in his bed. Leo looked at the clock that read 8 pm. He went to the kitchen and made grilled cheese, he brought them to the bed where Alex was lying. Alex looked around the room,

"Way to go Princy, I still have a house." Alex smiled at him. The grilled cheese was charcoal, but he still ate it. "Thank you."

Leo rummaged through the bag from the hospital.

"We need to tape you back up." Alex nodded in agreement. Leo started to wrap his shoulder, and Alex took a deep breath. "Sorry." He finished taping up Alex's shoulder and gently kissed it.

"The flight leaves at 3, let's try and get a little rest while we can." Leo nodded and went to go to the couch. Alex grabbed his hand.

"Now Prince, would I make someone of your prestige sleep on the couch?" He patted the bed next to him. Leo crawled over Alex carefully so as not to injure him further. Alex's bed was pushed against the wall with little room in front of it. In Leo's mind, this was the safest way to get in bed. He laid his head on the pillow next to Alex's and faced the wall. Alex took a deep breath as he draped his arm over Leo.

"I can protect you better in my arms." Leo gently snuggled

back into Alex and fell asleep. Alex tried to sleep but no matter how he lay he could not get comfortable.

* * *

The clock read midnight, and Alex was fed up. He forced himself out of the bed and used the wall as a crutch. He went to the kitchen and made eggs for Leo. He walked to the closet, packed some clothes, and put three guns in his bag. He put the file on top of the bag and made his way back to the bed. He sat on the edge of it and twisted through his pain.

"Leo.." Leo stirred a bit but didn't wake. Alex leaned down and tousled his hair out of his face. "Leo, come on." Leo sat up and was greeted by breakfast in bed. He looked at Alex worried,

"I could have made the food," Leo spoke with a yawn and Alex smiled.

"True, but I like my house." Leo ate the food while Alex sat next to him. "It's time to go."

Alex went to stand and Leo helped him up. Leo grabbed the bag Alex left by the door and flung it over his shoulder. They locked the door and headed outside for their Uber.

* * *

Alex and Leo arrived at the airport around 1:30am. When they got to the airport security a security guard met them with a wheelchair.

"No," Alex shouted at him.

"Come on Alex, for now. It's a big airport." Leo begged.

"I am not helpless, I can manage. We have plenty of time

to get there." Alex spoke, pushing the chair to the side and clenching Leo's shoulder.

They made their way inside. Leo was half asleep, and Alex was on high alert. He knew until they got in the air Leo wouldn't be safe. They were escorted by security to the front of the line. Leo walked through the metal detector. Alex put his gun and badge on the belt but couldn't walk on his own through it. Leo held him up as the machine went off. He grabbed his badge and put his gun back into the top of his pants.

They walked to the gate where they took their seats. Leo flagged a security guard and asked him to get them some coffee. The guard did so, seeing the shape Alex was in. Alex sipped his coffee watching everyone closely as they walked by them.

Soon the chairs began to fill around them and the flight attendants started speaking over the intercom.

"Now boarding flight 227 to Philadelphia International." Leo stood up and helped Alex.

"We will start with.." The Flight attendant paused. "Our Crown royalty members." Alex nudged Leo and they started walking. Alex didn't take his eyes off one guy who stared at them since they sat down. The guy reached into his pocket. Alex pushed Leo into the tunnel and yelled,

"Get on the plane." Alex pulled out his gun and pointed it at the man. "CIA get on the ground." The guy took his hand out of his pocket and raised it high. He quickly fell to the floor.

Two agents wearing black ran over and put the guy in cuffs before patting him down. They found two different guns and a fake security badge, which explained how he got through the TSA. Alex started to faint, he grabbed onto the wall. The flight attendant grabbed him and helped him to the tunnel.

She brought Alex to his seat next to Leo.

"First class, there is a first for everything," Alex thought to himself.

"What happened? You can barely walk again and you're shaking." Leo took Alex's hands in his. Leo noticed that his shoulder was wet as well. He rolled up Alex's sleeve and saw the bandage was red.

"I'm fine." Leo lifted the bandages gently and saw that Alex had popped some of the staples that were in his arm.

"Alex, what happened?" Alex grabbed the bottle of water that was there and took a sip, before turning back to Leo.

"Nothing Princy, you are safe."

Leo grabbed their little first aid kit and found some gauze. He took the bottle of antiseptic from Alex and poured it on the cloth. He gently rubbed his shoulder removing some of the blood. He then placed more gauze on the wound and added some tape to hold it in place. The plane started to get loaded. At the end of the line, a little boy with his mother walked onto the plane. He was holding onto his mother's hand. The boy stopped and waved at Alex. Alex smiled and waved back.

"When I grow up I wanna be a cool CIA agent like you." The boy said, smiling at him.

"Listen, buddy, if you work really hard you can do even more than that." The mother turned and picked him up, and looked at Alex.

"Thank you so much." Alex nodded and leaned back in his chair.

"So you do have a soft side?" Leo said to Alex. Alex turned and hit Leo in the chest.

"This is your captain speaking, we have been cleared for take off. We expect to land today at around nine tonight. We ask that until you are instructed otherwise remain seated and have your seat belts fastened. We will be serving meals and drinks shortly. Enjoy your flight."

The plane took off shortly after and they were miles in the air pretty quickly. Leo turned on his phone, connected to Wi-Fi, and checked the news. He put in one earbud so he could still hear Alex if need be.

"Still the threats continue to rain in. King Richard and Queen Sarah have not been out of their house in over a month. The threats are getting worse, and we just found out an assassination attempt was made on Prince Leonardo as well. Even out of the country, the royal family does not seem to be safe. There is still no word on the safety, and health of the young Prince..." Alex put his hand over the phone, and turned it off.

"Hey it's going to be a long flight, don't worry yourself. Your family is safe." Leo felt his eyes fill with tears. Alex put his arm around Leo and pulled him in close. "And I won't let anything happen to you."

"I may not really know them much, or ever get to see them very often, but they are my family, I love them. If anything happens..." Alex kissed Leo's head.

"Listen, those guards are good for two things at your castle. Protecting stuck-up rich people, and a good laugh." Leo shook his head.

"You always know what to say, don't you Alex? They sat there in silence for a bit. "It seems like you know everything about me. And don't say yeah it's my job too." Alex chuckled,

"Two weeks was far too long of a time alone with Janet I see." He paused, "Well what do you want to know?" Leo thought for a moment.

"Tell me about your family." Alex's smile left. He had not thought about them for a long time.

"My mother was never part of my life. She left when I was only a year old. She couldn't handle moving every year. My father was a member of the CIA. He was highly decorated, until…" Alex paused. "Until my sixteenth birthday. Every year my father made it special. He spent the whole day with me. He turned his phone off and took no work calls. It was the one time of the year we were a normal family.

That year he had been working on a highly classified project, his partner in training was Janet actually. I think she was around 20 at the time. We went out fishing that year." Alex closed his eyes remembering the scene. He could still smell the lake.

" I hated fishing, but I knew it made my Dad happy." Alex got a little choked up. "Janet tried to call him a hundred times that day. It was code Magenta. Someone was after him. They knew our exact location and when we would be there. Someone inside the agency. My father looked around the area and noticed that things were too peaceful, there were no birds and it was too quiet. He rowed the boat to go back to shore only an hour after being out there when we heard a loud bang. The next thing I remember I was in Janet's arms."

Leo looked at Alex and wiped away the tears falling down his face. "He never wanted me to join, but I wanted to keep his legacy alive. After that Janet took me in and raised me til I was 18. On my 18th birthday, I tracked down the man who killed my father. Janet caught me just before I…."

Alex was cut off by a kiss from Leo. "I'm so sorry, if I had known I would not have asked you to relive that. I can't even start to imagine." Alex folded down the tray in front of him and propped his phone on it.

"Let's watch a movie, I'll even let you pick Princy."

Eight

A New Start

"This is your captain speaking please remain seated as we will shortly start our descent to Philadelphia International. The time is now 8:50 pm, the temperature is 20 degrees. It is a beautiful night for a walk and the stars are bright. Thank you again for flying with us, and have a Merry Christmas. " Alex woke to the sound of the captain's voice, but Leo didn't move.

"Leo." Alex spoke half asleep, "We are landing soon." Leo sat back in his chair and looked outside. His breath was taken by the sight of all the stars out. The plane touched down and jerked around, it took everything in Alex not to scream from the pain. The aircraft came to a complete stop and Leo helped him to his feet. They exited the plane and walked through the tunnel. Leo clenched on to his hand,

"Ready for a new start?" Leo asked. Alex looked at him and smiled.

"Yeah."

They left the airport and hopped in a cab. Alex told them the address. They drove for about an hour and ended up in a small town. There were shops along the whole main street and small diners. It looked like some town out of a Hallmark Movie. Leo's face lit up; he dreamed of living somewhere like this. The car stopped in front of a modest-sized house with a white picket fence circling it. Alex couldn't hide his smile as he saw the wraparound porch which had two hand-made rocking chairs on it. As they walked to the door he let his hand graze the chair admiring the craftsmanship and finish.

Alex opened the door, and they were greeted by the smell of a Douglas fir. In the foyer, there was a huge tree lit with rainbow lights. It had been decorated with classic red, green, and white ornaments. There were rows of garland and on top a beautiful shining bright star. At the bottom of the tree was a small tree skirt around it that was red, and the tree stood in a sled holder. Alex looked over at Leo,

"Welcome home." Leo had the biggest smile on his face. This felt like a dream to him. It was everything he had ever written about in his journal. He loved every inch of the remodeled house. "You are watering the tree." He joked with Leo.

Alex and Leo's shoes were soaked from the snow outside so they took them off and walked into the living room. The fireplace was burning with a warm glow, and there were two stockings hung on it. One for each of them. Alex walked around the main floor with Leo as his crutch. The kitchen was huge. It had two ovens and a countertop stove. A center island with a marble top sat in the middle of it. There were benches on either side of it. There was a card on the counter as well. Leo noticed the card and grabbed it. He opened it up and saw it was from Janet. He handed it to Alex.

"Agent Twist, your father never wanted this life for you. Hell, I did not want this life for you. Your father built this house when he was your age. He always wanted to settle down and bring you here himself." Alex felt a tear roll down his cheek. *"I am so sad to see you go, but after your mission Alex, you are relieved of your duties. The only thing we ever agreed on is that you are not a killer, this job has changed you, and I want you to remember the sweet boy you are. You have to find yourself. I already saw a spark of that again the way you look at him. I have given you everything you need Alex, it's up to you now to make this home. While I will miss you much, I know you'll be happy. Merry Christmas Alex.."*

Love

Janet.

Alex tossed the note on the counter, and let himself cry, for the first time he felt like he had a family again. Yet at the same time, he felt like he just lost it all over again.

"Alex," Leo spoke, watching his reaction. Alex pushed back up to his feet.

"This was her plan all along. Damn, bitch is too smart for her own good." He smiled. Someone hung some fliers on the fridge that showed events going on in the town.

"Oh, it's a big tree-lighting event." Leo pointed. "Maybe if you're up for it we can go." Alex nodded. Leo was like a kid in a candy store. His eyes darted around the house. He walked to the other side of the stairs. There was a small sitting room with some fiction books all around. Each book by James Patterson. Alex's favorite author. Alex grabbed one of the books and opened it. "Dear Alex, may you find your way through the darkness and into the light. "James Patterson"

She really did think of everything. Alex and Leo made their way up the grand staircase slowly. Once up there they saw a huge sitting area that overlooked the main floor. There was a handmade pool table that had "Dom Twist" engraved on it. It was a table his dad made. Leo noticed the name and pointed it out to Alex.

"Did your dad . . .?" Alex nodded. They walked to the closed door and opened it.

"OH MY." Leo covered his mouth. Inside the room were paintings he only dreamed of seeing. Janet made a few calls as per Alex's request and made the room just as he wanted it to be. Sure they were all copies but he knew Leo would love it. In the center of the room was an easel with a small table next to it filled with paints and pencils. Behind it was a window that overlooked a huge backyard with a gazebo. A small couch sat in front of the window.

"Do you like it?" Alex asked Leo.

"Like it, Alex I love it. But how did they know? " Alex replied with a smile, "I made a call last night to Janet." Seeing Leo so happy, and relaxed for the first time since they met made Alex smile. It was as though every concern flew from his mind. Leo opened the case that was sitting on the table admiring the different shades that were there for him to choose from. He was thinking of all the endless possibilities.

"Alex, this is amazing. It's like my every dream came true."

Alex hunched over and grabbed his middle. The pain meds were starting to wear off.

"Leo…" He called out in pain. He felt himself about to fall over. Leo closed the case and ran over to Alex. With his arms wrapped around him, he guided them back out of the room and to the double doors he guessed were the bedroom.

He pushed them open and was surprised to find there was a canopy bed that took his breath away, simple but handmade. Leo sat Alex on the bed and took off his shirt, and pants, and guided him down gently. Leo went to the last room but it was locked. It completely piqued his curiosity. He tried to pick the lock with his card but it didn't work. He shrugged for now and joined Alex again. He pulled the blanket up a bit exposing silk sheets. He turned off the light and turned on the fireplace in their room.

Their room, he liked the sound of that. He laid down and moved close to Alex who was finally able to settle and relax.

* * *

Alex was woken up by the doorbell. He sat up and forced himself to get his pants on. He went downstairs with his gun in hand. He opened the chain and looked through the door hole. Standing there was a woman in her mid-thirties. She had cookies in her hand. He opened the door and hid the gun behind it.

"Hello," she said. "I made some cookies for you, our little way of welcoming you to town." Alex took the cookies and put them on the counter. She tried to look in the house, he could tell she was very curious and was dying to see inside. "We live right over there." She pointed at the house two doors down. Alex pulled the door open and invited her in. She did not think twice and walked in. Her jaw dropped, as she spun around looking at the house.

Alex walked into the kitchen and put the tray of cookies on the counter, before offering her a seat on the couch. Alex took a seat across from her.

"Your tree is amazing. I have never seen one so beautifully decorated before." Alex smiled,

"Thank you, It makes the place feel like a home, I was about to make some coffee. Can I get you anything?" She stood up, "That would be lovely". She followed Alex into the kitchen. "I'm Alex by the way. Alex Twist." It took her a moment to respond. "I'm Silvia, it's a pleasure to meet you." Alex started to look through the cabinets for the coffee, once he found it he made a pot. Alex sat at the island and put a cup down for her. He saw the note from Janet and quickly grabbed it and put it in his pocket.

"I moved here about five years ago," Sylvia started. "I was trying to purchase this home, it has been empty for so many years you know." She spoke with jealousy anything but hidden in her voice.

"I just found out my father left it to me in his will, he built it from scratch you know." She shook her head,

"I did not, but that is amazing." She drank her coffee and explained to Alex that the town is quite small, there are only about 200 people who live in it. So it is pretty quiet, and you get to know everyone quickly.

Leo woke up and heard the voices downstairs. He quickly dressed and made his way to the kitchen.

"Do you live here on your own?" She asked as Leo walked in from behind her. Alex smiled, looking at Leo, who chose to put on some slacks and slick his hair back. He had a tank top on with an open button-up.

"No." Leo walked around the counter to stand next to Alex. "Sylvia this is . . ." Her eyes lit up. She stood up and bowed.

"Your Highness, I am so sorry I didn't know." She stood back up.

"Is it okay if we keep "Your Highness" at a minimum? I don't want everyone to know who I am if they don't already." She nodded.

"It's truly an honor though." Leo was going to have some fun with this. He walked over, took her hand, and bowed, kissing it. They watched as she nearly fell over.

"Sylvia brought us some homemade cookies." Leo turned and saw Alex holding the platter in his hand. Leo grabbed one,

"Oh, did she?" He took a bite of it. "It's pretty good." He held the cookie up to Alex and he took a small bite of it.

"It is amazing Sylvia, you have to share the receipt." He watched as her face went red, and she stood again.

"Are you two together?" Leo looked at Alex. Alex smiled and nodded his head. She nearly screamed.

"I do have to be going. I have to bring my son to school soon." Leo and Alex smiled. Leo led her back to the door followed behind by Alex. He held the door open for her and she nearly screamed again. He closed the door behind her"

Well someone has a fan, Princy." Leo walked to Alex and kissed his cheek.

"Shush you. How are you feeling this morning?" Alex opened the bottle of pills in his pocket and took one.

"A bit better but still really hurt." Alex walked back to the kitchen. He turned to the pot of coffee again. He pulled a mug down, and Leo walked behind. He placed his arms on either side of him.

"What are the plans today?"

Alex turned around and handed him his coffee.

"Thought we could maybe walk around the town, or we could hang out here, and you can do some painting. I wouldn't mind seeing you work." Leo smiled, "that would be nice but on one condition."

"You have to model for me," Leo demanded.

"You got a deal." They finished their morning coffee and went upstairs. Alex walked to his closet and opened it up. Janet knew his style so he wanted to see what she had picked out for him. He grabbed a pair of jeans that had holes in the right leg and a sweater that had a distressed look to it. Alex pushed open the door after he changed and Leo was there speechless. "That looks great!", he grabbed a beanie and draped it over his head. "Now the outfit is complete. "

"Before anything, I need a haircut, I wanna look presentable when you paint me," Alex spoke looking into Leo's eyes.

"Fine, but you already look amazing Alex." Leo grabbed a 'Di Lusso jacket from his closet and was ready to go.

Leo and Alex headed out the door, their arms interlocked. Alex was able to walk a little easier. Alex locked the door and put the key in his pocket. Leo rested his head on his shoulder as they walked through town. They passed various small boutiques and vintage shops. Smells were all over as they walked down the main road. They could smell homemade soaps as they passed one shop, and before they even passed through it, they could smell sausage cooking. It was a nice feeling. Every person they passed stopped them to say hello and welcome them. It truly was a lovely town.

A pole was spinning with red and white stripes. They had found the local barber. They walked in and the bell chimed.

"Be with you in a minute." Leo and Alex took a seat on the chairs and waited. One of the ladies walked up, "Never seen either of you two in town before."

"We are new in town," Alex spoke clearly, and she nodded.

"Who wants to go first?" Leo stood up.

"Oh, what are you getting done?" Alex asked. Leo leaned down and kissed his cheek.

" I thought if I colored my hair it might be easier to blend in for us." Alex nodded. The lady grabbed some swatches and held them to Leo. He pointed at the red swatch, it was a reddish blond leaning more on the red side. She draped the cape over him and went in the back to mix the color. She came back and started to put it on his head. It didn't take more than 10 minutes.

She went over and grabbed Alex, and brought him to the chair next to Leo.

"What about you?" Alex took out his phone and showed her a photo of a wolf cut. She cut his hair with enough time to wash and style it. She brought Leo back and washed his hair. She proceeded to trim it a bit and style it so that it had more volume when he pushed it back. She walked them up to the counter and entered everything into the system.

"Okay, that comes to $60.00." Alex took out his wallet and paid the lady, then handed Leo the beanie to put it back on him. It still hurt to lift his arms at all. Leo placed the beanie on his head and smiled.

"You look great," Leo spoke as he brushed some hair behind Alex's ear.

"You don't look half bad yourself with red hair Princy."

They headed out the door and made their way across the street. Alex wanted to see the stores on the other side. There was a small grocery store, and next to it a jeweler who made their own jewelry. Alex stopped and tugged Leo's arm. He looked around at the beautiful options that were inside. Necklaces made of diamonds, and rings with all different colored gems. In the back corner was a small cabinet with earrings. Alex walked back there and took a look. Leo followed closely behind him. He saw Alex's eyes light up.

"See anything you like?" Leo asked, already knowing the answer. Alex was staring at the set of earrings that looked like swords. They were black with a bright red gem on the end of the handle.

"Hello." The jeweler said with a smile walking in from the back room. "Can I help you with anything?" Alex asked to see the set of earrings. The woman came over and opened the case. She took out the pair that Alex had his eyes glued to. She placed them on the counter and Alex picked them up admiring them. There were lines carved into the blades of the swords. There were smaller red gems along it as well made to look like blood.

"How much? " Leo asked. Alex turned the price tag over. $1,000 It read! Alex's jaw dropped. He backed up a bit from the counter and thanked her for letting him see them. The woman went to close the box they sat in.

"May I?" Leo asked, reaching his hand out for the box. She nodded and Leo took one out and held it up to Alex's ear.

"We will take them." She smiled and walked them to the counter.

"Are you sure?" Alex asked Leo.

"Of course, I'm sure they will look amazing on you."

Alex was starting to feel the pain in his chest again. He leaned over the counter.

"I love your ring if I may say so." The woman spoke, pointing at Alex's hand. He looked down at his hand and noticed Leo's ring. He puckered his face into a pout.

"Thank you." He turned to Leo and punched his chest. "When?" Leo smiled.

"At the hospital, you needed a reason to live, and I was being forced back home. I knew you would wake up, and wanted to make sure you remembered me." He rubbed the wolf pendant around his neck. Alex shook his head. Leo paid for the earrings and helped Alex put them in. Alex looked in the mirror and smiled.

"They go great with the new haircut, and bring out the sparkle in your eyes." Leo teased helping Alex put them in.

They left the jeweler and continued on their way home. Alex made one more stop and purchased a bouquet of flowers. He handpicked which ones he wanted. Leo stayed outside and called his family.

"Leonardo. How are you?" His mother spoke softly, holding back her tears. She wanted so badly to hold her son, to see his smile.

"I'm doing really well Mom. I colored my hair today. It matches yours, now." Alex wanted to give Leo some space as he guessed he was talking to his family, and he knew that wasn't always a walk in the park. So he stood close the door, watching him. Leo paced back and forth while talking to his mom. Alex gave Leo his space to talk to her and waited inside holding the flowers. Once Leo hung up the phone Alex walked out. He handed Leo the flowers.

"For you," Alex spoke, handing Leo the bag. Leo looked inside the bag and saw a bouquet of baby breath, three different color lilies, which was his favorite flower, and forget-me-nots.

Though the flowers are very different, and never seen together, it looked like they belonged.

"Lillies because I love them, but what are these other ones? Leo asked, pointing at the two-tone blue flowers.

"Those would be my favorite. Bluestars. They remind me

of the stars and what possibilities are out there. Alex points in the bag, and these are forget-me-nots. Because I never want to forget you, I never want you to forget me." Leo leaned down and kissed Alex.

"Never," Leo whispered to him.

Nine

A Simple Life

Alex and Leo removed their coats and hung them on the coat rack. They proceeded upstairs and into Leo's art studio. Alex sat on the couch while Leo put the flowers in the vase beside him.

"How should I pose?" Leo walked over to him and leaned him on his left side against the arm of the couch, He rested his head on his hand and laid the other across himself. "Paint me like one of your naked women, Princy." Alex impersonated Rose from Titanic. Leo smiled and went to the easel. He opened the case and started to paint.

"Can I ask you something?" Alex spoke, trying not to move too much. Leo nodded, continuing to paint. "Do you want to be King one day?" Alex asked.

"I'm not sure. I would love to live like this, to be free to do what I want. My father has sheltered me my whole life. I only really know how to be a prince. He always told me I was destined for it." He spoke impersonating his father. "I have to keep the bloodline in rule, Alex. My family worked hard to be where we are today." Alex never thought of it like that. He just assumed that it was handed to them. "It's up to me to keep their memory strong, and their traditions alive. The people depend on us, and it's my duty to them to rule."

Alex tilted his head a little more to see Leo behind the easel. "But Leo, what do you want?" Leo didn't answer right away, he was pondering.

"I want this. I want a home, not a castle. I want to be like everyone else, I want to be with you." Hearing that melted Alex's heart, but he knew he couldn't keep him from his family. "Would he be happier here with me?" Alex thought to himself. "Could he replace all he would be losing as a prince, as a King? Would it be selfish if he wanted him to stay here?"

"What about you Alex?" Leo asked.

"What about me?"

"Are you happy living in your apartment, working for the CIA? What do you wanna do?" Truthfully, Alex never really thought about it.

"I mean." He paused remembering the note from Janet. "That's all I know as well. I turned 18 and joined." He looked around the room and at Leo. "I could get used to a house and not some falling apart studio." Leo put his brush down.

"Alex. Come on, what do you want?" Alex was afraid to answer. He didn't want to say what he felt. How he wanted the same as Leo, he wanted to be here with him.

"I don't know what I would do if I stepped down, Leo."

Leo stood up and turned on the radio in the room, he lowered the volume a bit, before walking over to Alex. He extended his hand.

"Dance with me?" Alex took his hand and stood up. Leo slid his arms around Alex, who in turn rested his head on Leo's shoulder. Alex closed his eyes and swayed along with Leo.

"What do I want?" He looked up at Leo's blue eyes and smiled. "I… I want to be with you, Leo. Anywhere you are, wherever you go. If you're King or Prince. Whatever you decide to do, I want to protect you."

The song finished and Leo leaned down a bit and kissed Alex.

"I would love that." Alex looked up into his eyes,

"How's the painting coming there Princy." He went to walk over to it. Leo stopped him.

"No! You can't see it till it's done." He sat Alex back on the couch and continued to paint.

* * *

Leo finished painting Alex and moved on to the background, and Alex left the room. He went down to the kitchen to start making them dinner. He was very eager to cook something in the big kitchen they now had. He opened the fridge and saw fresh vegetables and chicken. He grabbed both and lightly buttered the pan. He chopped the food before starting to saute it. He let his mind wander off a bit while stirring the food around. He never believed in love at first sight.

"What is it about him? It feels so fast. His smile was so warm the first time I met him, even with everything going on it made me feel safe when it was my job to keep him safe." Alex thought.

The smell of garlic and chicken mixed with potatoes filled the house. The chicken was starting to brown and Leo snuck into the kitchen behind Alex.

"Well, doesn't that smell amazing?" He put his hands around Alex's waist. Alex took a spoon from the drawer beside him and scooped some of the sauce onto it. He turned and let Leo taste. "It tastes even better than it smells." Alex turned to him and asked,

"Can you grab some plates?"

Leo turned and opened up every cabinet looking for the plates. Alex turned and pulled the cabinet open that had see-through glass in it.

"In here." Leo grabbed two plates and brought them to Alex who spooned good helpings of food onto them.

They carried their plates to the dining room and sat across from each other, talking a little more while they ate. Alex learned that Leo has always wanted a dog, and Leo learned how Alex loves to do woodwork like his father did. Alex admitted to not being nearly as good, but Leo wanted to see it. They finished their food and brought the plates to the kitchen.

They were comfortably moving through the cleanup together. Alex boxed the remaining food up and Leo started to wash the dishes. Then, Leo dropped the first plate and it shattered. Alex ran over to him and checked his hand.

"You know you make it hard for me to do my job when I have to protect you from yourself." He smiled after making sure Leo was okay. Alex took all the glass out of the sink before letting Leo continue. Alex dried everything and put it away.

They walked to the living room, and Leo told Alex to stay put. He ran up the stairs. Leo shortly after came back down the stairs with his painting. He handed Alex the canvas. He turned it around to look at it and saw himself as he never did before. Leo captured everything from his freckles to the fine details on his earrings. The number of diamonds on the ring matched. The number of petals on each flower. He even captured the snow falling in the window. The lighting from the sun was perfect…

"My favorite part is your eyes, Alex. I can see how you really feel." Alex looked at his own eyes. He could feel that same sense of happiness he had experienced being there with him in the room.

Alex got up and went to the garage. He grabbed a hammer and some nails. He returned to the living room where he gingerly stood on a chair and hung the picture up above the fireplace. As he tried to carefully step down, he slipped and luckily landed in Leo's arms. He puckered his face into a pout.

"Falling for me Agent Twist?" Leo smugly smiled. Alex squinted.

"No, more like your clumsiness is rubbing off on me." Leo laughed and carried Alex to the couch and placed him down.

A timer started to go off in the kitchen. Leo went in, turned it off, and yelled to Alex, "What's the timer?"

"The oven Princy." Leo grabbed the pot holders off the counter and pulled down the oven door. His mouth started to water as inside he found a peach cobbler. Leo carefully took it out and placed it on the counter, turned off the oven, and rejoined Alex.

"Where did you learn to cook?" Alex smiled and changed the channel.

"Today on Master Chef." The Television played as Alex pointed to the television.

"A little of this, and Janet taught me. The cobbler was her recipe, I just made it better by adding a few extra ingredients." Leo smiled and put his arm around Alex. The fireplace was blazing in front of them. Alex picked up his feet onto the couch and covered up with the blanket that was hanging behind it. He tuned out the sound of the show and focused on the beating of Leo's heart.

* * *

Two weeks later the two woke up to the doorbell. Leo stayed in the room while Alex ran down the stairs. He was almost one hundred percent again. With his gun in hand, he looked through the peephole. He saw Janet standing there looking at her watch.

"Agent Twist I know you're right there," Alex smirked.

"And the color of the day is?" He yelled back to her. She took the key out of her pocket and opened the door fast. The door smacked Alex in the nose and he started to bleed a little.

"Red." He stood back holding his nose. "I brought the check with me this time. Christmas is almost here and the post is shit. I wanted to make sure you guys were doing okay." She took off her coat and sat on the couch.

"Sure, make yourself right at home. Can I get you anything?" Janet turned on the fireplace.

"Some coffee would be great. The flight here was horrid. And their coffee is worse than yours." Alex shot her a look and went to the kitchen. "I don't remember ordering a painting of you Alex?" She said knowing well where it came from. But she spoke loud enough for Alex to hear her. He came back out and handed her a cup. "I must say though Alex, you are glowing." She took a sip, "Yup just as bad as always." She put the cup on the table. "Are you two going to the tree lighting? I hear the town all gather for it." Alex nodded,

"Leo wants to go." He spoke with a smile.

Janet nodded. "It's Leo now. Exactly how close have you two gotten?" Alex felt his face flush red. "The painting really is amazing though. He has such talent." Alex looked up at it and said,

"Yeah, he does." Leo came down the stairs and Alex's face lit up. Janet stood.

"If you even think about bowing, so help me. . ."

"Maybe you two have been together too long." Janet joked as Leo was starting to sound American. "Leonardo. Nice to see you again." Leo walked up to her and hugged her. "This is all amazing Janet. The house is perfect."

"Shall we go out and grab breakfast.?" Janet asked, looking at the two. Leo was dressed and hair done, and Alex was still in his pajama bottoms and shirtless so he went to change.

"So Leo, Have you thought about going back home?" She asked, standing up and grabbing her coat.

"A little, but. . ." Alex came back down the stairs with his beanie on, and a pair of jeans and sweater.

"But. . .?" She repeated and followed his eye. "Oh." Janet tossed on her jacket and opened the door. They all headed down the street. Janet walked on one side of Leonardo and Alex on the other. Both of them were on high alert watching each person walk by, listening to conversations as they walked.

The walk was quiet, and Alex didn't hold Leo's hand this time. They turned into the Twisted Sisters, the local bakery that had amazing breakfast options. Alex and Leo sat on one side of the table while Janet sat on the other. Alex took Leo's hand under the table and watched as his face lit back up.

Denise came over. "Oh Alex, Leonardo who is your friend." Janet looked at her.

"Agent Johnson." Janet handed her the menu and replied, "What can I get for you?"

"I'll take coffee and one of the danishes please."

"The usual?" Denise asked Alex and Leo who nodded in response. Denise walked off, and Janet looked at them.

"Stop it," Alex told her.

"Stop what?" She knew exactly what he was talking about. She was profiling them, it was her strong suit at the agency. She was the best profiler, and Alex was the best undercover agent.

Denise came back with two cups of coffee, and a cup of tea for Leo.

"The food will be out shortly, love." She walked off.

"I spoke with your family today. Your mother and father are both missing you terribly." Leo rolled his eyes.

"So you spoke with my mother?" She nodded.

"You are spending too much time together." She joked again. "She does miss you, Leonardo." He tried to smile, but his eyes filled with tears.

"I miss her too, I'll be right back." Alex watched as he walked to the bathroom.

"You're not going to clear it?" Janet snapped. "It's a single-person bathroom, the light is out, the door opened and no one was in it." Alex sniped back to her. She squinted, and he turned back to her. "Let me do my job and you do yours. Why are you really here, Janet?"

"You do know me well." She pulled a file out of her jacket and slid it to Alex. He opened it and smiled as he read over the file. "They caught more of the mob after the royal family."

"That's good." Alex continued, thoughtfully.

"Alex there's more. The King is demanding that Leo come

back home. I managed to talk him down for now. But it's getting heated over there. He is worried sick. The threats are getting even worse. Has he seen anything on the news?" Alex shook his head,

"I have been trying to keep it all off his mind."

"Good," She spoke back.

"Janet, I do have a favor to ask. What are you doing on Christmas?" She shrugged. "Would you like to spend it with us?"

"What are you up to?" Janet smiled while questioning him. Alex took out a pen and wrote in the file. He slid it back to Janet. She opened it and took a glance.

"Mission accepted." She smiled at Alex after reading it and she could tell how much he cared for Leo. Leo rejoined them right before the food arrived.

Denise put the same pastry in front of Alex and Janet, and a stack of French toast in front of Leonardo and asked with a smile,

"Can I get you guys anything else?" Janet took out her card and handed it to her.

"No thank you." They all ate and left the bakery together.

"Alex, maybe you should talk to the owner, they can teach you how to make a decent cup of coffee." Janet joked and Alex kicked her from under the table. The three chatted about the beautiful small town, the house, and the weather while finishing their food for about an hour. When they were full and content they got up from the table and walked outside. The cool air hit their faces and made their eyes start to water.

"Well, this is where I leave you guys for now." Alex nodded and she gave them both a hug. "Look out for one another."

"Do you really have to go already?" Leo asked her.

"I know Alex can be a lot to handle but. . ." Alex nudged him.

"I have some business to attend to before I catch my flight back," Janet said. "Just got a new mission, the job keeps me on my feet." She turned and walked away, waving once more. Leo and Alex turned back around and headed home. Alex wrapped his arm around Leo's and rested his head on his shoulder for the walk.

Janet stopped and turned around once more to watch Alex. She smiled.

"He's finally happy." She spoke with a sigh of relief.

* * *

"Leo, are you almost ready?" Alex called up to him. Leo came down the stairs from his studio. Alex wiped some paint off his cheek. "You're always a mess," he said laughing. Leo grabbed his coat and they were off. They walked for 30 minutes to get to the center of town. Everyone from town was there. As they passed each little shop Alex noticed they were either in the process of closing or already closed.

It was freezing that night. Alex led Leo to a little stand where he got them some hot chocolate to warm their cold hands. On the stage was a group of kids singing Christmas carols. Leo was beaming as he looked at all the activity around them. He never got to do anything even close to this fun. There were roasted chestnuts over open fire being sold. There were stands for the local shops selling all kinds of festive decorations. He could smell meat pies in the distance.

As the evening wore on, the colder it got and Leo started shivering more. Alex moved behind him and held him close, before checking his watch. There were only two minutes left until the lighting. Leo turned into his embrace and laid his head on his chest.

The Mayor took the stage and his voice cheerfully boomed over the microphone, "Hello everyone, thank you all for coming out and spending the evening with us. It is times like this that I am so glad for the community we have here. Are you guys ready for the main event?" Everyone cheered. "Turn off the lights," the Mayor shouted. And all the street lights and park lamps went out. "HIT IT!" The Mayor shouted. The tree lit up, and all the decorations in the park went on as well. Alex looked behind them and all the lights in the street went red and green as well. There were decorations everywhere. "Merry Christmas everyone." As the mayor left the stage there were clapping and excited "ohs" and "ahs". When the excitement toned down everyone started to go their separate ways. Alex was enjoying the night so much he didn't want it to end, however, he could tell how cold Leo was. He took his hand and they headed back home.

Ten

A Royal Christmas

Alex's eyes snapped open and he stretched before sitting up to look down at Leo and smile. He leaned down and kissed his lips. "Merry Christmas Princy." Leo woke up and pulled him down into a hug. The two have gotten close in the past few weeks. Alex felt that there was nothing better than waking up next to Leo. After working at the CIA, it was nice to have something consistent in his life, and right now that was Leo. He smiled, slid his hand under his pillow, and held onto a small box.

"Merry Christmas, Alex." Leo kissed his cheek. Alex pulled himself back up and looked into Leo's eyes. The blanket was wrapped around Leo's waist exposing his shirtless chest. Alex gingerly balanced the box on his chest. Leo's face exploded into a huge smile, his eyes wide as he grabbed the box and sat up.

"What's this?" Leo asked, pulling the top off. Inside was a

ring made of silver painted black. It looked like a paintbrush that was bent around his finger. Diamonds make up the brush. Leo smiled looking at it, but hesitated taking it out as he looked at Alex waiting for an explanation.

"I'm not asking you to marry me, it is a promise ring." Leo took it out of the box and slid it onto his finger.

"And what exactly is the promise for?" Leo asked, looking at Alex, his eyes wide.

"A promise to always be there. To always protect you. Even after this mission ends, it's a promise to always…" He paused. Alex took a deep breath and was about to say the words he had never spoken to anyone. "To always love you." Leo smiled from ear to ear.

"Then Mr. Big Bad, secret agent, I accept." He kissed him deeply, pulling Leo into himself. Leo got out of bed and ran out of the room coming back with another canvas. He turned it around and showed Alex. "From our first date."

Alex looked at the painting, it had them both in it. Leo was kissing his cheek and Alex was smiling the biggest smile he could remember. Alex took the painting from him, and something fell from behind the canvas. Alex picked it up. It was a solid gold ring with diamonds around it. In the center was a forget-me-not.

"I, Prince Leonardo Cambrage of Britain promise to be by your side… Always. I promise to make you smile when you want to cry. I promise to love you unconditionally, and one day I hope to make you the happiest man alive." Alex put the painting on the bed, got up, and pulled Leo into a hug. He kissed him softly letting his lips linger for a moment on Leo's. Alex felt his heart start to flutter. It was the most romantic thing he had ever seen.

"You already do that." He spoke smiling and kissed him again while putting on the ring. He looked down at the painting, his heart feeling over full.

"Where should we hang it?" He asked Leo. Leo grabbed it and led him down to the grand stairs. He already had a spot for it. It had a light that hung down over it so there was always light on it. He hung it up.

"Well, what do you think?" Alex tilted his head.

"It's perfect." He hugged Leo and looked over at the clock sitting on the small table below the photo.

"Shit, is that the time?!," Alex spoke in a panic. Leo looked over at him.

"Yeah, why what's wrong." Alex rushed back to their room and quickly got ready.

"If we wanna eat what I had planned, we had to start cooking an hour ago." Alex quickly changed and tossed on the first thing he could find. He ended up in Leo's shirt and a pair of shorts. Leo grabbed Alex by the arm.

"It's okay if we eat a little late, let's enjoy the moment together." Alex nodded, grabbed an outfit from his closet, then showered and changed. Leo walked by him as he left the bathroom and entered after kissing his cheek.

Alex put on a nice blue button top but didn't button the first 5 buttons, and a pair of black slacks. He brushed his hair back and pulled it up, this had been the longest it had been, and he liked it that way. He put on his promise ring and the Royal ring on the middle finger of the other hand. He also put on one of the watches that were sitting on the counter and cracked the bathroom door open. Leo stopped and turned to Alex.

"Now doesn't that feel better, Alex? No need to rush, everything will work out." He held Alex by the arms and kissed him. "I'll be down after my shower." Alex took a deep breath and nodded his agreement before he headed down to the kitchen. He pulled out a turkey and started to prepare it. He set the oven and moved to chop all the vegetables he would need.

Just then the doorbell rang, and Alex ran over to it. He had a mixing bowl in hand, and his apron on. He opened the door, and Janet walked in with a hooded figure. Alex quickly put the bowl on the counter behind him that overlooked the living room and bowed.

"Your Majesty, I'm so glad you agreed to our invitation." The queen smiled and lifted Alex's head by gently lifting his chin.

"You do not need to bow, I am in your home, I am your guest, and I would never miss a chance to see my boy," she spoke softly. Alex led them to the main sitting area.

"May I get you anything?" He spoke standing straight.

"Really, relax Agent Twist, it's a holiday." The queen replied, laughing softly. Alex walked into the kitchen.

"If that is the case please call me Alex," Alex shouted back to her, and the queen and Janet followed. She took a seat at the small table in the kitchen.

"It already smells like Christmas here, Alex." Alex smiled, acknowledging her while mixing some ingredients.

Janet walked over to the counter.

"Anything I can do?" Alex handed her a grater and some carrots. "He joked with her, your mission if you choose to accept it is to grate. Grate like your life depends on it." Janet smiled and indeed grated like all their lives depended on it. Alex grabbed a glass and poured the queen a mimosa.

"May I help? I used to love cooking," the queen asked expectantly. Alex nodded gratefully and he joined them at the kitchen island. She picked up a peeler and started peeling some apples while humming softly to herself. It was quiet except for her humming which seemed to echo throughout the house.

"Alex, do you hear someone humming or am I losing my…" Leo turned the corner from the stairs and dropped a vase of flowers. His eyes instantly let out tears.

"Leonardo. Is that any way to greet your mother?" She held her arms out and walked over to him. Alex ran over to make sure he was okay. He kicked the pieces of glass to the side and started to clean it up.

"Mom…" Leo whispered as he let the tears fall down his face. She pulled him into a hug and he cried into her shoulder. Alex joined Janet in the kitchen. She elbowed him as they watched the two.

"Great call, Alex." Alex went to the foyer, pulled a gift from under the tree, and handed it to her.

"Merry Christmas, Janet." He spoke nicely to her for the first time in a long time and she smiled at him.

"You never said that to me, and actually meant it. Let's give them some space," Janet suggested, and Alex agreed. The queen and Leo went up to Leo's art studio and Janet and Alex went to the kitchen. Alex put the food into the oven and finished up the pie before joining Janet.

She waited for him before opening the present. She pulled the box top off and revealed a beautiful dancing diamond necklace, the light danced in and around it.

"I remember you used to always look at them when I lived with you, but could never afford one." She smiled and held it up for Alex to put it on her. He took off his apron and clasped it around her neck as she pulled her hair to the side.

"It's beautiful Alex. Thank you." She looked at him and noticed the ring on his finger. She pointed at it. "Something you want to tell me?" Alex covered his hand and blushed.

"It's from Leo." She leaned over the table and pulled his hand to her. She admired the simplicity, yet elegance of the ring.

"Did he…"

"No."

She nodded, "Then what is it?" Alex looked down at it and smiled.

"A promise," Alex spoke with a radiant glow around him.

She let his hand go. "The new painting is really nice." Alex felt his face flushing more and more.

"Another gift," Alex answered smiling. Janet poured herself a mimosa and folded her hands on the table. "You two seem to be getting really close, is it safe to call you an item at this point? Don't worry, I won't tell the agency." Alex smiled and leaned back in his chair.

"Yes."

* * *

"It's so good to see you, Mom," Leo said, offering her a seat on the couch in the studio. She looked around a bit before sitting. She admired the paintings that hung around the room. Mainly of flowers, and scenery.

"These are lovely, who made them?" Leo walked over to her.

"I did," Leo stated confidently as the queen took her seat.

"It's nice to know you got something from your mother other than her nose." She laughed and held her glass in one hand and patted the couch with the other.

"This is a lovely house. How have you been here in America?"

The queen questioned. Leo smiled shyly and replied,

"It's more of a home at this point, I have been good. Very, very good." The queen continued to smile, nodding slowly as she glanced down at the couch and said,

"Your Father was very against this trip you know," Leo nodded. "Things are still just as bad as when you left. The threats keep coming and there have been numerous attacks. I really want you to come back home, Leo." Leo nervously twisted the ring on his finger, and almost whispered,

"Mom, I." She raised her hand to silence him.

"Agent Twist seems to have recovered well." his mother said brightly. Leo nodded, smiling and hearing Alex's name. "Janet told me on the phone this was all his idea too. He seems like a sweet young man." Leo blushed a bit. "Can he protect you better than our Royal guards though?" The queen questioned her son's safety.

Leo did not think twice before speaking. "He is amazing at his job Mom, he has proven already he can, and on more than one occasion. Even when he could barely walk on his own." The queen smiled and Leo was falling right into her trap.

"And he takes care of you?" Leo felt anger rising as she continued her questions.

"We take care of each other," he replied sternly. She nodded looked at him squarely and asked,

"And he is the reason you don't want to come back to the castle?"

Leo took a deep breath, "No. I am not sure I want to be Prince." It was the first time he told his mother how he felt about it.

"You two look very happy together, how long do you think that will last?" It felt like a low blow and Leo felt a pain in his chest like never before.

"We will always be friends, he is merely doing his job. So what if we enjoy spending time together, isn't that what being friends is all about?" She looked at Leo for her final question.

"Do you love him?" Leo without thinking a moment answered immediately.

Leo stood and in a strong, raised voice said "Yes." She smiled.

"I just wanted to hear you say it, I saw the painting of you two in the hall. Leo dear, you've never looked so happy."

* * *

"Alex. Have you given any thought about the note I left you?" Alex was lost in his head and didn't hear her at first. Alex blinked and looked at Janet.

"I have." He spoke softly.

"I'm glad but care to tell me?" Alex got up and went to baist the turkey.

"I am going to be with Leo, no matter where he goes. Mission or not, I will protect him." Janet smiled. "There is the passion you need to have." She looked behind her to make sure no one was there. "But what will you do if he decides to stay here? Could you live with yourself knowing he chose you over the crown?" Alex turned to look at her after closing the oven.

"He doesn't want to be prince, but I'm ready no matter what." Janet's smile widened.

"I know you planned at least part of this, Janet. You assigned me to the case not because I was the best, but because you knew I would have to open up to keep him safe. You knew that I would have to let my guard down to get him to trust me.

But you were not expecting me to fall for him."

Janet folded her arms, "I had a feeling you would after I saw you look at him for the first time. But what do I know, it's not like I trained you and raised you or anything." Alex stood up, he saw a shadow run along the house. Janet stood just as fast. Alex looked up to the ceiling.

"Scorpion," Alex called to her. She nodded and ran to go upstairs. Alex pulled out his gun and cracked the back door.

* * *

"How long have you known Leo, that you were having feelings for him, and when were you going to tell your mother?" The Queen asked her son.

Leo closed his eyes. "I officially knew when he took me out for my birthday. But even before then the more time I spent with Alex the more I wanted to be with him. I was afraid of how you and Father would take it."

The queen gasped. "Leonardo, you think me, the queen, and more importantly your mother, would be so shallow as to be homophobic? We will save that for your father. Leo, I have known for a long time that being a prince was not meant for you. You are a dreamer, and if you choose to, you can abdicate. I will think no less of you. All I ever wanted was for you to be happy. I am just terrified that one person can't always be there to protect you. I value your safety a little more than your happiness."

"I have never felt safer than I do right now," the prince replied confidently. Just then Janet shouldered the door that Leo locked and busted it open. She tossed pillows on the ground.

"Get down." Janet watched out the window trying to locate

Alex.

"What's going on?" Leo asked. "Alex caught someone sneaking around the house." Leo went to get up and looked out the window. The queen grabbed his arm and whispered, "Do as she says." Leo nodded and stayed down.

Alex pushed the door open and held his gun at the ready. He circled the house and located four men in black suits standing on the side. He moved in closer.

"The queen is in there, along with the prince." One of the men said. He had no hair and hid his eyes behind sunglasses. Alex looked around and saw only four sets of tracks. Alex climbed a nearby tree and hit a button on his watch.

"Agent Twist to Mother Hen." Janet heard him talking to her from her necklace. She smiled, he learned so much from her that it even surprised her.

"Go ahead." She called back.

"The house is secure, if you hear anything inside the house, I failed. Permission to take out the targets."

"Granted Agent Twist, commence The Crowns Agent." Alex pulled his gun back out and took two deep breaths. He fired three shots, each finding their targets.

Three more men ran out of the woods.

"Three more men remain on the side of the building. I have no shot." Janet looked out the window and raised it. She fired a shot and killed the man where he stood.

"Agent Twist. Protect the Prince at all cost," Alex smiled, the last three men were running directly at the tree where he was. He slipped his feet between two branches and hung upside down, and pulled the second gun from its holster.

"Looking for me?" His eyes went wide, and he fired the remaining bullets.

"Agent Twist, come in. Agent Twist." Alex flipped down from the tree and started walking to the woods.

"Checking the perimeter, Mother Hen. Watch my six."

Alex walked through the trees following their footsteps and then headed back to the house.

"Targets eliminated, The crown is safe." He called Janet. Janet let out a sigh of relief and helped the queen and Leo to their feet. Leo looked at his mother and hugged her.

"Mom, I know he can protect me." She hugged him back and quietly said,

"I know he can." Alex went to the hose and washed his hands off. He opened the kitchen door as Janet was making a call, "Code white."

About thirty minutes passed, and agents showed up within the minute and cleaned the area, they took the bodies and cleared the blood. They explained to the neighbors what happened, and left.

Leo ran down the stairs and hugged Alex. He looked him up and down,

"Are you okay?" Alex nodded and looked back at the queen.

"Are you two okay?" Alex asked.

"We are." The queen reported. "And you will be happy to know I have decided to let Leonardo stay here as long as he wishes. You have proven to me that you can protect him. I know he is in good hands."

Leo turned to his mother, "You mean it, but the king?" Leo was excited to have his mother's blessing.

"I will handle your father." Janet turned the corner from the front door and she was talking to one of the agents.

"Yeah, I'm fine too. Thanks for asking Alex." The queen tried to cut the tension and asked, "The real question here is, is the turkey okay? " Alex quickly turned and took it out of the oven.

Eleven

Long Goodbyes

❧❦❧

Alex finished cooking and placed the food on the table. Leo started to set the table, and pour drinks. Janet sat at one side of the table next to the queen. Leo and Alex sat on the other. Alex and Leo dished out the food, smiling every time their eyes met. The queen leaned into Janet and whispered,

"You would never know how long they knew each other, and I have never seen Leo so happy." Janet held her hand over her plate so the two stopped putting food on it. She looked at the queen and whispered back, "I could definitely say the same about Alex." The two finally sat down after handing everything out.

"Your Majesty?" Alex questioned, "I was thinking it would be a good idea for Leonardo to sell some of his artwork. They are far too beautiful to only be in one house."

The Queen smiled. "I couldn't agree more." She looked at

Leo who was blushing at Alex's comment. "I must ask Alex," The queen dabbed her mouth with her napkin before placing it back onto her lap. "Do you intend to make every dream of my son's come true? You already turned him into an artist." Alex smiled, Leo must have told her he set up the studio.

"The skill is all him, I just put the brush in his hands." Leo took Alex's hand. "But as long as it is in my power, Your Majesty, I will make sure every dream he has comes true."

The queen smiled softly, and she turned and looked at Leo.

"Your father promised me the same thing." Leo squeezed Alex's hand. "Janet tells me your father built this place Alex, did you inherit any of his special skills?" The queen asked. He swallowed, and replied sheepishly,

"I dabbled a bit with woodworking and writing, but nothing special." She tilted her head,

"You're a writer? Let's hear something if you don't mind?" This also intrigued Janet who put her fork down for the first time since the food was put on the table.

"Yes Alex, let's hear something." Janet poked in.

Alex's face was redder than the apples in the bowl behind him. "With all due respect, I will have to decline. I have nothing prepared." The queen chuckled, "That is perfectly fine, make something up, we will not judge you too harshly." Alex put his fork down and knocked on the table lightly. He took a deep breath.

"My heart skips a beat when I hear you call my name, as my love for you is like flame. Growing more we give it life, yet I find myself with an internal strife. I have let my guard down, Will it cost the crown? I haven't a second thought that loving you is all I have ever sought."

Alex picked back up his fork and continued to eat.

Everyone else around the table gawked at him, their mouths hanging open.

"I never knew you could write Alex. Even after all these years, you managed to keep that a secret from me." Janette said smiling.

"You don't know everything, Janet," Alex replied teasing.

The queen dried her eyes, understanding the depth of what Alex must feel for her boy. "I'm glad you two have found each other. So many people go through life never knowing happiness or love." The queen spoke softly.

The four finished dinner, and Janet helped Alex begin cleaning up. She paused and turned to him, and handed him a key, a blood-stained key. "The extra room upstairs." Alex looked at her questioningly, then excused himself and ran up the stairs. Leo went to go after him but Janet grabbed his arm.

"He will need a moment." Janet insisted.

* * *

Alex opened the door, the room was empty with the exception of an old desk and a file sitting on it. Alex walked to the desk and brushed the dust off it. He picked up the file and opened it. He noticed the paper inside the file was written by his father.

Dear Janet,

They know where we are. The Crown knows but hasn't moved in to help. I fear today might be the last day I have to spend with Alex. All we needed was more time to figure out who the man in charge was. If the king had just shared the name it would all be over. Alex would still have a father and mother. I should have never protected the king. Everything that has happened has been my fault. He has lost so much already. I never noticed how bright the sky is. I think I will take my boy fishing today.

If anything should happen to me, protect him. Keep him away from this Janet. There is money in a secure account, enough to last him a good year or two. Make sure he gets back on his feet. When the time is right give him this.

Alex could see a spot on the paper where the key was once taped to. He turned to the next page and saw another note directed to himself.

Alex,

I am sorry for everything. This is never the life your mother or I wanted for you. But I know you're in good hands. Your mother was killed protecting us both. She took a bullet that was meant for me. She never walked away from you. She spent her last breath begging me to not tell you the truth. She didn't want you to grow up thinking her death was your fault, or with the same hatred we had for the King.

20 years ago Your mother and I were assigned to protect the crown. To be his secret agents on the inside. Our mission was to figure out the inside leak they had. Sadly we failed our mission, and the king paid the price. The castle got word we were there and blamed us for the death of the King. Trying to shield you, we moved every year. Yet I could tell that moving so much was keeping you from making friends and having meaningful relationships. I decided to stay put no matter what may happen. I am sorry it has left you an orphan, my son. I hope you can find it in your heart to forgive us, but we only ever wanted you to be happy, and safe.

I hope this letter brings you some kind of closure. Alexander Twist, remember you are very loved, and that we will always be there. Even if it is not in the flesh, we remain by your side.

Alex couldn't hold back the emotions anymore and began to cry. His tears soaked the paper.

* * *

Downstairs the queen and Janet took turns rinsing off some dishes while Leo bagged everything up. A loud thud echoed through from upstairs and Leo dropped the food. He went to run up. Janet tried to grab his arm. He turned and flipped Janet, and raced upstairs. The Queen knelt and helped Janet to her feet.

"Is it time?" The queen asked. Janet nodded and they walked up the stairs. "You told him?" The queen asked sternly. Janet looked at her solemnly before she responded, "You choose when and how to protect your boy, let me decide how to protect mine. He has the right to know the truth. There will be questions Sarah, be ready."

Leo turned the corner and found Alex on his knees leaning over the file.

"Alex," Leo called to him. Alex did not answer him. He knelt down next to Alex and put his arm over him, and Alex pulled away a bit. Leo was stunned at Alex's response. He looked down at the file and picked up the letters. He quickly read them as Janet and his mother walked into the room.

"Is this true?" Leo looked at his mother. "You guys knew and said nothing? This could have all been prevented!" Leo for the first time felt absolute hatred for his father.

"Leo, your father was still very young. We lost contact with them after they returned to the States." Janet knelt down next to Alex. He hugged her but never looked up.

The queen knelt before Alex. "I am so sorry Alex." She spoke softly. Alex reached his hand down and placed it on his gun. His whole life was a lie and for no reason. The letter did not bring him any closure, but this would.

"Alex," Janet spoke softly. "Breathe. If you do that you're not only hurting yourself."

Leo knelt down next to Alex, "Hey. Alex, I'm . . .." Alex let go of the gun, dried his eyes, and stood up.

"I am CIA Agent Twist. Badge number 55393. My mission is to protect the Prince." He walked out of the room leaving the three behind. Janet raced after him.

"Agent Twist," Janette shouted. Alex stopped and turned to her. "Alex, take a deep breath and think," pleaded Janet. Leo raced out and threw himself into Alex's arms. Alex hugged him tightly and buried his face in his neck. He couldn't keep a wall up against Leo. They knelt there for what seemed like a long time, but was really only a minute.

"I'm so sorry Alex," Leo whispered, rubbing his arm.

Janet knelt down next to Leo and Alex. "The king did not know everything. And what Sarah said is true. We cut off communication with them, not the other way around. He was still a prince, much like Leonardo. Alex looked up for the first time since he finished reading the note. Janet handed him a photo of himself, his father, and his mother. It was the first time he actually saw his mother. She had dark hair like him, and brown eyes just like his.

Sarah knelt back down. "We tried to call, to warn your father once we found out. Janet took the call."

Janette followed quickly, "And I called your father 1000 times that day. But you know how he was on your birthday."

"It still hurts, everything I ever knew, was. . ." Alex shook his head and stood up. He dried his eyes, and after thinking about it for a little bit, he smiled. He did feel loved, not only Janet, and Leo, but for the first time in 20 years, he knew his mother loved him. He hugged Janet, and whispered, "Thank you."

Alex sighed, "My father was right, for the first time I finally have closure. And he was right about something else, I was in great hands." He looked at Janet,

"Thank you for everything. I'm stepping down as Agent 55393 after this mission. With your permission." He looked Janet in the eyes and she nodded and smiled, a tear falling down her cheek.

"We are losing the best agent we ever had," she replied proudly. Alex took Janet's hand, "And are gaining the son you never did." Alex hugged Janet, then turned to the Queen and took a breath. "Thank you for trying to save my family. Now I will do the same and keep yours safe." She nodded and smiled. Sarah and Janet went back downstairs, made a cup of tea, and could be heard talking quietly.

Alex walked back to the empty room. Leo followed behind him. "Alex?"

Alex turned back to Leo. "I gave up on this past a long time ago. I was so angry with everyone around me. Especially Janet. I never forgave her." He walked to Leo. "I don't want to be angry anymore. This is all history. I am loved, I know that now." He went on, "I might have lost my family a long time ago, but I have chosen my new one." Alex walked to Leo and kissed him. "I am letting go of everything in this room that once held me back." With that, Alex took Leo's hand and they walked out of the room, locked the door again, and sat down against it.

"Alex, I'm here for you." Alex leaned his head on Leo's

shoulder and took deep breaths.

"Part of me is glad I get to choose my own family, and the people I want to be around." He looked up at Leo. "I never said it yet but Leo, I love you."

* * *

Some time had passed, and it was starting to get late. Alex took Leo's hand. "Come on, we have dessert to dish out." Alex and Leo joined the queen and Janet downstairs. Janet had been sitting down on the couch with a bag of ice on her back. The queen was sitting in the rocking chair rocking gently back and forth.

Alex looked at Janet, "Everything okay?" He asked, seeing the ice. She sat up stiffly. "If your boyfriend ever flips me again we are going to have some issues." Alex let out a chuckle.

"You were right Alex, it's about the stance, not strength." Leo quoted Alex. Alex smiled, and looked back at Janet,

"He flipped you?" Alex laughed harder.

"Shut up, I can still kick your ass." Alex turned and extended a hand to the queen, "Your Majesty, can I speak with you please?" The queen glanced at Leo, then willingly took his hand and allowed Alex to walk her into the kitchen.

Alex took a deep breath, " Your Majesty, I may not be accustomed to your traditions, or even have much to offer Leonardo. But I would like your blessing that even after this mission is over, if he should choose to stay in America he will be allowed." The queen looked at Alex, with intrigue.

"Is that all Agent Twist?" The queen asked with a smile, and Alex shook his head.

"I don't know when I will see you again, but I would like

your blessing to be with Leonardo." Her smile got bigger.

"And what if he should choose to move back home?" The queen asked.

"Then I will follow him." The queen walked over to Alex and kissed his head.

"You already have my blessing, Alex. He is happier than he has ever been. You have made so many dreams come true already, I can't wait to see what comes next!"

With that, the queen turned to walk back to the living room but turned back around. She took her ring off her finger and handed it to Alex.

"Should you ever decide to settle down with him, please . . ." She placed it in Alex's hand and closed it with her own.

"It is the only thing I have that hasn't come from the crown. It was my mother's. I am sure you can both enjoy that." Alex smiled and bowed to the Queen. She returned the bow and walked back to the room to join the others.

* * *

The four sat around the fireplace and talked for four more hours. They spoke about how things were going in America, and what the next plans were for the Crown, and the Queen spoke about her next visit to see Leo. She even dreamed out loud about living in a small town like this one. Janet checked her watch and was surprised when she saw it read 5:30 AM. She stood up and looked over at the queen.

"Sarah, it's time." The queen swallowed hard and stood. She grabbed her coat and gave Leo a tight hug.

"I'm going to miss you, my sweet angel." She whispered into his ear.

"I'm going to miss you too," Leo spoke back to her through his sobbing. Janet walked over to Alex and smiled.

"You did well Alex." She put her arm around him. Alex swung both his arms around her.

"Don't stay away for too long," Alex demanded. Janet nodded and walked to the door.

"We must be going." She spoke softly, placing her hand on Sarah's back. Leo let go and walked back next to Alex. The queen walked to Alex and hugged him,

"You keep my boy safe." She demanded softly in his ear.

Leo rested his head on his shoulder and watched as the two walked out the door.

Alex took Leo's hand and walked with him up the stairs.

"It's been a long day, let's get some sleep," Alex suggested. Leo nodded and walked beside him.

Once in the comfort of their room, Alex kissed Leo and started to remove his shirt. Leo then sat on the bed, and Alex walked over to sit next to him.

"Thank you for this Alex, it was so good to see her." Alex turned and kissed him.

"Merry Christmas." Leo lay down and turned to face where Alex would be lying, but he did not lie right down. Instead, he walked to a small safe and opened it. He put the ring from Sarah inside. Leo watched as Alex removed his shirt and pants before laying beside him. Alex laid on his back, and Leo moved in close to him. He rested his head on his chest and smiled. Alex's arm lay behind Leo and held him close. The two shortly after drifted off to sleep.

Twelve

A Taste of Happiness

The next few weeks felt like a dream. They spent a quiet New Year together, just sitting in front of the fireplace, snuggled on the couch under a comfy throw just talking and learning more about each other. It was peaceful and neither one of them wanted it to change.

Leo signed Alex up for a bake-off. He wanted Alex to see that he was a good cook because it was starting to seem that Leo telling him was just a habit. They have had a few neighbors come over and everyone seemed to love his food. Yet he knew Alex had his doubts about it. They spent the past month working on his recipe for the peach cobbler. They finally figured out the right ingredients and were ready.

"Leo pass me the cinnamon please," Alex called to him. He was stirring the batter together. Leo passed him the spice and started to sift the flour into the pan. After making four cobblers the two hugged each other. They were ready for tomorrow.

They went up to their room and got in bed both exhausted from their day of baking. Leo fell onto the bed after removing his clothes. He laid on top of the blanket enjoying the breeze from the fan above him. Alex felt himself blush as he looked down at Leo and all he had to offer. He stripped and lay on the bed the same way as Leo. Their heads side by side. Leo looked over to Alex.

"Are you ready to win tomorrow?" He questioned Alex who rolled onto his side and looked at Leo.

"If I win it's only because I had your help." He spoke softly and kissed Leo.

Leo looked up and smiled at the sight of Alex naked. He crawled onto the bed and pulled Alex on top of him.

"Is it too early to celebrate?" He asked Alex, kissing his neck and running his hand down his chest to his waist.

"I think, just this once it is okay to celebrate early." He leaned down and kissed Leo.

* * *

The next morning Leo woke up with a start and pushed Alex out of the bed. They were running behind schedule. Leo ran to the bathroom and showered last night's residue off himself. He dressed in a sweater and khaki slacks. As soon as Leo was done in the shower, Alex jumped in after him, kissing his shoulder in passing. He put on a pair of black jeans and a red sweater that was loose-fitting and had holes along the sleeves.

The two ran down to the kitchen and grabbed the cobblers before racing out the front door. They made their way to the town square and found their table. Alex lit the burners and set the trays up. As they started to warm, the smell of peaches and cinnamon filled the air around them. Soon, they were surrounded by people who wanted a taste of what smelled so good.

Anyone who took a bite of the cobbler smiled in appreciation of the warm, gooey goodness, and Leo enjoyed seeing the light in Alex's eyes as he served everyone with a big smile. He looked so happy, and it seemed to come so naturally to him. Leo hugged Alex once they cleared the line, and they were out of food.

Alex slid his hand under the tray, pulled out one more piece of cobbler, and looked at Leo.

"You have not eaten anything today." He said holding a spoonful of cobbler out to him. Leo leaned in and ate the cobbler from Alex. He smiled, savoring all their hard work. It really was amazing.

The judges were at the podium about to announce the winner and Leo dragged Alex to the stage. He hugged him hoping for the best.

"In third place is Silvia with her sugar cookies." Everyone clapped as Sylvia took the stage. "In second place are Twisted Sisters and their blueberry danishes. And in first place Leonardo, and Alex with their to die for Peach Cobbler." Everyone clapped and Leo jumped up and down and hugged Alex.

"We did it." He kissed Alex and they went on stage. The judges handed them a blue ribbon and everyone patted them on the back or shook their hands congratulating them before they went their separate ways. The two headed back home to relax and savor their accomplishment. They decided on a horror movie, Leo snuggled into Alex's arms. The sun had completely set, and the jump scares made Leo snuggle into Alex as close as he possibly could.

"So now that we won, do we get to celebrate again?" Leo asked beggingly.

"We most certainly do." Alex picked up Leo and carried him to their room.

* * *

The snow outside had melted, and birds filled the air of the small town. Alex stirred first that morning in bed, feeling a chill in the room he got up and closed the window. He grabbed a sweatshirt, put it on walked over to Leo, and nudged him before kissing him. "You didn't close the window again." Alex sat on the edge of the bed. Leo sat up and stretched, allowing the blanket to fall to his waist. Alex smiled looking at Leo's chiseled chest. There was a mark on it.

"Oops," Alex whispered and Leo looked down.

"Really?" He tilted his head questioningly. Alex stood up and walked to Leo's closet.

"Today is your big day, are you ready?" Leo stood and walked over to him, he wrapped his arms around Alex's brushing his hair to one side so he could rest his head on his shoulder. Alex grabbed a black suit and turned to Leo. He had not realized Leo hadn't put anything back on till now.

He handed him the suit. "Go get ready, I'll make you something to eat." Alex put on a bathrobe and went down to the kitchen. Leo smiled watching him leave then made his way to the bathroom and filled the tub with water.

Down in the kitchen Alex cracked some eggs open and began to scramble them. He was preparing a simple meal this morning since they were pressed on time. He plated the eggs and went to get Leo. He pushed the bathroom door open and walked in.

"Babe, your breakfast is done." Leo was just wrapping up his relaxing bath and stood up. Even though Alex had seen him naked several times he still got flustered. Leo knew this and enjoyed the effect he had on him. He wrapped a towel around himself and walked to Alex.

Alex stared as the water slid down his chest, and Leo smiled.

"Do you know what today is?" Alex asked as he closed his eyes. He thought about the first time he really saw Leo. He had just gotten out of the pool and walked to him with water falling down his chest. Leo nodded,

"A year since we first met." He lifted Alex's head and kissed him gently. "Alex, if you keep staring we are going to be late." Alex gently punched his chest and turned on the shower. He took off his robe and hung it on the door before stepping into the shower. Leo is dressed in a black blazer with a white t-shirt. He put on Alex's necklace that hung over the white shirt. He put on his trousers and headed down to the kitchen to eat.

Leo looked around in the kitchen and could tell Alex had not eaten yet. He smirked and made him some eggs as well, then sat and ate while listening for the water to turn off. He turned and waited for Alex expectantly. He came down the stairs wearing a mesh shirt that he had a blazer over that covered his chest and scars. He had on a pair of black casual pants and a pair of boots with two heels to them. Leo looked on appreciatively as Alex joined him in the kitchen.

"Did you not eat?" He asked, pointing at the eggs on the plate. "I made you breakfast." Alex looked around the kitchen,

"And we still have a house." He joked while walking to Leo

and kissed him. He grabbed the plate of food and started to eat it. He smiled at Leo.

"Your cooking is getting better." Leo smiled and kissed his cheek. "I have a good teacher." Alex finished eating, ignoring the shells in the eggs as he smiled to himself. He put the plate into the sink and grabbed Leo. They went up to his art studio and started to grab his paintings. They made a pile in the foyer of them.

The doorbell rang, and Leo walked to the living room. Alex put a hand on his gun and peeked through the door. He pulled the door open, and two men stood there in front of them in purple jumpsuits. Alex pointed at the canvases they had stacked on the ground and the men started to load them onto a truck. One of the men came back and grabbed a canvas that was wrapped in a purple blanket.

"Not that one," Leo called out, to stop him. The men double-checked they hadn't missed anything and left heading down the road. Leo propped the canvas up against the stairs and took Alex's hand.

"Shall we get going?" Alex nodded and locked the front door.

They piled into Alex's car and followed behind the truck. They drove through town seeing that almost every shop had been closed for the day and made it to Central Park. There were tents set up everywhere, and tables all about. Vendors came in from other towns as well. There were lines of food trucks and all different kinds of sellers of various things. Leo took a minute before getting out of the car. His leg was shaking, and he was toying with his hands. Alex took his hand in his.

"Do you think they will sell, Alex?"

Alex leaned over and gently kissed his hand. "A painting

made by you, Princy? Of course, they will." Alex got out of the car and opened the door for Leo. After he got out, Alex straightened Leo's blazer, pushed his hair back, and said,

"Looking as good as you do, you will be the talk of the market." Leo smiled, looked at him affectionately, and quipped back,

"Careful they might just end up auctioning me off if I look that good." Alex laughed, took his hand, and said "Over my dead body" as they started to head into the market.

As they made their way to the booth that the delivery men had set up with all the canvases they curiously looked at all the treasures around them. They had hung some larger canvases on the back of the tent. On either side were paintings of flowers, and in the center, were two paintings, one of the royal castle and one of their home. Various-sized canvases were also laid out on tables. A banner that read Crown Paintings was draped on the table inviting people in. Alex and Leo took their seats and sipped some coffee waiting for the fair to actually start.

A couple walked by and stopped to look at Leo's work. They went through the smaller stack of paintings and settled on one of the gardens with a bridge that would be used to walk over it.

"How much?" they asked, holding up the eight-by-ten canvas. Leo smiled and told them "Fifty dollars." They happily handed him the money.

"Your work is amazing Mr..." The man paused waiting for a name.

"Leonardo," he spoke back. The man smiled. I knew you looked familiar. He waved and walked away.

Leo turned to Alex smiling from ear to ear, "I made my

first sale!" Alex hugged him. "The first of many. I told you, you have some real talent, Princy." All through the day Leo's paintings continued to sell until almost everything they had brought was gone. He had sold about 50 paintings in one day! A taller woman in a business suit stopped by their tent as they were starting to clean up and take down the last few paintings that were still hung in the tent. She had her black hair tied up into a knot, and very professional-looking glasses on. She pointed to the paintings behind them and asked,

"How much for these?" Leo turned around to see what was left there and looked back at her.

"Which one ma'am," Leo asked. The lady looked offended by the question and replied rather haughtily,

"All of them." She reached into her pocket and pulled out a small business card. I'm the curator of the local museum, I assume you both have had the chance to go." Leo shook his head.

"We have not had the chance." She scoffed and replied, "Well, you simply must go." Leo turned back to the paintings assessing which ones they were discussing, and their size and told the curator,

"One thousand for all four." She pulled out an envelope and handed it to him.

"Make sure you come by and see your paintings displayed in the museum. I'm sure you will be quite impressed. Can you have them delivered?" Leo nodded and said, "Yes, of course. Thank you very much." then took down the paintings. The curator walked away, and Leo looked to Alex, his eyes wide, and said,

"I sold everything?" Alex smiled at him, "And got into a museum all in one day." Alex was so proud of him, and he had no idea how to show or say it. He kissed him tenderly.

"Look at you gone from a prince to a hideaway, to an artist," Alex said smiling.

" You forgot one thing there, Alex," Leo responded.

"And what's that?"

Leo smiled. " I went from prince to hideaway, to the happiest man alive, to an artist." He leaned in and kissed him tenderly.

"Let's go home, there is a new movie I wanted to check out with you."

The sun was setting as the two drove back to their house with the windows down enjoying the fresh air. Once they made it back to the house Leo went inside and plopped onto the couch. He had never talked to so many people in one day and it took a toll on his mind. He wanted to watch this movie with Alex, but he also just wanted to climb into bed. Leo kicked his feet up on the table and turned on the television. Alex went into the kitchen before following Leo.

"Close your eyes," Alex said. "I made something new and want you to try it." Leo closed his eyes. Alex took off his blazer and rested it on the back of a chair in the kitchen before he grabbed a small cup, and spoon and went to sit next to Leo. He took a small spoonful of the substance from the cup and said,

"Open up." Leo opened his eyes, and Alex guided the spoon into his mouth.

Leo was greeted by a rich and sweet chocolate mousse. "Oh my gosh, it's great Alex." Leo turned to him hoping for another sweet spoonful and said,

"I think that when this is all said and done you should open your own fine dining restaurant here. Everything you make is just amazing."

Leo and Alex watched the movie Leo had been talking about for days. About an hour into the movie once the ads started Leo got up and grabbed the canvas that they had left behind earlier.

"I hope you don't mind, but I have been working on this for a few weeks, and I want you to have it. I know tomorrow is your birthday, but I didn't want to wait." Alex smiled and took it. He turned it around. Looking back at him was a family portrait of him, his father, and his mother. Leo had taken the photo Janet gave to Alex, and aged his parents, making their features still the same, but he added some gray hair, and small details so they aged along with Alex. Tears started streaming down Alex's face as he stared at the painting. His family. He knew that they were always there, watching him grow, but having something like this . . . was more than he could have ever hoped for. When he had taken a deep breath and settled himself, Alex quietly stood and hung the painting then joined Leo back on the couch.

"Thank you. That is the best gift you could have given me." He kissed Leo softly and held him tightly, savoring this moment and wondering how he had gotten so lucky. Alex grabbed the blanket and covered them both. As they lay there together watching the movie, Leo caressed Alex's arm up and down through the mesh shirt with his thumb and kissed his head every so often. Even though it was Alex's job to protect Leo, nothing made him feel safer in the world than being in Leo's arms.

Alex, much like his own father, had a thing where he would not look at his phone if he was spending time with Leo. It was his way of making sure that Leo had all his attention. His phone rang a few times that night but he never bothered to see who it was. Shortly after the movie ended they went up to bed arm in arm.

The next morning Alex and Leo went around to the local shops picking up supplies, and groceries. They drove by a run-down restaurant.

"Alex, pull over quickly." Alex didn't notice the building or the reason he was pulling over. Leo got out of the car and examined the building. Alex followed after him as Leo peeked inside. He was imagining a restaurant bouncing with business. He looked at Alex, his face lit up with excitement.

"This would be perfect for you, you have to do it." Leo started insisting. Alex just smiled, he couldn't see things as easily through the dreamer's eyes as Leo could.

"I don't know," Alex said as he looked over the building, and through the windows while rubbing his hand through his hair. Leo pointed at the broken-down bar,

"I could be there making drinks, and over there you would greet the guests as they come in." He spoke pointing at the fallen-over counter, "We could do it together, it could be fun." Leo's romantic view of life always made Alex smile.

"Maybe one day, but for now I have a job to do." He took Leo in his arms. "And you keep my hands pretty busy at the moment." Leo blushed, taking that statement in more than one way. "Not here." He said embarrassed. "At least think about it for me okay?" Alex nodded his head in agreement and the two returned to the car. Before they headed home they had to stop at the little corner market. Leo stopped at the television behind the counter as Alex went to grab a few things

"Today's news in Britain, an interview with Queen Sarah." Leo watched closely. He had not spoken to his mother since

Christmas, he had only overheard conversations Alex had on the phone with Janet, so he didn't know how bad or good things really were. "Tell us, Your Majesty, how are you and the King handling all these new threats? It seems we have more reports every day about attempts on the lives of the royal family. Has there been any discussion of abdicating the crown?"

His mother sat high in the chair next to the reporter. She had on a white business suit. Her hair was braided and pulled up into a knot and her crown sparkled brightly from the studio lights.

"We have taken these threats very seriously. No one is allowed in the castle, and after this meeting, no one is permitted to leave it. As you know, the last attack was the closest they have gotten." The reporter sat up in her seat. She could sense a good story, like a snake tracking its prey.

" Are you referring to yesterday's meeting about the proposed increase in taxes?" The queen did not bat an eye.

"We are committed to continue to make improvements to our already strong country. We must have a strong economy to make sure every citizen of this great country is not only treated fairly but has all they need including good jobs and decent healthcare which is why we are still debating the legislation that would raise taxes. We want to make sure that it affects everyone equally, and will not hinder…"

Alex made it back to the counter carrying a container of laundry soap, and fabric sheets and looked up at the television. He saw the queen's crown, and the royal guard racing to her. Alex tried to tug on Leo's arm to tell him he was ready and to get him away from the television. Leo however was glued to it. The queen was tackled to the ground moments before three guards and the reporter were shot. Leo darted away from the television. Alex pulled him out of the corner store and back into the car. He stood in the door of the car looking down at Leo.

Leo felt his heart break in two as he just watched his own mother almost die.

"When will this all end, Alex?" he muttered.

"Things always get worse before they get better, Leo. You just need to have hope." Leo looked up at him.

"I want to go back. If anything happens to my family I want to be there." Alex felt a tear roll down his face.

"I can't protect you there right now. They are not letting the CIA help anymore." Leo felt his heart break even more.

"I can't do it, I am not as strong as you are Alex." Alex knelt down and looked up at Leo. "You're right Leo, you are stronger." He pushed himself to his feet.

"If you want to go back, I'll be right by your side, every step of the way." Leo dried his eyes.

"But you just said." Alex took out his badge and tossed it on the back seat.

"I quit." Alex proclaimed. Leo let out a small sigh and hugged him. "You would do that for me?" Alex got into the car, " I would do so much more, Princy."

Thirteen

Going Home

When Alex and Leo pulled up to their house, Leo noticed there was a car out front. He looked at Alex, and asked, "Are you expecting someone?" Alex shook his head. He parked the car a bit from the house. He took out a gun and handed it to Leo. Alex walked to the car and put his hand on the hood, it was still hot. So, they haven't been here long. Since he'd only brought one gun with them on their outing, all Alex had after giving Leo his gun was a knife. As he inched closer to the door he twirled the knife so it laid against his arm.

They made it to the door, and Alex put his hand on the knob, the door was already cracked open. Alex held his hand over his lips telling Leo to not make a sound. Leo stayed right next to Alex, his hand resting on his back. Alex pushed the door open carefully searching the room before walking in. Alex led

Leo around the first floor of the house, nothing seemed to be missing, and it wasn't trashed. The house looked just as they left it. With the main floor secure Leo stayed hidden in the kitchen corner while Alex went up the stairs and went to their room. He checked all the closets and the bathroom. No one was in them. As he came out of the bathroom there was a gun pointed at him.

Alex quickly bashed the hand holding the gun into the doorframe and disarmed them while turning the gun on them. He turned the corner to see Janet. "You're lucky I didn't shoot," Alex and Janet both said.

Alex hollered down, "Leo it's okay, it's only Janet. We'll be right down." Leo put Alex's gun on the table and made some coffee for Janet.

"Has he seen?" Janette anxiously asked. Alex nodded,

"He wants to go back." Alex looked down at the bed, in a flash he remembered all the nights they had spent holding each other. Janet took a deep breath. "That is why I am here. The agency wanted me to tell you that they can not allow you to travel with him, if he goes back your mission is over." Alex figured that would be the case and thought about that every night Leo was in his arms. Once his mission was over, he was out of the CIA. Out of the only thing he had ever known. He just thought that when it happened he would not be left in the house all alone.

"Alex," Janet grabbed a new file from her coat, "The President is requesting your protection. He has seen the work you have done on your current mission. The agency has approved it, you are to ship it out tomorrow." Alex did not take the file from her. He took a seat on the bed and picked up a photo of himself and Leo from the bedside table. Alex closed his eyes and felt tears rolling down his face.

"I can be just like my father." Alex thought out loud not knowing that Leo was standing in the doorway behind Janet.

Alex put down the photo and reached into his pocket.

"Janet, I quit." He handed her his badge. "I am going back with Leo. I may not have the help of the CIA, but I am not done protecting him. I am not done loving him. I will not turn my back on him." Janet smiled, she wasn't surprised, but she was happy he was finally letting go of the past.

"Your parents would be so proud of you." Alex looked up at her.

"How do you know?" Janet started to walk to Alex and Leo slipped into his art studio. "Because Alex, I am," she said, hugging him and taking his badge. She handed him a different envelope. He opened it and saw two tickets for a flight to London, along with a civilian passport for him.

Alex smiled and slid it into his pocket. He stood up and hugged her.

"You knew what I was going to pick," Alex asked and she nodded,

"You have one last mission Alex, not from the agency but from me. Your mission is to find your happiness. If you choose to be there or here, I will always find a way to see you. Also, while you are there, if you need any help, call me. I will be on the next flight." Janet spoke softly, and Alex nodded. He hugged her again, wondering where he would have been without her.

"I'm going to miss you," Alex spoke as he saw Leo turn the corner and walk into the room. He saw Alex in tears and Janet holding his badge.

"Are you sure, Alex? Are you sure you won't regret this?"

Leo asked, looking worried. Alex dried his eyes and walked over to him.

"I am not sure of anything other than that I love you." He kissed him and pulled the suitcases out of the closet. Janet helped them pack and placed four new guns inside the bag for Alex. She placed his bulletproof vest from his time in the field as well.

"The CIA has agreed to let you carry on the plane since it will only be you two."

"You better use this. That is an order." Leo chose his favorite clothing from the closet, as did Alex. He also packed four suits as well.

"I am going to have to look the part, aren't I?" Alex asked, and Janet smiled.

"Yes, you will need to dress like an agent even though you are not one."

Janet went down to the car to start it up, saying,

"I'll meet you two outside." on her way out. Alex and Leo took their suitcases and headed down the stairs. Leo looked around the house one last time taking it all in. Alex felt like he was losing his one chance of happiness. He turned and held Leo for a moment.

"It will still be here if you choose to come back." He kissed him, and they headed out the door and into the back seat of Janet's car.

"It will be a nineteen-hour flight," Janet spoke, trying to break the somber silence. "I sprung to get you both first-class tickets so you'll be comfortable."

"Thank you, Janet," Leo responded gratefully. He had such mixed feelings swirling around his head he was thankful for Janet's help. Janet walked them to the gate having flashed her badge to the TSA agent. She hugged Leo,

"Promise me you will keep him out of trouble. We both know how he is." Janet spoke directly to Leo. Leo nodded as she turned to Alex. She hugged him tightly,

"Remember your training, stay safe and come back home." For the first time, Alex saw Janet cry. He couldn't help but think things were worse in London than she had led him to believe. Alex looked at her and smiled.

"Big bad Janet does have a heart." He spoke softly so no one would hear him. Janet smiled sadly then turned and walked away.

Alex took a seat next to Leo and rested his head on his shoulder. Leo put his arms around Alex.

"We take off in a few hours. We should rest a bit," Leo suggested hoping Alex would actually close his eyes. Alex shook his head.

"Not till we are in the air and you are safe, Princy." Alex slid down Leo's chest and rested his head on his lap.

"I will only ask one more time," Leo said, looking down at Alex. "Are you sure this is going to make you happy, giving up your badge, and coming to London?" Alex did not even hesitate,

"I don't mind drinking fancy tea with you. I am sure of one thing, Princy. My happiness is wherever you are, and I will pay the price to have that no matter what it is," Alex spoke looking up at him. Leo smiled and bent down to kiss him.

The next few hours seemed to drag along as they waited for their flight to start boarding. Leo spent the time running his fingers through Alex's hair. Alex had turned onto his side facing away from Leo, to keep an eye out. No one joined them that day in the waiting area as London had closed the airports.

They were taking every step to keep the King and Queen safe. Alex's eyes were starting to get heavy, as he fought the sleep he so desperately needed.

Leo, on the other hand, was far too anxious to sleep. His leg was held still by Alex's head. He focused on it so he did not bounce him. He couldn't wait to land and see his mother again, but was terrified of landing and what would follow after. While it was completely legal in the country to be gay and be married, his father still had the mindset of the old ways.

"Now boarding flight 5J7 to London. This is our no overlay trip so get ready for a long flight," The stewardess called over the intercom. Alex sat up and rubbed his eyes before stretching. As they were called to board for first class Leo stood and started walking to the tunnel. His mind was a fog of emotions that he could not see his way through. Alex grabbed both the carry-on bags and caught up with him. Leo snapped back to reality and rested his head on Alex's. "Thanks."

"Princy it's a long flight, don't let yourself get lost." Leo nodded.

* * *

The flight had taken off, and the two were the only passengers on the plane. The flight attendant brought them over some coffee and bagels. Alex made coffee for them both and handed Leo the cup. Leo was looking out the window before turning back to Alex to grab the coffee.

"Alex, promise me something." Alex looked up from his phone.

"What's that, Princy?" Leo turned in his seat and took Alex's hands.

"Promise me you won't die for me." Alex swallowed hard. "Leo…"

"Promise me, Alex, that if anything happens we will always be like this. That we can always come back home together."

Alex smiled, "Leo, you are always welcome both in my home and in my heart." He closed his eyes and kissed him softly. "Nothing can change that." Leo looked back out the window.

"We will see if he feels the same way after meeting my father." He muttered to himself.

Alex took out a pen and started making notes on the napkin that came with the coffee.

"Leo, do you know anything about the legislation your father was fighting, and trying to improve on?" Leo looked back at him and down at the notes he was taking. He was mapping the men who attempted to kill us, and a line that led to a mystery man. He included the man who also killed his mother and father on the list as well.

"Do you think it's all connected?" Leo asked, surprised. Alex shook his head.

"I am not sure right now, but I have a hunch that it is. Why else would the king not want any CIA assistance?" Leo told him everything he knew about the legislation, and even though there was not much to go on, Alex appreciated it. He folded the napkin and placed it back into his pocket.

Leo found the flight to London a lot longer than it needed to be. He could feel every minute that passed by. His mind was in a fog with worry about what awaited him back home. They were in the air for about ten hours, and he kept getting up to walk around the plane. Finally, Alex got up and walked in front of him. He grabbed his arm and looked into his eyes.

"You need to sleep," Alex said, looking at the bags under

Leo's eyes. He pulled him back to their seats. He grabbed a blanket from the cabinet where he saw the flight attendants kept them and covered Leo.

Leo rested his head on Alex but was unable to escape the turmoil inside his mind. Alex began to hum the same song he heard Leo's mother hum at Christmas. It was a soothing song that sounded like a lullaby. Leo's legs stopped tapping and he kissed Alex's cheek before falling asleep in his arms.

"I will keep you safe, no matter the cost." Alex kissed his head.

* * *

There was one hour left before they landed, and Alex had woken up from the turbulence. He stood up and grabbed his suitcase from the overhead bin. He closed the privacy curtain and opened the suitcase. He changed and put the case back up before going into the bathroom. He splashed some water onto his face and pulled up his hair into a ponytail, before walking back to his seat.

While he was gone, Leo woke up and started to drink some coffee Alex left on the tray for him. He looked out the window as they were flying over the Castle. He closed his eyes and thought about his prison life schedule.

"Maybe this time it will be different with him there." Leo wanted to bring Alex home, to show him the country, and the beauty that hid inside it. "I never wanted to force him into this war zone." He spoke out loud.

Alex pushed open the curtain, "You didn't." Leo turned and saw Alex standing there in a black suit that complemented his body. The only jewelry he had on was his promise ring. He had taken out his earrings, and taken off his watch and bracelets. His hair was pulled up tight. Leo stood up and looked Alex up and down.

"You look…" He found himself at a loss for words.

"Dorky?" Alex said, finishing his sentence laughing. Leo brushed a piece of hair from Alex's face over his ear, kissed him, and said,

"Amazing."

Alex opened his eyes and smiled. "Who knew this old thing would still fit? I had to wear it before I got into the undercover department." Leo smiled,

"Well, you look great in it." Leo sat back down while Alex slid three guns into their holsters and put his bag back up into the compartment. He joined Leo as they put on their seatbelts and readied for the landing. Alex put his arm around Leo and whispered to him,

"Welcome home." Leo laid his head on his shoulder and wished he could say it was nice to be back, but as the plane got close to land, he could feel his freedom drifting away. He knew the minute they touched down, they would try to drag him back into the same old routine again.

Fourteen

Not So Warm Welcomes

The plane landed and royal guards filled the tunnel. They grabbed Leo and rushed him in the middle of them. His hand was pulled from Alex's. He was right, his freedom was gone. Leo tried to stand but was pushed forward by the men.

"The king orders, to move your highness." Leo closed his eyes and walked forward with the guards. Alex grabbed their bags and caught up with them. He forced his way into the circle and grabbed Leo's hand.

"It's okay." The guards marched them through the tunnel and to a helicopter that was ready for takeoff. Leo was trying to speak to Alex, who was unable to hear him. Leo was being shoved by the guards to the helicopter. Alex had enough. He put his hand into his pocket and pulled out his gun and fired it into the air. The guards stopped and pointed their weapons at Alex. Leo wrapped Alex in his arms.

141

"Put them down. Or shoot the Prince too." The guards lowered their weapons. "Give us space." The guards fanned out. "I do not need the protection of the royal guard." He shouted so they could all hear him. "You are all dismissed." The general walked to the prince. "Is that an order, Your Highness." Leo looked at Alex. "Yes." They all walked away.

"Are you crazy?" Leo looked at Alex laughing.

"Do you really have to ask?" Alex responded by laughing. They got into the helicopter, and it took off.

As they flew over the country Leo pointed down at spots he saw in movies and magazines that he wanted to see in person. Places where he wanted to take Alex. Alex could not help but look at Leo lovingly as he shared more of his dreams with him. He kissed Leo gently as they came up to the palace. The helicopter landed in the garden and Sarah was standing in the front doorway. Once it landed and the blades stopped, she ran to the plane.

The royal guard stood along the path the queen ran down. Alex hopped out of the plane and helped Leo down. The queen instantly hugged him, and Alex. She looked at Alex and brushed off his blazer.

"Don't you look spiffy?" She whispered to him.

Leo smiled at his mother's approval. She looked down at Leo's hands looking to see if Alex finally asked him yet or not. Alex reached into the helicopter and grabbed their bags. Leo waited for him, and the three walked into the palace. Leo felt the same way he used to; seeing the bland walls, and the lack of color made him regret coming back. He knew nothing had changed.

"Your father requests your presence in thirty minutes." Leo nodded and turned right as his mother walked towards the main hall. Alex followed behind him. Leo turned into his room and sat on the bed. Alex put the bags inside the room and walked over to him.

"Everything okay?" Alex asked, sitting beside him.

"I guess I was just hoping that something would have changed here. That I would not just be barked orders to follow. I was hoping to be greeted with open arms by my father who has not seen me in over a year. But no. He thought like a king and instead ordered me to him." Alex hugged him. "Just once I want him to treat me as his son and not the Prince."

Alex rubbed his back trying to soothe him. Leo got up and went to change into his boring navy blue suit. Alex looked around his room a bit, admiring the small doodles on scrap paper that were lying around. Leo walked back out of the bathroom, and to the dresser where his crown sat. He picked it up and sighed looking at it. Alex walked over to Leo, he put his arms around his waist and Leo turned to face him.

"I regret coming back here." Alex took the crown from him and wiped away the tears falling from his face.

"You only just got here, maybe you are the one needed here to make the change." He placed the crown on his head. "You are the best-looking prince I have ever seen." He leaned in and kissed his cheek. "Cinderella's prince charming couldn't hold a candle to mine." Leo smiled a bit before going to kiss him. Alex pulled back for a moment.

" Wait, if I kiss the prince does he turn into a frog?" Leo finally laughed, and Alex kissed him. Alex backed away a bit and headed for the door. "Come on, Princy, the King awaits."

Leo walked out the door and took Alex's hand. They walked through the maze of a palace and down a flight of stairs. Alex raced Leo down the flight of stairs. Leo was a few stairs behind him, and Alex turned around and picked him up to put him down the last few.

Behind them was a large wooden door. Leo was smiling again, he forgot everything that was so awful about the palace. Alex kissed him and the doors swung open. The Queen and King were sitting on their thrones and saw the two by the stairs. The queen cleared her throat, and Alex and Leo took a step apart. Leo felt his face turn red, and Alex was the exact same shade. They walked into the main hall. Leo bowed before his father, and Alex followed his lead.

"At least you're on time today." The king didn't bother to stand. Alex looked at Leo from the corner of his eye. He saw the smile fade from his face.

"Yes, Your Majesty. I have gotten better at that." Leo spoke not looking up.

"Have you finally decided to grace London with your presence? Have you had enough playing around in the West?" The king shouted to them. Leo did not respond to him. He stayed bowed and held back his tears. Alex looked up and saw the king still sitting, and Sarah looking helpless. "I have ordered you to return months ago, and yet you defied me. Now you have returned, expecting us to welcome you in, and brought the CIA with you. Do you have no faith in our ways anymore?"

Alex looked back at Leo who was no longer able to hide his tears. Alex stood up and met the king's gaze. He walked up to him. The guards in the room rushed to stand before the king.

"You hide behind your men, while your son has faced danger head-on. You hide in this palace instead of doing what the country needs. He has been more of a king than you have. You are letting whoever is making these threats win. You show your hand before the game has even started." Alex shouted back at the king. Leo stood up and his eyes went wide. "With all due respect, Your Majesty." He looked over at Sarah, and back to the King. " You have become power hungry. My father used to speak so highly of you. How do you talk to him about your goals as king? How you would look after the small people. Have you forgotten all that?" Alex questioned the king.

The king walked down the stairs and through the guards. He walked right to Alex and looked at him. Alex saw the vein in his forehead throbbing. His eyes widened and he walked back up to Sarah.

"You didn't tell me." She looked back at him.

"Would you have listened?" Sarah snapped back. The king sighed.

"Agent Twist." Alex looked up at him again. "It's just Alex now. I have cut all ties with the CIA. You see, he followed your ridiculous rules." Alex walked back to Leo who still was bowing.

"Thank you," he whispered so only Alex would hear him.

The king cleared his throat. "You are too both to be in your rooms by sunset, you are due to eat every meal with yourself and your mother. You are to not leave the palace grounds without the guard." The king started to demand his orders from Leo.

"I can guard him myself." Alex cut the king off.

"Mr. Twist, that is twice now you have interrupted me. Do not make it a third." The king reprimanded. "You are to not leave the palace grounds without the guard and furthermore you are to return to your Prince duties. You may leave."

Leo stood up and looked at his mother, before turning around to walk out the room. Alex took his hand, and Leo turned back to his father.

"Your Majesty, I have two requests." Leo's voice was broken and defeated.

"Oh really?" The king stood shouting.

"Hear him out." The queen put her hand on his chest. "Do not make me lose my son again." She pleaded with the king.

Leo held onto Alex's hand tighter. "Alex is to be with me at all times." The king made a face but nodded.

"The second?" The king asked, slightly intrigued. It was the first time Leo ever stood up to him.

Leo looked at Alex. "You accept my refusal of the crown. I did not return to be the prince you want me to be. I returned to be your son." Leo took off his crown, placed it on the floor of the room, and walked out.

"Leonardo." The king called out to him. Leo stopped and turned around to face the king.

" Take your crown, I do not accept. You will be Prince, you will continue the royal name. Your friend may stay with you." Alex picked up the crown and the king's eyes went wide. It was disrespectful for anyone outside the royal family to touch the crown.

"Take it for now Leo." Alex pleaded looking him in the eyes.

"The kingdom needs its prince!" The king shouted at the top of his lungs. Leo held the crown in his hand.

"And its prince needs his freedom," Leo demanded.

The king walked down and pushed the guards apart; he stood face-to-face with Leonardo.

"I fear you have spent too much time in the West, and have forgotten what respect is. The king raised his hand and brought it down to slap Leonardo. Alex caught it before it connected. Alex shook his head.

"You will not lay a hand on him." Being that close to Alex he realized how much he looked like his father. He pulled his arm free.

"You're just like your father with no respect for our ways."

"Respect is something that is earned, not thrust upon oneself because of a title," Leo spoke up to the king. "I will wear your crown for now, but know I will not be the prince you want, I will not be attending any more royal classes, and I will not be accompanied by the guards through my home. I have all the protection I need." Leo took Alex's hand in his own and smiled. " And one last thing, he is not just a friend, Father.." Leo bowed to his mother. He took Alex and left the room. The guards bowed to Leo as they closed the doors.

Leo sighed as the doors shut and hugged Alex.

"Just once I want to be his son." Alex hugged him tight and the doors to the room opened and Sarah walked out.

"Leonardo." Leo dried his eyes and bowed to his mother. "Forgive your father, he is under a lot of-" Leo cut her off.

"He tried to strike me, do not try to protect him. He will never see me as a son, will he?" Leo questioned and his mother looked down.

"One day, he will, Leo. Right now he has a lot of pressure and things on his plate."

Leo looked at his mother.

"All he cares about is the crown, even before all this started. Raising me to be friendless, alone, only knowing Sebastian and barely even knowing you. He forced the old ways down my throat, how to walk, how to talk. Mom, it's not me." Leo spoke and all his frustrations were coming out. Leo walked away and took off to his room. Alex looked at Sarah.

"I'll talk to him."

Alex followed Leo up to his room and caught the door before it slammed shut.

"FUCK!" Alex yelled as his hand was smashed in the solid oak door. Leo turned to see Alex standing there at the door holding his hand.

"Alex, I'm so sorry." He rushed over to him and looked at his hand. It was already swollen and purple.

"I'm okay." Alex took Leo's crown off him with his other hand and placed it on the dresser where it was originally. Leo gently kissed the hand he crushed. "Compared to you shooting me, this is nothing. But Princy, do you think I can borrow one of the suits of armor to be around you?" Alex asked sarcastically.

Leo smiled a bit at Alex's stupid attempt at a joke.

"You know, for a smart ass, you are corny as all hell." Alex nudged him with his shoulder.

"That may be so but it made you smile still." Alex kissed his cheek.

"You know, you shouldn't come down on your mom so hard, she is stuck in the middle, and is trying her best to keep her family together." Leo nodded,

"I know." Leo lay down in bed and looked up at the ceiling. Alex lay next to him.

"Did I make the right choice coming back here? We were so happy in our home together, no one to worry about, nothing to bother us." Alex rolled to face Leo.

"I am not sure, but we are still together, and I am still happy." Leo rolled and laid his head on Alex.

"What do I do with my father?" Alex smiled,

"If it was me I would defy him every step of the way. But give him a little more time. Maybe being back and not being so stuck on a schedule, will give you time to show him that person I fell in love with." Leo sat up and looked at Alex.

"I hope you're right." Alex leaned up and kissed him.

"If I'm not then I will just kidnap you and start a war." He spoke, smiling at his prince.

Fifteen

Just One Drop

Leo and Alex ended up falling asleep, still jet-lagged from the flight. A loud knock came from the door before it opened.

"Leonardo, your father is waiting for you for dinner." Alex sat up and shook Leo awake. Leo looked at his watch.

"Shit," Leo shouted, and Alex jolted up. "We are thirty minutes late. He is going to kill me." Leo quickly got his shoes on and raced to the door followed by Alex.

Sarah and the King were sitting at a table that was far too big for only the four of them. Leo ran into the room and took his seat. Butlers came and dished out the food to everyone, and they began to eat.

"I am sorry for being late, Your Majesty," Leo spoke softly, avoiding his father's eye contact. His father did not say a word, instead, he looked at Sarah. A few minutes passed, and his father put down his fork.

"Leonardo, I have thought about what you said and talked it over with your mother. I still do not accept your refusal of the crown, however it is nice to have you back home. I can overlook some tardiness, and Mr. Twist's outburst." The king spoke softly. Leonardo was not buying it, he shook his head.

"Mr. Twist, what is the purpose of your time here in London?" The king asked Alex, trying to start a conversation at the table. Alex nearly choked on the piece of turkey he was eating. He took a gulp of water that was on the table.

"I am here to support Leonardo, and to protect him." The king tilted his head.

"But I thought you said you left the CIA." The king questioned his true purpose.

"That is correct, Your Majesty, I have. I have no backup and no connection to them whatsoever. I have followed Leonardo here and still protect him because…." He looked to Leonardo, who nodded. "Because I love him."

The king who at that time was taking a sip of his wine began to choke on it.

"I see, and you think you can protect him better than our whole royal guard?" Alex was about to take a bite of some peas that were on his plate when he noticed the smell was off. He learned it from training with Janet.

"Stop eating," Alex shouted, and everyone dropped their forks. Alex stood behind Leonardo who he saw eating the peas. He immediately started to do the Heimlich on him. Leonardo lost his meal on the table.

"What is the meaning of this?" The king shouted.

"Your Majesty, the food has been poisoned." Leo turned and hugged Alex.

"Don't hug me yet, it's already entered your system." He

grabbed his napkin and wrote down a list of medications he needed. "Can you get these, I need to get Leo back to his room." Alex picked up Leo, carried him to his room, and laid him in bed. His body was already starting to clam up. Sarah ran into the room after them.

"Will he be okay," she asked, handing him the medications he asked for.

"If I caught it sooner I would be sure that he would be, but right now," Alex dried his eyes, and pushed some hair back from Leo's face. "I'm so sorry, Leo, I failed you." He whispered. The Queen looked at her boy who was pale, and went back to Alex.

"There is still hope right?" She pleaded, and Alex nodded.

"There is a chance, but this was an inside job, Sarah. I am going to find out who did this." He leaned down and kissed Leo's head. "Hold on Princy."

"Alex, please allow my men time to question everyone inside." The queen begged.

Sebastian entered the room,

"Is the young lord going to be okay?" Sarah turned to him,

"He is strong, he will pull through this." Sebastian moved closer to the bed,

"What caused this, what could have acted so soon?" Alex looked up to Sebastian and the Queen. The queen asked Sebastian to leave, saying that his assistance was not needed at the moment.

"Hemlock," Alex whispered to her. You can't smell it or taste it. Even the smallest pinch of it is enough to kill someone.

"How did you know it was in the peas?" She then nodded, "Janet." "We need to clean out his system and fast, these medications should make him very sick. Sick enough to empty out his whole stomach. Call a trusted doctor and have him here as soon as possible. We need to pump his stomach. The longer he waits the worse he will get."

Sarah ran from the room and made phone calls. Alex held a bucket for Leo as he threw up again.

"Leo, this will get worse before it gets better. But I need you to hold on okay?" Leo nodded and kept eye contact with Alex. Alex put the bucket down and took his hand. He felt his head with the other. He was starting to burn up. He looked at Leo,

"Leo, listen. This is very important. How much did you eat?" Leo spoke very faintly,

"I am not sure, maybe 5 spoons." Alex nodded and kissed his head. "Where the fuck is the doctor?" Alex shouted and Sarah ran into the room.

"He is about 2 minutes out."

There was nothing more Alex could do than watch the love of his life die in front of his eyes. He squeezed Leo's hand every couple of seconds to make sure he had the strength to squeeze back. The doctor ran into the room led by the king.

"My boy...." He cried out. Sarah stood and walked to the door. To stand by the king.

"What is it?" The doctor asked.

"Hemlock." The doctor prepared to pump Leo's stomach,

"I think we just made it." The doctor handed Alex a thermometer, to hold to Leo's head.

"Prince, I need you to hold very still, this will be uncomfortable, and very painful." The doctor slid a tube down Leo's throat and began to pump all the contents.

Leo screamed and held onto Alex's hand squeezing. The Queen could not watch and had to leave the room.

"Richard, what are we going to do, we can't keep risking our lives," She pointed back to the room, "and the life of our only son." The king, for the first time in years, showed he was a human and hugged his wife who cried on his shoulder.

The doctor removed the tube from Leo, who passed out during the procedure. Alex laid his head on his chest and listened to his breathing. It was returning to normal. The doctor gave Alex a bottle of pills.

"He will need to take this three times a day. But he will be okay. You, my dear boy, are a hero." The doctor left the room and was escorted by guards out of the palace. The king was the first to enter. He sat next to the bed on the chair the doctor had been using.

"Is he going to be okay?"

Alex nodded, "Some medications for a while but he will recover." The king sat back in his chair.

"Can you stay with him?" Alex asked the king. He nodded. Alex ran out of the room and spotted the queen.

"What staff have worked here the longest?" Alex asked her.

"I'm not sure, I would say maybe Sebastian, or Mary, the housekeeper." Alex unconsciously growled, "How long have they both worked here?"

"Sebastian's worked here for nearly 50 years."

Alex undid his jacket, "And where is his room?"

"The third floor, first door on the right." Alex pulled out his gun and raced up to the third floor. He kicked the door in. Sebastian was not in there, but he noticed Hemlock growing under a heat lamp. He put on gloves and cut some from the branches. He returned to the main floor and called the king out of the room. Holding the hemlock in hand, he looked at the two.

"No, he wouldn't." The king's face turned redder than the

guard's uniform.

"GUARDS." He shouted and two showed up. "Has anyone left the castle?" The guard swallowed hard.

"Only Sebastian, who said it was by your order, had documents and everything." They handed the king the documents. The signature looked just like his own. How long has he been plotting against us? The king took Alex and went back to Sebastian's room.

They went inside and began to search it.

"Your Majesty, you may want to see this," Alex spoke after opening the closet door. There were letters, from someone named J, and photos of his parents with x's over them. The previous King's face also had an X over it.

"If he has worked here for so long, why did he wait till now to attack us directly?" The king questioned.

"ALEX, RICHARD!" The queen shouted from downstairs.

"Probably waiting for the orders. Whoever J is, wants to wait and see your next plan as king, and now you gave him the chance he needed. Hiding in the palace, there was only one option left. Attack from the inside."

The king sat on the bed, "You were right. I put my family in danger, and if you weren't here they would be…" The king started to tear up.

"But they are not, and they need you now. Go." The king stood and took the order. He walked back down to the room and took his wife's hand.

Alex finished searching the room, there was an envelope on the desk that had the imprint of money on it, and a list of names. Each name on the list has already been killed by either the guard or himself back in the States. So he was the hitman. He worked here for 50 years, why did he suddenly slip up?

Alex decided to scope the room one more time. He noticed that the hemlock plant was not the same one that was used in the food. "This wasn't him," Alex spoke, confused.

Alex raced back down the stairs and pulled the king outside. "It wasn't Sebastian. At least not this time. Do you see the small petals of the hemlock we found in his room, it doesn't match the kind Leo ate. He might have been planning something but this wasn't him. He ran when he found out I knew what almost killed Leo, but it's not the same hemlock."

"Alex," Leo called out in a daze. The queen turned to Alex.

"He is calling for you."

"We can talk more later, Your Majesty." He walked into the room and sat beside Leo.

"Must you always play my hero? I'm the prince, when do I get to save you?" Alex picked up his hand and kissed it.

"You saved me a year ago by coming into my life. I have to talk to your father a little more, then I'll be back, okay?"

Leo shook his head a small bit, his neck still sore from the tube.

"I am going to find out who is trying to kill you all," He looked at the king. "To answer your question from earlier, as you know from working with my parents, yes I can do a better job of protecting him than the royal guards ever could." The king did not say a word, he truly believed that Leo could not be in better hands and the queen was in agreement.

"Is there anything we can do for him?" The queen asked. Alex looked back at Leo.

"Some tea can help numb the pain he is feeling in his throat." Sarah left to get some tea.

"Mr. Twist, I am glad my son has met you." Alex turned to the king,

"Your Majesty, that is what he needs to hear. He needs to know that you see him as a son, and not just a prince to you." The king swallowed and went to walk in. "Not tonight, it will mean more tomorrow. If you do it now he will only think you feel bad." The king nodded and understood what Alex was talking about.

"Someone knew that Sebastian had hemlock growing in his room, and knew about his past. They tried to frame him. That is all I know at the moment." Leo coughed a bit from the room. "I am going to try and make Leo comfortable. We can talk more in the morning."

The king agreed and walked to his chambers.

"Please let Sarah know where I am." Alex nodded and turned into the room. He walked to Leo and sat next to him. Leo coughed and spit blood into the bucket.

"Am I dying?" He asked softly. "It only feels that way Princy, you can't get away from me that easily." Leo smiled and coughed again.

Alex undid the buttons on Leo's shirt and took it off him. He undid his pants and pulled them down before covering him up. He looked at Leo lying there. "I'm going to find out who did this, Leo." Leo grabbed his hand.

"Lay with me," Leo begged, and Alex nodded and lay next to him.

A few moments later, Sarah came back with some tea. She placed it on the stand next to Leo.

"I made your favorite. Some green tea with a dash of sugar and honey." Leo smiled and took a sip. It burned as it went down his throat and he wanted to scream. His eyes went wide. "Is it too hot?" she asked. "I brought some ice as well." Leo shook his head.

"It's going to be hard to eat, drink, and talk for a few days, Leo. The doctor gave you some medications to help with the pain." Alex spoke to Leo who nodded.

"The tea will help numb it a little as well." Sarah spoke softly, "I will let you get some rest." Sarah leaned down and hugged Leo. She waved Alex to her.

"Again you save him. We are so lucky to have you in our lives, and I could not wish that my son found anyone more special. I am going to talk to his father about you too. Make him understand." Leo smiled,

"I think he already does," Alex spoke proudly. She nodded.

"Goodnight, Alex, and thank you."

Alex took off his blazer, and let his hair out of the ponytail. He lay next to Leo and watched him fall asleep. Once Leo passed out he was going back to work. He was not going to stop until he had a name. Until he had the person responsible for almost taking Leo's life. Alex took out his phone and texted Janet about what had happened. She called moments later.

"Is he okay?" Janet asked.

"He will be. He needs rest though right now." Alex whispered back to her.

"And the king and queen?"

"They are fine and didn't ingest anything."

"You checked Sebastian's room?" Janet asked.

"Of course I did, I may not be an agent but I still know to be one."

"Good, keep an eye on him. parents never trusted him."

"Janet, he killed the king and my father."

"You're sure?"

"More sure than anything Janet, but he didn't do this. He ran the minute he heard it was hemlock, but the plants didn't match. Someone is framing him, but we do not know who. There are no leads. I am at a dead end. Tomorrow I will meet with the king about the assassination attempt. I am going to convince him to allow outside help, can I count on you?"

"Of course you can, if you get the go from the king, I will be there on the next flight. But listen, there were a lot of threats to the kingdom back then, most of which are still out there. It can be any one of them. You need to watch your back, you can't trust anyone. You need to set a trap."

Alex looked down at the papers in front of him.

"How can I set up a trap when I don't know who to trap?"

"You know where to start, find Sebastian, let the past catch up with him." Alex smiled and felt a small amount of evil stirring inside him.

"You mean to show him that he made the biggest mistake by not taking me out years ago." Janet could hear his tone change back to how he used to be.

"Don't get lost in the past though Alex, remember what you have now," Janet spoke softly, hoping that Alex would remember the sleeping price.

"Alex," Leo called out in his sleep. Alex hung up with Janet and walked over to him.

"I'm here, Leo," Alex spoke softly and took his hand.

"Alex, lookout," Leo yelled sitting up. He started coughing up blood again. He turned to Alex in tears.

"What is it, Leo?" Alex questioned him.

"Nothing, it's just a nightmare." Alex laid back in bed with Leo. He pulled him close and kissed him.

"Go to sleep, Princy. We have a long day tomorrow. We are going to spend it together, it will be just like before. I promise." Leo slid closer to Alex.

"I like the sound of that," Leo spoke, smiling in a soft voice. He kissed Alex.

"Thank you again for saving my life. I guess you are my knight in shining armor, aren't you?" Alex smiled.

"If that is what you want me to be then sure. Let me get changed." Alex spoke partially sarcastically, and Leo smiled.

"Shut up and kiss me," Leo demanded. Alex did not hesitate to kiss his Prince once more. He stripped and lay in bed for the night. Alex held Leo and watched as he slept. He was afraid of closing his eyes. Leo wasn't safe until this person was caught. He had to figure out a way to get the king to let Janet back in after so many years. Perhaps he could talk to the Queen first. Leo woke again and looked at Alex.

"Are you going to sleep tonight?" Leo was starting to worry again.

"I will now, Princy." Alex was true to his word and closed his eyes. He let himself drift off as Leo slept in his arms.

Before completely falling asleep he kissed Leo again, "I love you."

The Deserved Welcome Home

The next morning Alex woke early. He sat up and looked down at Leo. Leo's skin was still pale, but he no longer had a fever. He went to the bathroom and got Leo some water. He returned to the bed and placed the water on the end table. Leo's eyes slowly opened, and saw Alex there beside him.

"I'm alive?" Leo's voice was raspy and winded. Alex nodded back to him. "I wish I was dead, it would hurt less." Alex crushed the medicine from the doctor and mixed it into his water. He handed Leo the glass. Leo took a small sip before spitting it out. "That's disgusting. I think you're the one trying to poison me."

"Shut up and drink it. It will help, I promise." Leo drank the mixture and made a more disgusted face with each sip. He finished the glass and put it on the table next to him.

"Other than the pain in my throat, I feel okay," Leo said,

rubbing his neck.

"Well, I am very glad to hear that," Alex spoke softly and leaned down to kiss him. Their lips were only inches apart and his bedroom door flung open. Leo's father was standing in the doorway. Alex made a pouty face before turning to see the King.

"How is he, is my boy okay?" Leo sat up confused. His mind started to race. Did he just call him his boy? Alex got out of bed and walked out of the room. He turned back to them before he left,

"I'll give you two some time to talk."

* * *

Alex walked down the main hall to the kitchen. Sarah was there. He stopped and bowed to her.

"Your Majesty," He spoke. Sarah turned to him and smiled.

"What brings you to the kitchen, Alex? We could have brought food to the room for you and Leo." She spoke softly.

"With all due respect, I do not trust your cooks at this moment." Alex looked around the kitchen, opening cabinets.

"Can I help you find something?" Sarah offered.

"A blender would be great." Sarah opened the cabinet below her and pulled one out. Alex began to add fruits and yogurt to it.

"I have not had a smoothie in years." Sarah spoke, "Could I possibly have one as well if it is not too much trouble?" Alex nodded and smiled. He poured her a cup and made a second batch.

* * *

The king sat at the foot of Leo's bed and looked at his son.

"I am so sorry, Leonardo." He spoke trying to keep hold of himself, "Alex was right, you were right. I put my own family in danger. For what? Power, the crown, money."

Leo sat up in the bed and looked at his father.

"You know all I ever wanted was for you to be a father to me. Not just my king." Leo took a breath and swallowed. The pain was a lot. "I only ever wanted to be a prince so that you would see me as your son. I tried to do everything to make you happy and see me. I tried to be happy with this sheltered life you built for me, but nothing I ever did seemed to be enough for you. Do you know what it's like to grow up without friends, to never have experienced heartbreak or your first kiss?" The king looked away from Alex. and started to pace back and forth.

"I do, I used to stay in this room myself. When my father ruled, he forbade me to talk to anyone he thought was a peasant." He stopped and looked at Leo. "It wasn't until Alex's parents came to help us that I had a friend. By that time I was twenty-nine. It was the same time I met your mother. I convinced your grandfather to let us have a great ball like they did in the movies."

"Then why did you do the same thing to me that he did to you?" Leo asked, staring at his father, and waiting for an answer.

"It was never my intention, I wanted to protect you from something like this happening. I knew as King they would do anything to hurt me. So I built up this wall, but I see now that doing so has only made it worse. My own son hates me."

"I never hated you. I just needed to hear that you cared for me. That you loved me." The king walked over to the bed and hugged his son for the first time.

"I do love you, Leonardo. And I want you to be happy. If that means going West and being with Alex, so be it. I will miss you terribly, but I know you will be safer there than if I kept you in a prison here." Leo smiled and hugged his father back. "I'm so glad you're okay, my boy. I love you, Leonardo, I am so proud of the man you have become."

* * *

Alex finished making the second batch of smoothies. He poured them into small glasses and brought them up to Leo's room. He walked in as the king was hugging Leo. Alex cleared his throat and walked in along with Sarah.

"I made you a smoothie, it shouldn't hurt too much to drink, and it will taste better than the medicine." Leo smiled and took the smoothie. "For your sake, Alex, it better taste better." He sipped on it while the King hugged Sarah.

"From this day, Sarah, Leonardo, I will be a changed man. I will be the king, a husband, and a father." Leo smiled and Sarah kissed his cheek. "That reminds me, Alex, we need to talk about our next move." Leo frowned a bit, and Alex stopped the King who was about to walk out of the room.

"With all due respect Your Majesty, the recent events have reminded me how short life is, and I would like to spend the day with Leonardo. Would it be okay if we spoke tonight?" Alex proposed. He still didn't know how to convince the king to let Janet or the CIA help with matters in the palace, and he wanted to hold onto the moments he could with Leonardo.

The king nodded in agreement. "Then we will meet tonight, in the main hall." He took Sarah by the hand. "I think I shall do the same and spend the day with my beautiful wife. You're right Mr. Twist, life is too short to always be worried. But stay on the castle grounds." The King escorted Sarah out of the room, and Alex closed the door behind them.

"Of course, Your Majesty." He turned back to Leo and got in bed next to him. He took the smoothie out of his hands and placed it back on the end table. He put his arms to either side of Leo and held himself over him. "Now where were we?" Leo smiled and put his arms around Alex.

"I believe you were just about to kiss your prince." Leo pulled Alex into him and let himself be taken by the passion of the kiss.

* * *

Alex rolled out of the bed and kissed Alex. "I am going to get cleaned up. Drink your smoothie," Alex demanded from Leo. Leo watched as Alex bent down to grab his underwear and slip them on before walking to the bathroom. He admired his back muscles. Alex walked with a pep to his step, and he bounced back and forth. Leo smiled as he laid back in bed, the blanket just over his waist. He grabbed the smoothie and finished it. He got out of the bed and walked to the bathroom. He knocked on the door before walking in.

Alex was behind the glass of the shower and the fog was enough to keep him covered from the leering eyes of Leonardo. Leo pulled the door open and stepped inside with Alex. Leo kissed his neck and watched as Alex changed shades. Their bodies were pressed against each other, and Alex turned to face him. His hands rested on Leo's chest. He leaned his head down on him.

"I want to be happy like this forever." He whispered to himself. Leo lifted Alex's head and kissed him.

Alex stepped to the side, and let Leo into the water. Alex watched as Leo tilted his head back in the water and his body became saturated. He couldn't help but run his hands down his chest. He was able to feel Leo's heart racing. Leo handed Alex a loofa,

"Do you mind washing my back for me?" He asked, planting a kiss on Alex's neck. Alex washed Leo's back and noticed for the first time the amount of muscle he had in his back. He spent a little longer washing it, to admire his prince more. Leo turned around to Alex. "You okay there?" Alex shook his head and smiled.

"Yeah you're just dirty, Princy." Leo smiled, pulled him close, and kissed him.

* * *

They finished their shower, and Alex grabbed a towel for Leo. Leo dried off and bent in front of Alex, pressing up against him. Alex pressed his lips into a pout.

"Get dressed," Alex spoke while pointing to the door. Leo walked out of the bathroom and went to his closet. He put on one of his suits. Alex walked out of the bathroom in his towel and sat on the bed. He checked his phone to see if Janet had responded with any thoughts on how to convince the King, but there was nothing. He turned and leaned back onto his arms. He looked down at his bag and saw the ring from Leo's mother. Leo walked over to Alex and leaned into him. He gently kissed his head.

"Are you getting dressed today?" Leo asked. Alex held out his hand for Leo to help him up.

"Are you sure you want me to, Princy?" Alex teased and dressed in another black suit. Leo watched as he walked to the bathroom and started to pull his hair up.

"What are the plans today?" Leo called out to him. Alex was holding the hair tie in his mouth while he smoothed his hair back.

"I was thinking you could show me around the palace, maybe we could find a spot to be alone for a bit. There is something I want to talk to you about." Alex called out to Leo while finished pulling his hair up, and started to put in his earrings. He turned back and walked to Leo. "Well, how do I look?"

Leo smiled at the sight of Alex. He sat on the bed and pulled him onto his lap.

"Like a beautiful knight in shining armor." Alex grabbed Leo's crown and put it on his head.

"Good because I have a very attractive prince to protect." They kissed and went to leave the room. Alex let go of Leo's hand and ran back to the bedside. He knelt down and grabbed the ring from the bag and placed it inside the pocket on the inside of the blazer. He hurried back to Leo and took his hand.

Leo showed Alex around the palace but was eager to get outside of it. There were so many memories inside that he wanted to forget. Once outside he slowed down. He took Alex to the far north corner of the palace. There was an old oak tree that had a tire swing on it, a small bench, and a lake. Leo led Alex over a small bridge to the tree.

"When I was younger my mom used to bring me out here, and push me on that." he pointed at the tire and smiled. "I remember crying to her about my days, and she sang to me till I felt better." He walked over and sat on the tire. Alex looked at him and gave him a push. Leo chuckled but hopped off hearing the tree crack. "The old oak might be a little too old now." He chuckled.

Alex walked over to Leo and swept him off his feet. He carried him to the bench nearby.

"Leo," Alex spoke looking down at his hand and seeing the promise ring he gave him. "In the past year, I have learned a lot. I learned that life is really short and that I do not want to live without you in mine." Leo smiled listening to Alex. "I want to be this happy forever." Alex looked up at the sky and thought to himself. Why is this so damn hard? "Since you came into my life, nothing has been the same. I want to be with you forever, Leo." Alex got down on his knee and put his hand in his pocket.

Leo put his hand over his mouth, and his eyes started to water. The queen and king were out for a walk and saw Alex getting down on his knee. The queen held her arm out to stop the king in his tracks before they were seen.

"Leo, you have made me the happiest man in the world, in just one year. Whether we stay here in this big palace, and you become King or we return home to our simple life. I want to be by your side, even though you have tried to shoot me. I may not have much to offer you. I can offer you happiness, a heart that will only beat for you, and a person who will love you unconditionally for years to come. I can promise to protect you forever and spend every second thinking of only you. Will you be my Prince Charming, even though I'm just a Cinder Fella" Leo smiled from ear to ear fighting back his tears. "Leo, will you marry me?"

Leo shook his head yes, and let Alex slip the ring on his finger. Alex stood up and Leo jumped into his arms. His own arms draped around Alex's neck. He kissed him and Alex spun him around.

"Yes. I will be your Prince Charming forever." Alex put him back on the ground, and Leo stared at his new ring. The queen ran over the bridge and hugged the two of them.

"Welcome to the family, Alex." She spoke. Once she backed away, Leo grabbed Alex's hand and placed the other on the inside of his elbow. He laid his head on his shoulder and kissed him softly. "I love you and always will." Alex handed the queen his phone and asked her to take a photo of them.

They stood in front of the oak tree. Alex picked up Leo and held him in his arms. He kissed him, and Leo held onto his neck. The ring is shown more than the crown in the photo. The queen handed Alex back his phone and showed them the photo.

"You better paint this one, Princy." Leo smiled at him.

"You know I will," Leo spoke, watching as his father walked over to them. His father inched closer, very straight-faced. He was face-to-face with Leo.

"Congratulations, Leo." He said, nudging his arm. "I'm very happy for you both."

Leo hugged his father. The four sat around the peaceful area and ate a lunch that the queen had prepared for them. She made a smoothie for Leo, and some ham sandwiches for Alex and themselves.

"What kind of wedding do you two want?" The queen asked she was very excited to plan the wedding. Alex smiled and looked at his fiancé.

"It doesn't matter to me as long Leo is there." Leo smiled.

"I want a royal wedding. I want everything." Leo's father's eyes widened as he remembered the cost of his own royal wedding. He smiled though and nodded.

"It will be the best royal wedding of all." He spoke. "No cost is too high." He looked at Sarah, "Please keep it cheaper than ours." He joked.

They talked a bit and Sarah stood up.

"Come on Leo, let's go look through some magazines and pick things out." No one could tell who was more excited for the wedding, his mother or Leo. Leo took her hand though and turned back to Alex.

"Are you coming along?"

"I'm going to keep Alex here for a little. Gotta have that Father of the Groom talk," the King said. Leo nodded and kissed Alex goodbye.

"Be nice Dad." Leo walked away with his mother with his hand held out in front of him admiring his new ring. It looked amazing on top of the promise ring Alex gave him.

Seventeen

Time To Attack Back

Alex sat on the bench next to the king.

"What is the plan? How to fight back against a person we can't see." The king said, sighing. "How do we protect our family?"

"That one is easy. Live bait." Alex said softly. The king stood up and looked at him.

"You want to use my family as bait?" The king shouted.

"No. Me."

"I don't understand." The king spoke, sitting back down.

"We set the scene, host a press conference that is going make sure you only announce Agent Twist. As far as anyone here knows, that name ended with my parents. Sebastian had no idea who I was even looking at me. He doesn't know that he has left some webs in the closet." The king nodded as he was starting to follow. "I will need a backup of my choosing."

"What did you have in mind?" The king sat back on the

bench.

"Only one agent I truly trust. I want Janet to join us." Alex held his phone in his hand, with her contact pulled up.

"Make the call. She is welcome back." The king nodded and started to walk back to the palace.

"Nothing better happen to you though Alex. Leonardo would never forgive either of us. He is already going to hate this plan as it is. I will make the calls to the press. They will want to meet tomorrow. I will tell them we have opened our doors again to our friends at the CIA, and to speak on the partnership we have with Agent Twist."

Alex nodded knowing well enough Leo would hate it. That is why he hasn't told him yet. It bothered him keeping the secret from Leo and knew he would need to tell him as soon as possible. But first, he had to call Janet and make sure she would be there by morning. Alex dialed the phone and waited for Janet to pick up.

"Alex. Are you okay?" He heard from the other line.

"We have the green light, the trap is set, and missions start tomorrow at 0400."

"Got it, I will be there." Janet went to hang up the phone, but Alex managed to catch her.

"You have one other mission, Agent Johnson. And it might be the most important mission of all."

"And what is that?"

"To walk me down the aisle, Janet. I'm getting married."

"I will gladly accept that mission, Congratulations." Alex could hear the smile in Janet's voice.

Janet hung up the phone and Alex walked back to the palace. He smiled. "I'm engaged to the Prince." He shouted not thinking of who might be around to hear. He didn't care if anyone heard either. He ran to the palace and entered. He ran up the stairs and back to their room. Leo was not in there though. Alex started to search for the big castle for him. Eventually one of the housekeepers stopped him.

"Mr. Twist? Are you lost?" She asked him.

"A little, do you know where the royal family is?"

She nodded, "The king is in his office, the queen and prince are in the dining hall." Alex ran to the dining hall and saw the table was covered with pictures of venues, flowers, cakes, and suits. Alex walked into the room and bowed.

"Your Majesty," Alex spoke and the queen shook her head.

"Would you cut that out already? You are family, family does not bow. At least not to me." She said smiling.

"May I steal the prince?" Leo sat behind the queen shaking his head vigorously. The queen looked at the table.

"I guess we can put a pause on this for now, but we do have so much to plan."

"Thank you," Alex said graciously. Leo stood up and scurried next to Leo. He grabbed his hand and they left the room.

"Thank you." Leo sighed out. "That was exhausting." Leo fell into Alex's arms. Alex swept him off his feet and carried him to their room. He laid him on the couch in the room, took off, and started untying his shoes. "I had no idea what I was getting into when I said yes." Leo quickly sat up. "That came out differently than how I meant it. I wanna marry you, I do."

"Relax Princy, I knew what you meant," Alex spoke crawling over Leo. He kissed him and looked him in the eyes. "There is something I need to tell you."

Leo walked over to the closet mirror and started to undress. "What's up, babe?" Leo asked, undoing the buttons on his shirt.

"I figured out a way to draw out Sebastian." Alex swallowed

hard.

"I knew you would, so that's not really news." He turned to face Alex removing his shirt.

"In order to get him to come out, we needed live bait in a sense."

"NO," Leo shouted and walked over to Alex, instantly regretting it he started to rub his throat. "You just proposed you are not going on a suicide mission. I won't have it Alex." Alex got off the couch and walked over to Leo.

"It's to protect you, and my new family. I'm not asking, but I do want you there. Janet is on her way as well, I will have a backup. We have everything planned out, your father has agreed to it." Leo grabbed and put back on his shirt, and headed for the door.

"Then I will talk to him and change his mind," Leo spoke upset.

"Leo, listen to me." Alex grabbed his arm, pulled him back into the room, and closed the door. "You know Janet would never let anything happen to me, and we can't get married till things calm down around here," Alex spoke softly.

"Alex we just got engaged, this finally no longer feels like a dream to me. All of it. I love you, I only just got you. I don't wanna lose you." Leo let himself fall into Alex. So many thoughts flew through his mind. Alex picked him up and put him on the bed.

"If anything should happen to me. I want you to be the last person I see. Please promise you will be there." Alex begged Leo.

"You know I will be Alex." Leo moved into him. "But you will be okay, right? Is it completely safe?" Leo asked him. His voice broke between words. Alex looked down into Leo's eyes.

"Every mission has its risks, but this one should work without anyone getting hurt. This will not be my last mission. After all, I still have a wedding to attend." Alex spoke softly.

Leo looked up at him. "I don't like it all, but at least we will have Janet here to make sure you don't kill yourself, but until she gets here, I want you to be with me," Leo demanded from Alex. He hated not knowing if this would be the last day he had with him.

"I gave it some thought, and opening a restaurant would be nice. Just being able to settle down with you, now that sounds like a dream come true." Alex spoke dreaming of what might be.

Leo kissed him softly, "It sounds like a plan." Alex got up and locked the door so no one could interrupt them.

"I think we should celebrate the engagement."

"I'm sure my mom is planning that party already," Leo suggested to him.

Alex walked back over to the bed letting his hair down.

"Not exactly what I had in mind. What do you say? I take the lead this time?" Alex spoke in a raspy voice. Leo felt himself blush as Alex stripped and got back in bed with him.

* * *

It was approaching nine at night, Leo and Alex were lying in bed talking and staring into one anther's eyes. Alex climbed on top of Leo and held himself up kissing him. The door flung open and he quickly rolled off Leo.

"Maybe I should have knocked first?" Janet asked. Alex and Leo's faces were both bright red.

"You think, Janet?!" Alex yelled back at her. Janet had her

hand over her eyes to give them some privacy. Alex leaned down, grabbed his pants, and got dressed under the blanket. Leo remained frozen in shock and embarrassment.

"You really had to pick the locks, did you?" "Alex walked over to her, scolding her. Alex sat her facing away from Leo, and he finally mustered up the courage to reach down and grab his pants. He joined them after dressing and listened as Alex fully explained the plan to her.

"Not a bad idea, Alex. You're a chip off the old block." Janet brushed her shoulders off. "Sounds like one of my plans." Janet hugged them both and then went to find her room. "I'll see you boys in the morning. Don't get too frisky, we have work to do."

Janet left the room and closed the door behind her.

Leo let out a sigh of relief,

"After hearing it fully I feel a lot better."

Alex walked to the bed, grabbed one of Leo's pills, and handed it to him. He didn't bother to fight with him and took it. He grabbed Leo and walked him to the bathroom. He pushed the door open and turned on the tub. He grabbed the rose petals from the counter and sprinkled them into it. Alex remembered seeing bottles of champagne for them and some chocolates from the queen on the coffee table and went out of the room to grab them.

When he returned Leo was sitting in the 72-inch double-person jacuzzi tub. Alex popped open the champagne and joined him in it before pouring two glasses. He handed one to Leo.

"To new beginnings," Alex raised his glass to Leo.

"And a happy life." They clinked glasses, both took a sip, and put the glasses down next to the tub. Alex turned off the lights and lit a few candles in the room for them. He opened the box of chocolates which had chocolate strawberries in it. He took one and held it out to Leo. Leo moved forward and took a bite. Alex ate the rest. He leaned forward and kissed Leo. His tongue slid inside his mouth this time. While kissing him he got onto his lap.

"You have changed my life for the better Princy, thank you."

"And you have given me a taste of freedom, and I want more of it," Leo spoke with hunger in his voice. He pulled Alex back down into him.

They dried each other off, and Leo pushed Alex into the wall. He kissed and nibbled on his neck.

"I swear if one more person walks in tonight imma use your gun." He picked Alex up, kissing him. Alex's legs wrapped around him as he carried him back to the bed. He gently placed him down and leaned over him.

"One more time before bed?" Leo questioned.

"Do you even have to ask?" Alex wrapped his arms around Leo's neck.

* * *

Some time later the two lay in bed. Alex held Leo close and fell asleep. Leo was not so lucky. The thought of Alex being there with everyone looking at him, not knowing how the plan would end kept him up. The endless possibilities sent him into a panic attack. His legs started shaking, and his breath became shallow. Alex stirred and opened his eyes.

"What is it, Princy?" Alex whispered to him.

"Alex, I'm worried, please don't do it." He begged him.

"Leo, I understand you're scared. But I will be okay," He put his hand under Leo's chin and lifted it. "We will be together for a very long time, our story does not end tomorrow. I promise." Alex spoke softly. Hearing him promise meant a lot to Leo. Alex, in the time they have been together, has never once broken a promise to him. No matter how small it was.

"I'll try and sleep. I promise." Leo spoke back.

"Good because now I will not sleep until I know you are." Alex kissed him. Leo slowly started to settle and drift off to sleep listening to the sound of Alex's heart.

Eighteen

Let The World Know

Leo woke up before Alex the next morning. He dressed and went to the kitchen. He tried to remember everything Alex taught him. He started whisking together the ingredients for pancakes. He smiled remembering the first time Alex made them for him. He put in so many chocolate chips it tasted more like a dessert than a breakfast.

"I like it better with chocolate in them." He could hear Alex's voice in his head. "Come on, try them for me Leo."

Leo added some chocolate chips into them, and some pieces of banana, since he knew it was Alex's favorite fruit. He poured it on the skillet and could swear he felt Alex's hand over his. If he closed his eyes it felt like they were back in their small house. Leo opened his eyes and watched the batter start to bubble. He flipped them and let out a sigh of relief, they were golden brown and not burnt. He counted to himself so the other side would not burn as well.

Once he had a stack of pancakes he made coffee for them. He smiled thinking about the first time he made Alex's coffee. He put way too much sugar in it and Alex had spit the coffee all over the table. Even though he was tempted to do it again to get the same reaction out of him, he only put in two cubes of sugar. He placed everything on a tray and stood there leaning over it.

His eyes filled with tears as he thought about his nightmare from last night. He saw Alex being shot right in front of him, his love died in his arms. He was so afraid of this happening at the press conference and hated knowing that there was nothing he could do to change Alex's mind. Leo dried his eyes and looked around the kitchen. He put a single long-stem rose in a vase, before carrying it back up to his room.

He placed the tray on the table next to the bed and leaned over Alex. He kissed him and Alex's eyes opened. He smiled looking up at Leo.

"Good morning, Princy." Alex looked at Leo and could tell he had been crying. He hugged him tight. "I am going to be okay."

"But what if you're not? What if something happens?" Leo spoke softly.

"The only thing you need to worry about, Leo, is what if you oversleep on our wedding day," Alex spoke, lifting Leo's head so his eyes would match his. "Don't focus on things you can't control."

Leo nodded and handed Alex the tray of food. Alex looked down at it.

"It looks perfect, Leo."

"What could I say, I had a pretty alright teacher," Leo joked and Alex nudged him.

Leo smiled as Alex cut into them. He was hoping that they were cooked right in the middle. He felt like he was waiting for the judge's critique and Alex was Gordan Ramsey. Alex looked up at him.

"These are the best pancakes I have ever had." Alex kissed him. "They are definitely going to be on the menu when we open that restaurant." Leo smiled once Alex finished the food then stood and extended his hand.

"We should probably go get showered and dressed before someone walks in on us," Leo suggested looking back at the door. Alex nodded and went to the bathroom with Alex. Leo started the shower and held the door open for Alex, who bowed to him and stepped into the shower. Leo watched as Alex let the water run down his hair and back. He took every detail in. He wanted to remember this moment forever. He grabbed the shampoo, then leaned into Alex and kissed him. He started to scrub his hair. Alex's eyes closed, enjoying the sensation.

He rinsed his hair out and looked at Leo. He pulled him close, kissing him and spinning him so he was in the water. He returned the favor and washed his lover. The two stepped out of the shower and dried off. They hung up their towels and walked out of the shower. Leo froze and covered up his neither reign with his hands.

"I thought I said don't get too frisky." Janet jokes, sitting in the room waiting for them. She had been dressed in a purple blouse, pearls, and blue jeans The outfit was finished with a pair of black heels. Alex pushed Leo to the side and stood in front of him, mimicking his gesture, and covering himself up. He walked back to push Leo into the bathroom.

Alex turned and put on a pair of boxers, and looked over at Janet.

"We need to have a talk about boundaries." He scowled at her through his teeth. "I can't believe you would just come, let alone sit there and wait for us. You couldn't come back?"

Janet stood up and walked around the room admiring the art that hung around. She turned back to Alex and tossed his suit at him.

"I could have just come into the bathroom and dragged you both out. The king wants to see us immediately." Janet repeated the king's orders. Alex grabbed Leo's clothing and handed it to him through the door. Alex dressed and Janet pointed at his bag that still had the bulletproof vest in it.

"You better put that on." She demanded from him. Alex ignored her request and pulled up his hair. He put on his promise ring from Leo, and the Royal family ring as well.

Leo walked out of the room and avoided eye contact with Janet. He put on his gold watch, and tie. He was shaking, still worried about the events planned for the day. Alex walked over to him and tied it for him. Alex pushed back some of Leo's hair and smiled at him. Janet was walking out the door and called back to them.

"We are in the dining hall." Janet barked and closed the door behind her.

Alex grabbed his bag and put it on the bed. He turned to Leo and took off his blazer. He slid his hand into the bag and pulled out the bulletproof vest. He kissed Leo and slid the vest on him. He started to zipper it up when Leo pulled away.

"You need this more than me. I want you to wear it today please," Leo requested.

"I will feel better knowing it is on you," Alex suggested to him. He zippered it and kissed his cheek. "You're still the prince, and you need to be protected at all times. Plus he may want me dead when he finds out who I am, but you're still the main target for someone else." Leo nodded and hugged him.

"Fine, but if anything happens you get out of there okay? No heroics." Leo ordered Alex.

"Promise."

* * *

Leo and Alex walked into the dining hall. Leo sat next to his mother, and Alex sat next to him. The king clapped his hands and the butlers brought out breakfast. The table was lined with eggs, toast, sausage, and pancakes. The five ate breakfast in silence. Leo's fear was shared by them all. Sarah did not want her son to be left heartbroken. The king felt the worry from his wife and placed his hand over hers on the table. Janet sat staring at Alex.

The new head butler came into the room. "

Your Majesty's, the limo has arrived." The five stood up went outside and climbed into the limo. Alex sat between Janet and Leo and the king and queen sat on the other side.

"This better work," Janet whispered to Alex who nodded and took Leo's hand.

"It will."

* * *

The limo came to a stop, Alex took his gun out and handed it to Leo.

"I know you won't let anything happen to me." Leo took

it and slipped it into the waist of his pants. He kissed Alex's hand. The two stepped out of the limo after the King and Queen, and Janet ended the trail of them. Leo and Alex did not hold hands or kiss outside of the limo. They both knew there would be a time to talk about them, and this was not it.

They were greeted by a lady who had on a red suit. Her hair was unkempt and had dark rings around her eyes.

"We will start in three minutes. We will have everyone walk out together, pose for the camera then everyone but the king will take their seats." She started barking out orders and looked at Janet. "And you are?"

"Press channel 5," she flashed a press badge and the producer waved her in. Janet went in and took a seat in the middle of the crowd. Alex watched as she walked and sat down so he knew exactly where she was. The producer started to count down from 5. She got to one and pushed Alex in first, followed by Leo, the Queen, and then the King.

Alex walked out from behind the curtain first. There were flashes in every direction from the press, and people shouting questions at him. He found himself a little lightheaded having so many eyes on him. He went from being undercover all the time, and now he is the center of attention. He walked behind the podium keeping eye contact with Janet, before glancing around the bleachers. Nothing looked out of the ordinary yet. Leo walked out and joined next to him.

"You okay?" Leo asked him. Alex slightly shook his head to the side. Leo reached over and let his pinky brush against his hand. He noticed that his stance eased a bit. Leo rubbed his hand while his mom and father took the stage. They posed for a few photos before taking their seats in the front row.

The king cleared his voice, "Ladies and Gentlemen, thank

you for your time today. As you all know we have been under attack. Someone threatened my family, and in the challenge of protecting them I closed us off to our friends at the CIA, I have closed our borders to travel. I fear it has only hurt our beautiful country. I hope you can find it in your heart to forgive my rash and horrible decision. It is now that we have decided it is time to fight back and take back what is ours." The king made a fist and brought it down on the podium. "The CIA has joined us today, and they will be here until we find the culprit and bring them to justice. Please join me in welcoming Agent Alex Twist. The child of my old friends at the CIA Don Twist, and Liza Twist."

The king stepped to the side of the podium and clapped. The press joined the king in clapping. Alex stood from his chair and walked onto the stage. He bowed to the King and turned to the press. The king took the empty seat next to Leo. Leo felt his heart racing faster than it ever has. He held his hand over his chest. He was starting to have a panic attack. His eyes were glued to Alex and he started to speak.

"Thank you, Your Majesty. It is my pleasure to be here on loan from America." Alex looked around the crowd. "It is the goal of the CIA, not only to protect the royal family but to make sure whoever started all this will come to justice. Thirty years ago the CIA loaned the royal family to my Father." He paused for a moment. "My mother, and Agent Johnson, and although things did not go as planned, their mission did not stop with them." Alex watched as Janet stood awaiting any orders. She moved out of the crowd and looked around.

"I have worked on this case." Alex spotted Sebastian, he put down a bag and started to put together a sniper. "Although my parents are no longer here, I carry out the name and legacy.

And although it has cost so many lives, I will protect the royal family even if it costs me my life. As for our plans at the CIA, we will fly more agents from the **West**, and we will bring swift justice and aid. We, at the CIA, always **look up**, and know exactly where and when an attack will come from."

Janet nodded and looked up at the bleachers, she started to run towards the west side of the auditorium. She saw Sebastian lining up his shot. She pulled out her gun and held it to his head. "Pull that trigger and it will be the last thing you ever do. You won't even have the pleasure of seeing that bullet hit him."

Sebastien let go of the trigger and held his hands up. Janet took the butt of the gun and bashed it into his head hard enough that he passed out. She cuffed him and looked down at Alex. She nodded to him.

"Overall we want you to know that the Royal family is under the protection of the CIA, and nothing will happen to them this time." The king stood back up and walked to the podium. He held open his arms and invited his family on stage with him. He put his arms around them and posed for another photo.

"We open the floor now for questions." The king called out and looked at the press raising their hands. He pointed to a lady in the front row.

"Prince Leo, it has been over a year since anyone has seen you. What was it like in the West? Is this the same agent who nearly died protecting you?"

Leo walked to the podium and took a breath. He adjusted the microphone. There was instant gossip among the press.

"Look at his hand, He's engaged, to who, where was that announcement?" Leo could hear them all.

"My time in the West was enjoyable. They did a wonderful job protecting me. The CIA loaned me the best agent they had." He tried to fight the smile he felt forming on his face. "Agent Twist has been my personal guard for the past year, and yes he almost died for me. The CIA is here to help, it's time to forget the past and move forward."

Leo pointed to someone in the middle of the crowd. And they stood up.

"Are you engaged, is there going to be a royal wedding?"

Leo looked down at this hand and realized he used it to adjust the mic. There was no way anyone would miss the ring. He looked to his father who nodded. Leo looked around the room and saw Alex who was still looking up at Janet. He followed Alex's eyes and saw Janet standing in the back with one foot on Sebastian's chest. He saw her bend down as he bashed him in the head again with her gun.

Leo held his hand behind him and reached for Alex, who took it and walked to stand next to Leo. "Over the past year I have grown close to Agent Twist, and look forward to the day I get to marry him." Leo, relieved they caught Sebastian, was able to relax. He kissed Alex's cheek, and the press took hundreds of photos. Alex put his arm around Leo.

"Agent Twist, will you give up the CIA?"

"Prince Leonardo, will you give up the crown?"

"Will Agent Twist become a prince?"

There were so many questions the press had, it was the first royal wedding for many of them. It was a huge story that they all wanted. The royal guard went up to Janet and took Sebastian off her hands. She walked down the bleachers and joined the press.

"Agent Twist, will you settle down with the prince and live

happily ever after?" Janet shouted up to them louder than the rest. Leo's face went red from all the questions and he turned away and hid his face in Alex's shoulder.

Alex held up his hand. "No further questions at this time please." Alex shot Janet a look and escorted Leo off the stage and back to the car. The king and queen followed behind them and Janet took the rear. She kept her gun at the ready once they left the building and looked around before getting into the car.

She sat in the car with her gun on her lap. She looked at Alex and whispered in his ear. "Code Ivory." Alex turned and saw a BMW with tinted windows following them. Every turn they took the car was tailing them.

Alex looked to the king and the queen and took Leo's hand.

"Call the palace, we have trouble. We are being followed," Alex demanded from the king. The king did as Alex suggested to him.

They pulled up to the palace and there was a group of guards there to take the queen and King in. Alex got out of the car and put his hand in the car for Leo to take. Janet got out closely after him. She rushed him into the house.

Alex walked to the palace gates where the BMW was parked. He walked out of the gate and knocked on the window of the car with the butt of his gun. He couldn't see through the windows even that close to the car. The window did not roll down. Alex punched through the window with his gun. The car was empty, and there was no one he could see anywhere around. He shot the tires of the car, so it could not be moved before opening the door. Looking inside he only found a coffee and an empty notebook that had pages torn out of it. He grabbed the notebook and joined everyone inside.

Nineteen

A Breakthrough

Alex joined the King, Queen, and Janet in the sitting room. He looked at Janet and shook his head. "The car was empty" He spoke defeated.

"I figured as much, Once we question Sebastian we should learn more," Janet promised.

"We are not talking to him. The royal guards can only do so much, the same with you, Janet. He thinks I am still in the CIA, and that I will also have limits. But there is nothing holding me back from getting the answers I want."

"Alex no, you are too close, this involves your parents, let's not go back down that path again." Janet tried to convince him.

"Let me talk to him."

Leo walked into the room and sat on Alex's lap. "It's not about my parents, it's about my family now." He spoke, squeezing Leo. "I am not going back down that path again. I have a light in the darkness now."

The King stood up, "You will both speak to him. If things do not go as intended then Alex may have his time with Sebastian alone." He ordered the two. Janet and Alex agreed to his terms. "The guards have been questioning him and have had no luck yet. They have stopped for the day. I have ordered them to get no meals or drinks for him so that should give you some leverage for tomorrow morning."

He took his wife's hand and they left the room. Janet crossed her legs and let her posture slip, turning to Alex and Leo.

"So I hear you two got engaged?" Janet questioned, trying to lighten the mood. Leo held out his hand and Janet's jaw dropped. "It's beautiful." She looked at Alex. "Have you guys thought about what the plans are next, after the wedding?" Leo nodded and laid his head on Alex's shoulder.

"Opening a restaurant together back home," Leo spoke with so much joy in his voice. Janet stood up,

"Oh, I will have to make sure to stop by and try out the food. Sorry, I need a smoke, and to get out of these heels." She walked outside the front door and closed it behind her. Leo stood and helped Alex up.

"I am going to head to our room, and get changed, don't be long. You don't want to miss the show right?" Leo kissed his cheek and ran his finger down his chest. He turned and Alex watched as he walked up the stairs to their room.

Alex walked out and joined Janet.

"What did you find in the car?" Janet questioned Alex, who pulled the notebook out of his pocket and handed it to her. They both looked over the area looking for anything out of the ordinary. She took the book from him and started to look through it. She pulled out her pencil and pulled a page from the back of the book. She laid it on top and scribbled along the page. They looked together at the note.

The Royal family thinks they won by capturing Sebastian. They think that just because the CIA is here, they are safe again. Let us send them a little reminder we are not to be messed with... I think a nice explosion will do. J.

Alex and Janet looked at each other and ran inside the palace. Janet ran to the King and Queen to alert them. Alex ran up the stairs. He burst through the door and ran to Leo. He pulled him away from the window. That he was looking out of. The car exploded, and shrapnel was sent flying. Alex pulled Leo to the ground once his window started to shatter. Alex used himself as a shield. Just as fast as things happened they stopped. Alex took a deep breath and stood up. He helped Leo to his feet.

Leo stared at Alex, "I thought I said no heroics." Leo spoke, sternly looking at Alex's torn suit.

"I'm sorry Princy, can you ever forgive me?" Alex replied leaning in and kissing him.

"I guess I can, just this once." He kissed him back. He took off Alex's blazer and saw he was bleeding. He ran to the bathroom and grabbed some cleaning pads. Alex took off his shirt, and Leo cleaned the scrapes and scratches. He shook his head as Alex squinted from the pain. A knock came on their door. Leo walked over and opened it. His father pushed his way in and looked out the broken window. He saw their limo had exploded as well as the car by the gate.

The king put his hand on his head. "I thought this was going to help, not make things worse." He shouted as he turned around and looked at Alex and Janet. "I knew it was a mistake to let you two be here. My family could have died, my son nearly died again. I want you both on the next flight back to America."

"NO." Leo stood up and looked at his father. "If you can't see what is really going on here, then maybe you need to step down as King."

The king's eyes widened, Sarah walked over to the two and stood next to Leonardo.

"He is right, dear. It's okay to be scared, but how is going backward going to help now?"

"Well then what do you suggest?" He spoke looking at Alex and Janet.

Janet walked into the room and let her hand rest on Alex's shoulder.

"Let us protect you, We move out of the palace for now, we go somewhere no one will ever think of looking for us. There is a little hotel up the road. We go there, get some rooms, and remain there. Give us at least three days, Your Majesty." Janet bowed before him, " Let us figure this out."

"I don't like it," The king barked back.

Leo knelt down next to Alex and continued to clean the wounds.

"I am going to see Sebastian now." Alex's blood was boiling. Knowing that if he was just a few seconds later there would have been no wedding. He would have lost his love. He put his hand on Leo's cheek. Leo closed his eyes and laid his head in his hand. " I'm getting answers today."

The king left the room with the queen. Alex stood up and went to his bag. He changed out of his suit.

"Alex I know what you're thinking, I have seen that look before," Janet shouted at him. "Do not do this."

Alex pulled his hair up and looked at her. "You're not

stopping me this time, Janet." He dumped his bag on the bed. He grabbed a pair of brass knuckles, a small knife, and two more guns. He slipped the brass knuckles into his pocket, and the knife into a holder on his back belt loop. He walked over to Leo's closet and grabbed a leather coat from it. He turned to Leo,

"Is my dad's bike still here?" Leo nodded. Alex kissed him and headed out the door. "You better protect him, Janet," Alex spoke to her, giving an order.

Alex ran down the stairs and into the garage. His dad's bike sat under a tarp. He ripped the tarp off it and was in awe. It was still in mint condition; the flames didn't have a scratch on them. It was just like how his father used to talk about it. He hot-wired it and sped out of the garage. Leo watched as Alex sped out the gate.

* * *

Alex pulled up to the prison where they were holding Sebastian. He parked the bike and kicked the doors open. He walked right through the security and pushed a guard who got in his way to the side. His eyes were set on the last holding cell. The guards unlocked the gate and it slid open. Sebastian tried to make a run for it and ran right into Alex's fist. He shoved him back into the stall.

"How do you wanna do this, the easy way or the hard way?" Alex cracked his neck and knuckles at the same time. "I am really hoping you pick the hard way," Alex spoke with seriousness in a voice that sent shivers up the guard's body.

"I won't say a word," Sebastian yelled.

"Oh good, this will be fun then." Sebastian stood up and ran at Alex, he reached behind him and grabbed the knife from him. He attempted to stab him, but found his arm caught by Alex. Alex turned and flipped him over his shoulder, then jerked and popped his arm out of its socket. Sebastian dropped the knife.

"You can't do this," Sebastian cried out in pain. "The CIA will never let you get away with this."

Alex laughed in return and looked down as he stood over him. "I'm not with the CIA anymore." He punched him in the face, breaking his nose. "I am completely rouge now." Alex threatened and raised his eyebrows. Alex kicked him in the ribs and he heard something crack again.

"Do you remember the message that came back to you about the guy who killed my father for you? How I beat him within an ounce of his life?" Sebastian did not answer but his face went ghost white. "You won't be so lucky. You not only killed my family but threatened my love as well. I'm always one step ahead of you." Alex stepped back and Roundhouse kicked Sebastian.

"He trusted you, he saw you as a friend." Sebastian coughed up some blood.

"I never wished any harm to Leonardo." Alex knelt down and looked him in the eyes. He was speaking the truth.

"Then who did? Why are you protecting them, Sebastian? You're already here for life for killing the previous king."

Sebastian was having trouble breathing with Alex's knee on his chest. He headbutted Alex and busted his lip. Alex could feel the cut on his lip and see the blood falling from it. Alex put the brass knuckles back on and punched him in the face again. He watched as Sebastian's cheek instantly swelled.

"Who are you protecting? Who is J?" Alex punched him

again. Sebastian was having a hard time keeping his eyes open.

"He is just a name," Sebastian spoke through the screams of pain.

"What do you mean he is just a name?"

"I never met him, he always sent letters, we met on the dark web."

Alex got off him, "Sebastian, that's not good enough. I have seen the letters, I know you two met so stop lying to me. I know the hemlock wasn't yours either. Who was it?

"When we met he was wearing a hood. I could not see him clearly. As for the hemlock, I don't know."

Alex hated it but he was telling the truth. "Where did you send the letters to? You had an address… Give it to me."

Sebastian thought about it. "If I give you that, he will kill me."

Alex pulled out his gun and pointed it at him. "If you don't, I will kill you. I wouldn't take my chances on the guards protecting you over this missing bullet." He held the gun directly against his head.

Sebastion screamed for the guards who did not come to his aid. "You killed the king and nearly started a war. Do you think they are going to stop me, the one protecting the Prince? I will only ask one more time. An address?" Alex demanded and tilted his head.

Sebastian swallowed hard, "595 Bridge Way Blvd." Alex put the gun back into its holder. "If you are lying to me I will be back and you will regret it. Guard!" Alex yelled and the gate opened. Sebastian grabbed the knife off the floor and flung it at Alex. It cut the side of his face. He knelt down and grabbed it. He turned and threw it back at Sebastian. It landed on the shoulder of the arm Alex did not break. Alex walked back out of the prison and told the guards he had a knife.

He went outside and called Janet.

"Alex, are you okay?" Janet asked after worrying for hours. "Leo has had four panic attacks already, you can't just leave him like that. You said nothing, he thinks you're out there killing a man." Janet heard the sink going and Alex washing his hands. "You didn't."

"595 Bridge Way Blvd, we move in three days. Tell Leo I will be back in a few minutes. Have him pack us clothing. We are moving the family tonight."

Alex hung up the phone and looked in the mirror at the cut on his face. It was pretty deep; he knew it would need stitches.

* * *

Leo finished packing his bags along with Alex's. He sat by the broken window waiting for Alex to return. He saw a headlight shine through the gate and raced downstairs. He waited in the doorway. His heart was racing a mile per minute. Alex parked the bike by the stairs and Leo ran down to him. Alex got off the bike and Leo jumped into his arms. "If you ever pull a stunt like this again you better come back dead because if not I'm going to kill you myself," Leo spoke crying. He hugged Alex and felt blood fall onto his cheek. He looked up and saw Alex's gash. "What happened?" Alex took his hand and looked him in the eye.

"I protected my prince, and got answers." They walked into the house and up to their room. Alex pulled out a small first aid kit from under the bed. "Is your hand steady?" Leo nodded, and Alex handed him a needle and thread.

"I can't hurt you." Alex put the needle in his hands.

"You won't hurt me," Alex whispered to him.

Leo burnt the needle and started to sew up his cheek. "Are you okay?" Alex nodded and continued. He tied it off and just in time because Janet kicked the door in.

"If you hang up on me one more time Alex." She pulled out her gun. "I swear I will shoot you."

"Relax Mom. I got the information we needed, and he isn't dead, just in a lot of pain." Alex spoke sarcastically to her. Janet holstered her gun.

"Three days we move in. What do we do till then?"

Alex looked at Leo. "Till then we move the family to a hotel where you guard the queen and king along with the royal guard. As for me, I'm showing my prince his country." He looked at Leo. "I am taking you to see the sights you never got to see. And if anyone tries anything they will regret it." Alex watched as Leo's face lit up.

"The king won't like it, Alex."

"The king will deal with me. The prince deserves to know what his country has to offer."

"I will have to deal with who?" The king walked into the room. The queen was right behind him.

"Janet says you got the answers you needed, and that in due time whoever this J is will be under wraps, and things can return to normal." Alex smiled.

"Told you my plan would work, " Alex said smugly. "Are you both packed and ready to go, the less time we are here the better. The queen held up their bags.

"It will be nice to get out of the palace for a change, almost like a second honeymoon dear." She kissed the king's cheek.

"Yes well…" He turned and kissed her.

"The queen and King will ride with me, Alex. Are you and

Leo riding along as well?"

Alex shook his head no, "We are going on a little adventure, we'll meet you there."

The three walked out and pulled out of the garage.

Alex turned to Leo, "But first you're not wearing that suit." Alex handed him a bag of clothing he just bought on the way home and he went to the bathroom to change.

Twenty

Adventure Awaits

Leo opened the bag of clothing and pulled out a new T-shirt and a pair of blue faded jeans. He slipped into them and pushed his hair back. He took a look at his reflection fast in the mirror and sprayed his cologne on. He smiled at the idea of an adventure with Alex. He didn't want to keep him waiting. He opened the door and walked out.

He smiled as he walked to Alex. "Janet took our bag right?" Leo asked him. Alex nodded and took his hand. Leo ran holding Alex's hand down the stairs. "What are we doing tonight?"

"It's a surprise." They made it outside and to the bike. Alex handed Leo the helmet and pulled his hair up. Leo put it on and lifted the visor. He was nervous because he had never ridden a motorcycle before. Alex mounted the bike and held it steady for Leo to get on. Leo managed to get onto the bike and wrapped his arms around Alex's waist.

"Is this okay?" Alex turned back to face him before they took off. He nodded and kissed his nose through the visor. Alex started the bike and took off. Leo's grip tightened around Alex's waist, He enjoyed feeling the wind on his skin. He took the helmet and put it in the compartment of the bike. Alex saw him in the rearview mirror and smiled. Leo loved the feel of the air blowing through his hair. He was smiling and watching as the nightlife and lights flew by.

"Do you trust me?" Alex yelled back to him.

"You know I do," Leo yelled. Alex nodded, jerked the handlebars up, and heard Leo yells behind him. He was enjoying the thrill. He was on an adrenaline rush, but he loved the feeling. He felt free again, something he had not felt since they arrived back in London.

Alex drove them to the Eye of London. They parked the bike and got in line. Leo started to shiver as the nights were cool and damp. They stood in line waiting to get on. Alex took off his coat and draped it around him. Leo grabbed the coat while keeping his arms crossed. He was living in one of his romance books. He might have been the prince, but to him, Alex was the prince. He made him so happy every moment he could.

The line moved faster than they had expected and when they made it to the front of the line the guards bowed. Leo and Alex walked in, and the guards closed the door. They got their own cart since he was the prince. They sat on the bench while they made their way to the top.

Leo smiled thinking about his birthday last year. "Remember when you took me out on my birthday?" Leo asked, and Alex nodded.

"You came over and sat next to me, I looked into your eyes, and was instantly hypnotized. The lights danced in them much like they were tonight. I remember I was about to kiss you when the ride started again." Alex laid back on the bench and watched as they were slowly climbing higher. Leo lay next to him and looked up at him. He laid his head on his chest and listened to the beating. "I love you, Alex," Leo spoke softly.

"I love you too, Leonardo." They lay together staring into each other's eyes. Leo moved in closer and kissed him. About ten minutes later, the two sat up. Alex watched as Leo's face lit up. Leo stood up and was watching all the lights of the city. Alex stood behind him and held him close, rubbing his arms to keep him warm. They made it to the top of the Eye. Leo looked out over the city and smiled.

"This is all yours, Princy. Are you really sure you want to give it all up to just be with me?" Alex asked him. He wanted to make sure he really wanted this. Leo turned from the city view and looked at Alex.

"There is no doubt in my mind. This is nice to look at, and I would not mind coming back to see it. But I can only see my life with you, Alex. This all means nothing to me. All that matters to me is being with you. Don't ever doubt that. I decided I wanted a simple life with you. I want that white picket fence, I want a family of our own. I love you, Alex Twist."

Alex never thought about kids, but he did like the sound of having a family with Leo. Alex smiled and hugged his prince. The ride was starting to go back down. Alex held onto Leo as his life depended on it. The ride came to a stop and the two interlocked arms and walked off.

"What do you say we go and grab some food?" Alex asked as his stomach started to growl. Leo smiled and looked at Alex.

"Wherever you wanna go, I'll follow you."

Alex took his hand and led him over to a small 50's dinner. They walked inside and music was playing. The floor had black and white tiling. There was a jukebox in the corner. "Seat yourself, Hun," A waitress called from the bar." Alex and Leo walked over to a booth. The seats were blue with white stripes, and the table was white metal. Alex sat across from Leo and took his hand. There was a plastic one-page menu on the table. The two looked it over before the waitress came over.

Her hair was red and pulled up, she wore a blue 50's dress and was on rollerblades.

"What can I start you two love birds off with?" She spoke looking down at her pad.

"I'll take a root beer float with two straws." She nodded and scribbled on her pad before rolling off. She rolled back with their drink. Leo took a sip and smiled. He never had something like that before. It wasn't something that the king would allow in the palace. He dipped his finger in the whipped cream and plopped it on Alex's nose, who in return smiled and did the same. He leaned in and licked the whipped cream off his nose.

"I'll be right back." Alex got up and went to the jukebox. He scrolled through the song options. He slipped a quarter into the machine and pressed H7. He walked back to Leo, extended his hand, and bowed. "May I have this dance?" Leo took his hand and began to dance. Alex sang to Leo along with the jukebox.

Alex started to sing "Can't Help Falling In Love With You" By Elvis as the two swung to slow music. Leo rested his head on Alex's shoulder. The waitress leaned against the bar watching the two.

"Take my hand," Alex continued to sing and Leo looked up and kissed him. The two danced the whole song before taking their seats again.

The waitress came over, "Do you two know what you want to eat?"

They both ordered burgers and she left. Leo looked at Alex.

"You never cease to amaze me. You sing like an angel. Is there anything you can't do, Alex?"

"There is one thing. I could never stop loving you." Leo smiled at how corny his fiancé was. The two talked a bit until the food arrived. They ate and paid the waitress.

"We close in 10 minutes guys." She called from the bar.

"What do you say, Leo, one more dance?" Leo nodded.

"Always." He smiled and put a quarter in the jukebox. He put on, "Put Your Head on My Shoulder". The two danced while Alex again sang to Leo. The song came to an end and Alex bowed to Leo. He took his hand and led him out of the restaurant. They made their way back to the bike.

Alex drove them to the hotel where they were going to meet with Janet, the King and Queen. It was already going on midnight, and he knew they were about to get ripped apart by one of the three.

* * *

Alex parked the bike and stepped off before helping Leo off. Leo was so tired that he was stumbling into Alex as they walked into the Hotel. They walked to the front counter and the lady at the front desk noticed Leo. She bowed and handed him the room key. We closed off the whole floor for you and your family, Your Highness." Alex took the room key and looked at the number. He led Leo to the elevator and held him up while they stood inside it. Once the door opened Alex picked him up and carried him to their room.

Alex pushed the door open and placed Leo on the bed. He turned and locked the door. He went to the bathroom and started the tub before stripping Leo and himself and carrying him to it. He placed Leo into the water. Leo let out a sigh of relief and the warm water felt great on his cold skin. He looked at Alex as he stepped into the tub. He grabbed the washcloth and started to wash his chest. The two soaked for a bit in the tub, before getting out they dried off and went to the beds.

Leo lay in bed while Alex took down his hair, He ordered them some room service for dessert. He lay next to Leo and held him close. A few minutes after he got in bed a knock came from the door. "Room service." Alex walked over and cracked the door enough to grab the cheesecakes. He turned and lay next to Leo. He fed Leo the cheesecake. He smiled softly, watching Leo enjoying the cake. He looked over at the time and saw that it was one in the morning. He turned off the lights and lay down. Leo rolled and straddled Alex. He leaned down and kissed him.

He adjusted as things began to grow. "My knight in shining armor by daylight, and my sweet lover by sunset." He balanced on his knees and kissed Alex's neck. "Thank you for another amazing date." Alex's hips started to buck up into Leo. Leo started to press down onto him. "What do you say? We have a little more dessert."

Alex smiled. "You don't have to ask me twice," Alex spoke, ready to give in to his every desire. Leo leaned down and kissed Alex's neck and kissed his lips softly. He kissed down his chest and to his hips. Alex reached over to the end table and turned off the lights.

He laid back and sunk into his pillows. He clenched the blankets as pleasure overcame him. His eyes closed as he reached the climax of the night. Leo came back up and kissed his cheek. Alex flipped Leo over and started to kiss his neck. He made sure to leave a little mark as he kissed down to his collarbone. "I love you, Leonardo." He inched closer, planting kisses softly as he did. Leo's hips bucked up to Alex as his hands slipped down his legs. Leo's knees were bent, and the blanket lay right on top of Alex's neck. Alex came back up to the pillows.

Leo rolled over to face Alex. He closed his eyes and drifted off. Alex stayed awake a bit longer listening to his soft breath. He hated closing his eyes and letting nights like this end. He closed his eyes and let his exhaustion win. His eyes drifted closed and his breaths matched Leo's. His last thought was what Leo said on the London Eye. He could see himself having a child with him, living in that small house with a picket fence, and living happily.

"I love you, Leonardo." He let his lips roll off as he fell asleep.

Twenty-One

A Day To Remember

Leo yawned and rolled over to face Alex. He smiled and put his arm around him. He looked over his shoulder and saw the alarm clock read six am. He sat up in bed and looked around. He got up and stretched before walking to the bathroom. He looked in the mirror and saw the love bite left on his collarbone. He put his hand over it and smiled.

He moved his head to the side to look back at Alex. He admired his chest and his strong jawline. He turned around and lifted the blanket, before straddling Alex. He leaned down and kissed him. Alex swung his arms around Leo's neck and pulled him into himself.

"Should we meet your parents for breakfast?" Alex looked up at him. "I mean we should show them you're alive before I steal you away for the day again." Leo smiled and nodded, he got off Alex and leaned against the door to the bathroom.

"Maybe we should shower first?" Alex stood up and walked

over to him. He put his arms on either side of Leo's head. "You could take advantage of me in the shower as well," Leo suggested tilting his head and exposing his neck. "Something a little quick?" Leo questioned, last night left him wanting more. They walked into the bathroom and locked the door behind them.

* * *

In the lobby Janet was making coffee, She sipped it and made a disgusted face. It was even worse than the coffee Alex made her. She made a plate of food and sat next to the king and queen who were already eating.

"Have you heard from Alex or Leo?" The queen questioned Janet.

"I have not, Your Majesty." She responded after swallowing her food. "I am sure they are okay though."

"I wish they would have at least called when they got in last night." The queen worried, looking around the corner hoping they would be joining them. Janet sat back in her chair and sipped more coffee. They were a little busy last night, she thought to herself. Her room was right next to theirs, and she heard everything. She had to blast her television to drown the two out.

Alex and Leo turned the corner shortly after, holding hands. Leo walked over to the queen and hugged her.

"Mom, the London Eye is beautiful at night." Leo smiled and kissed her cheek.

"Isn't it Leo? I remember when your father took me there for the first time." The queen started reminiscing with the King. Leo took a seat next to his mother and listened to her story of their time on the London Eye. Alex was at the breakfast bar preparing a plate for himself and Leo. Janet walked over to him and leaned against the bar. She kept her eyes glued to the royal family.

"You two got in late last night. Was it a nice night?" Alex was stuffing his face with some toast while making more for Leo.

"It was a night I won't forget," Alex responded to her. "You know, the city lights look amazing through his eyes," Alex told her.

"Can you two maybe keep it down tonight?" Janet asked. Alex's face turned as red as the ketchup on his plate.

"How much did you hear?" Alex asked her.

"Enough to know that Leo is a screamer." Janet joked with him. "Sounds like you know what you're doing when it's in between the sheets." Alex shoved her gently, trying to hide how embarrassed he was. "What are your plans today with the prince?" She asked, taking a look at Alex before turning back to the family.

"I'm not sure yet, kind of playing it all by ear." He grabbed the two plates and walked back to Leo. He put the plate in front of him and sat across from him, next to Janet.

Alex handed Leo a cup of coffee. "You have to try this, it is a little different." Leo took a sip and smiled. He enjoyed the new coffee flavor.

"What's in it that is making it so sweet?"

"A mix of hot chocolate, and hazelnut coffee. It took me forever to find the right mixture of the two." Leo took his hand and smiled.

"Well, you better add this to the menu too," Leo demanded.

The king cleared his voice and looked over at the two boys.

"What are your plans today? I know Alex wants to treat you to a day in the town."

"I was thinking of taking a walk around Hyde Park," Alex spoke, through his bites of breakfast.

"Do you think we could tag along? It's been years since he took me out anywhere." She said, giving him a look. "Don't worry, we won't hover."

Alex smiled and looked at Leo. "It's up to you," he whispered.

"Yeah, Mom, join us. We've never had a family outing together."

"At least for a little bit, I would like some alone time with your father today. With the exception of Janet protecting us that is." The king nodded in agreement.

"It would be nice to spend some time together as a family. After all, soon we will all be family." Leo smiled at his father's statement and looked down at the ring sitting on his finger.

The family finished their food. Alex and Leo saddled up on the bike. Alex kicked the bike on and turned to Janet who rolled down her window.

"Race you there." Jeannette nodded, and Alex sped off with Leo holding on to him. He popped the front wheel up, and Leo screamed out again. Alex raced through the traffic swaying between the cars and cutting through alleys.

Leo loved the rush, and it gave him a reason to hold on tighter to him. He rested his chin on Alex's shoulder and kissed him.

"Can it go any faster?" Leo screamed at him. Alex cranked the bike and tossed it at high speed. Leo enjoyed it at first, but it became hard for him to breathe. He was not sure if it was due to the cold windy air hitting his face or an anxiety attack. He patted Alex's chest and Alex slowed down. He came to a stop and got off the bike. Alex turned to Leo and helped him to his feet.

Alex looked around; it was not the best part of town to be in. The shops were closed and had broken windows, street lamps were busted and glass remained on the ground around them. Alex took off his jacket and laid it down against the wall before helping Leo down. Alex knelt in front of him and looked into his eyes.

"Deep breath, Leo," Alex spoke softly to him. Leo nodded and took a few deep breaths.

Alex stood up and texted Janet that they were going to be a little late while Leo continued his deep breaths. Leo heard footsteps approaching, but Alex was too distracted to notice it. A man grabbed Alex from behind and held a gun against his head. Alex did not move a muscle. He was too focused on Leo who had his head down. He was unable to reach for his gun or break out of the man's hold without being shot.

"Don't scream or he gets it." Leo looked up and quickly got to his feet and raised his hands in the air. "Let him go please," Leo begged, acting like he was trying to catch his breath still.

"Put your wallet and jewelry on the ground." The man barked orders. Leo reached behind himself and grabbed Alex's gun.

"You let him, g..go," Leo stumbled on his words. But pointed the gun at the man. Alex noticed the line of sight. *I'm getting shot again*, he thought. The man pointed the gun at Leo.

Alex knew that was his queue. He flipped the man over his shoulder and grabbed his gun. Leo placed his back in the holster and ran over to Alex. "Get on the bike, Leo." Leo did exactly as instructed. Alex walked over and grabbed his jacket. He tossed it to Leo who caught it and put it on. Alex held the man at gunpoint as he got back onto the bike and started it up. Alex drove down the road a mile before tossing the gun to the side.

"You okay, Leo?" Leo kissed Alex's cheek before answering him.

"I'm fine." Leo held onto Alex who took it easy the rest of the way to the park.

* * *

Alex hopped off the bike and helped Leo down. He looked at Leo and smiled. "See, you got to be the hero today." Leo smiled at him and pulled him into a kiss. The two held hands and walked through the park and met up with Janet and the royal family.

The queen and king stood against a tree while Janet was taking a photo of them. The blended family walked towards the river and sat on a bench. The queen opened a paper bag and handed Leo some food to feed the ducks. Janet looked over to Alex.

"What happened?" Janet questioned Alex, fearing the answer he might give her.

"Not really sure, I think it was too much wind for Leo to handle. He lost his breath, we just pulled over for a second for him to catch it again." Alex paused for a moment. "Oh, and we were held up at gunpoint." Janet slapped Alex's head.

"You were what?"

"It was an everyday robbery. Don't worry, Leo handled it." Janet nodded her head.

"Are you training him?" She asked.

"No, I do not want this kind of life for him. He is learning just by being around me though." He looked over at Leo. "This needs to end soon Janet, He deserves a normal and happy life. He deserves so much more than running and hiding. He is a jewel that deserves to show off."

"Or do you mean you want this to end, so that you two can get married, and you can finally put all this behind you?" Janet questioned. Alex thought about it. Not needing to pick up his gun again, coming home from work and Leo sitting on the porch waiting for him.

"It would be nice, Janet." Alex took out his phone and looked at Leo, "I want tonight to be perfect. Can you make sure that there are no threats at all tonight, Janet?" She nodded and Alex walked away to make a call.

Leo fed the ducks with his mother and father, he was smiling and enjoying the time spent with them. It was the first time in years they did something as a family. He took in every moment, holding onto the memories. Leo looked around and ran over to Alex who was just hanging up his phone.

"Everything okay, Alex?" Leo asked as he got to him. Alex put his arm around him, "It certainly is, Princy." Alex kissed him softly. Leo smiled.

"I had the most amazing dream last night, can I tell you about it?" Leo asked. Alex took his hand and led him to a tree nearby where they sat against it. Alex put his arm around Leo and leaned into him.

"We were back at the house, we had a beautiful little girl. We were so happy. It will come to be right? We will be happy, there won't be any threats at some point right?"

Alex looked down at him, "Yes. I promise." Alex took Leo's hand. I will make sure that dream becomes reality." Alex took his backpack off and pulled out some grapes he had taken from the breakfast buffet. Leo laid his head on Alex's lap who fed them to him. Leo lay there eating, and taking in the memory. Alex's eyes locked with his. He put his arm around Alex's head. "Do you know how happy you make me?"

"Remind me." Alex smiled looking down at him. He pulled him down into himself and kissed him softly. "Oh, I will later." The two chuckled and stood up. They rejoined the family and continued to walk down the path, and back around to the cars. The sun was starting to set. Leo couldn't believe that they spent the whole day at the park. Time flew by so fast and he enjoyed it. It was nice to get out and forget everything going on.

It was a taste of what life can be. He looked at his mom who was laying her head on the king's shoulder. He felt like it definitely rekindled their love, and he had Alex to thank for it.

$$* * *$$

The king and queen went to their room and Janet went to hers. Leo and Alex followed behind them and turned into theirs. Alex looked at Leo. "I have a romantic night planned for us. Why don't you go get ready, I'll be back in 20 minutes." Leo nodded and kissed Alex as he left the room. Leo smiled and fell on the bed. He felt like a girl who just had her first kiss. He smiled so hard his face was starting to hurt. He showered and dried his hair. He styled it this time instead of just brushing it back.

He dressed in a simple sweater and pair of jeans, he put on Alex's coat. He started to rummage through his bag and sprayed his Versace Red Jeans spray on his neck. While waiting for Alex to return he kept going to the mirror to fix his hair.

He wanted everything to be perfect tonight.

A knock came from the door and Leo ran over to it. He peeked through the peephole and smiled. Alex was standing there, he had his hair down, and the earrings he bought him were in his ears. He smiled as his heart started to beat faster. He looked over the outfit he had on. Alex was wearing a pair of black faded and torn jeans, and the mesh shirt he wore for his first selling event.

Leo opened the door and stood leaning against the door frame. "Well, look at you," Leo spoke, smiling at his man. He pulled Alex into him and kissed him. Alex was taken in by the spray again but snapped himself out of it. He grabbed his hands and looked into his eyes.

"You trust me?" Alex asked him, whispering in his ear. The whisper sent chills down Leo's arms.

"I will always trust you, Alex." Leo took a black bandanna out of his pocket and tied it around his eyes. Alex led him up the stairs to the roof. He removed the blindfold and Leo was in awe of what he saw.

There were rose petals all around the roof of the hotel. A small metal table with two glasses and two covered plates waiting for them. He turned to Alex with his eyes sparkling.

"It's perfect." Leo barely got out. Alex walked him to the table and pulled his chair out for him. He pushed him into the table and took his seat across from him. He uncovered their plates.

"Sorry, the menu was slim," The plates had spaghetti and sausage on them. Leo smiled and took a piece of bread from the center of the table.

"It's perfect, Alex." He grabbed his hand and looked him in the eyes. "Are you sure I haven't just dreamed you up? You're everything I ever wanted, and so much more."

The two finished eating and Alex turned on a small radio. He picked Leo up out of the chair and held him for a moment.

"Leo, you have changed me. You knocked down every wall I ever put up around my heart." He placed Leo on his feet. The two started to dance, Leo's hands rested on his chest, and he looked up into his eyes. "You came to me in a very dark time and shined a light into my life. I will give you the world." Alex slipped his hand around Leo's waist, "I love you more than anything in this world." Alex whispered, kissing Leo's cheek. Leo felt his heart fluttering, he didn't want this night to end. He wanted to stay in his arms forever. He wanted to live in that moment for the rest of his life. He ignored the cold air, nothing could bother him. Alex picked him up and carried him back inside the hotel. Leo let his arms draped around his neck, never taking his eyes off him.

Twenty-Two

One Last Day

Leo was gently shaken awake by Alex. He groaned, still tired from the amount of exercise from the night before. Leo moved in closer to Alex and kissed his chest, keeping his eyes closed. He was anything but motivated to get out of bed. Alex leaned down and kissed the top of his head.

"Should I treat you to a bed-in-breakfast today?" Leo shook his head yes and pulled the blanket over his head to hide from the sun coming in through the red curtains. Alex smiled at his sleepy prince and dressed. He met up with Janet downstairs. He had an unusual pep to his step that morning and Janet picked that right up. She handed him a coffee and let him take a sip before she spoke.

"So, when the agency said you were their best undercover agent, I don't think that this is what they had in mind. Although I think the Prince would definitely agree to you being the best UNDERCOVER agent." Alex did not blush this time, he smiled and looked at her.

"You could always ask them to move your room, you know." She smacked her lips and grabbed some breakfast.

"We need to talk about tomorrow, Alex." Alex put down the coffee and the smile left his face. He knew he had to talk about the plan, and what they were going to do, but he also dreaded it. All it did was remind him that the perfect time with Leo was only an illusion. That there was still danger out there.

"I know." Alex's voice lowered, and he was back in agent mode again.

"The royal guard is planning on surrounding the house and will wait on my command to enter. You can not be involved though, Alex." Janet told him. He looked at her.

"Do you really think you can stop me?" Alex threatened. "They are after my fiancé."

"Oh I know I can't and if I am going into unknown territory, there is no other agent I want by my side." Janet nudged him. "I would never stop you, just have to say I told you not to." Janet smiled. "I'll take the front and you take the back like always." Alex nodded in agreement. "Are you taking him out today?"

"I am thinking about it, but actually I think I might want to just spend most of the day with him here, just hold him and take everything in, just in case anything should go wrong tomorrow. I want to make sure his last memory of us is one he will hold on to forever." Janet mocked throwing up.

"When did my bad ass agent son become a romantic?" Janet asked. "Around the same time you locked me up with a prince." Alex hugged her and she enjoyed the moment together. He backed up and showed her the keys to her car. "I'ma borrow this okay?" He grabbed the plate of food and ran to the elevator. "Thanks, love you bye."

* * *

Alex knocked three times on the door before walking in. He looked down at Leo who was still in bed. The blanket hung low by his waist, his arms were up over his head. Alex found himself smiling. He started to think about tying him up the next time they decided to make love. Alex held his hands over Leo's and leaned down to kiss him. Leo's eyes opened and he moaned out.

"I have a tie if you wanna do that," Leo spoke blushing. Leo looked to the table where the food was sitting, and back to Alex. He bit down on his lower lip, "I am hungry, are you gonna give me breakfast or am I supposed to eat dessert first?" Leo asked Alex.

"You tell me, Princy, what do you want?"

Leo thrust up into Alex kicking him up. It allowed a little leverage which he used to roll over and push Alex under himself. "Look how fast the tables can turn. Leo held Alex's hand down and kissed his neck. He tied his hands up and sat up. He reached over and took a bite of toast.

Alex smiled and slipped out of the tie. He spread his legs to either side of Leo and held him. Leo slipped some eggs onto the fork and fed Alex. Alex rubbed Leo's arms while he ate. Once the plate was empty, he pushed it further back on the table. He turned back around and pushed Alex onto his back. "I think I fall in love with you more every day, Alex."

"I feel the exact same, Princy." He leaned up and kissed him. "I have something very special planned today, are you ready to start your day now sleepy head?" Leo stuck his tongue out at him, and Alex took that as an invite for a quick makeout session.

They readied for the day. Leo had a pair of white slacks on and a simple purple T-shirt. Alex had put on a pair of blue faded jeans and a black T-shirt. They held hands and walked out of the room. They piled into Janet's rental and started driving down the road.

"So where are we going?" Leo asked, staring out the window.

"If you must know, I found a cute little farm I wanted to check out with you." Leo took his hand and turned on the radio.

"I've been thinking about the wedding." Leo looked over at Alex.

"What did you have in mind?" Alex asked.

"I want to make sure that we both walk down the aisle. I want to make sure that we both get our moment to shine." Leo picked up his hand and kissed it. "I think Mom and I managed to pick everything else out, except for what song we are going to dance to." Alex grabbed his phone and searched for a song. He played it on the radio. "I Don't Want to Miss a Thing" by Aerosmith started to play.

"I was thinking about this song. It completely describes how I feel about you." Alex started to sing along with it. He paused for a moment and when he did Leo started to sing. The two listened to the song. Once it ended Leo leaned over and kissed Alex's cheek.

"It's perfect." Leo started to yawn he still wasn't fully awake yet.

"Why don't you take a little nap? I will wake you up when we get there," Alex suggested to him.

"I think I might just do that."

* * *

Alex turned the corner and put his hand on Leo's leg. He gently squeezed it, and Leo woke up. Leo rubbed his eyes and looked around. They were driving through a dirt path and trees circled them. They pulled up to a huge barn-style house. It was freshly painted red, with pure oak window frames. Alex parked the car and ran over to open Leo's door. He extended his hand and helped Leo out of the car.

A woman in her fifties came out of the house. "Are you Alex?" She shouted to them. Her hair was pulled up, she was wearing a pair of jeans and a plaid button-up.

"Yes Ma'am," Alex called back to her. She flagged them over and they entered the gate. She led them to the barn where there were two horses with saddles on them. "We can walk or ride, it's up to you."

Leo looked at Alex, "I've never ridden a horse," Alex confessed to him.

Leo smiled, "Then we will ride there." Leo got on the horse with no issue and extended his hand to Alex. Alex felt his heart racing and took Leo's hand. He pulled him up on the horse. The lady got on her horse and led it out of the barn. Leo gently shook the reins and the horse jerked. Alex squeezed onto Leo.

The lady looked back and smiled at the two. "Yeah," she yelled and her horse picked up speed. Leo followed her lead, and their horse caught up. Alex was starting to loosen his grip, and his hair flew in the wind. They came to a stop shortly after another barn. As they pulled up they heard barking coming from inside. The lady got off her horse. Alex watched her and tried to do the same. He lost his grip on Leo and landed on the ground. Leo chuckled and got off the horse. He picked Alex back up and brushed off the dirt and hay from his back.

The lady flagged them over to the barn. Leo and Alex walked in. They were surrounded by a litter of Australian Shepherd puppies. Leo sat down and played with them while Alex spoke to the dog breeder. Leo was mauled by different colored puppies. They teamed up against him and knocked him onto his back

"Alex I could use some backup," Leo called to Alex. The lady laughed and turned to Alex.

"I'll give you guys some time to play." She walked away from the barn and Alex joined Leo on the ground. The puppies were climbing all over them and Alex watched as Leo held them and played with them. Alex sat down next to Leo, and one of the dogs came over to him. he climbed up on Alex's shirt and started to lick his face.

"If you had a dog, what would you name him?" Alex asked Leo.

One of the puppies tried to climb up Leo's shirt and tumbled back down to his lap. He picked up the dog and looked into his sky-blue eyes. "Maybe Skittles," Leo spoke laughing as the dog licked his face. The puppy seemed to have liked the idea. The puppy was primarily black, with a white chest and legs, his snout was white and his head was black, with a white line down the middle. His hind legs were tan. Leo stood up holding him.

"Isn't he just so adorable?" Leo asked, holding him up to Alex's face. The dog licked him and Alex smiled. The dog had the same sense of adventure as his last.

"Is he the one, Leo?" Leo turned to Alex. "You mean we are

getting one?"

Alex nodded and Leo ran up to him and kissed him. He nodded, crying. It was his first pet, and it felt like they were finally moving past everything scary in the world.

"I love him and I love you, Alex." They walked back to the barn since the lady took the second horse with her when she left and Skittles walked in between them. They made it back to the car and Alex opened the door for Leo. Leo bent down and picked up the puppy before getting in. The dog fell right asleep on his lap. Alex got in and started the car.

"Oh great, he is already a sleepy head like you, Princy." Alex poked fun at him, and they made their way back to the city.

* * *

Alex pulled up to a local pet store and turned the car off. He leaned over and kissed Leo awake. They went into the store and Leo held the puppy close. Alex grabbed a cart. As they walked around the store they started filling the cart with everything they would need to take care of him. They walked to the checkout and the cashier started to ring them up. Leo walked over to the badge engraver and started working on Skittles's name tag.

"That will be four hundred fifty-three pounds." The man spoke and Alex put his card in the machine. He grabbed the bags and joined Leo by the machine. He took the blue-collar out of the bag and put it on the puppy. Leo did not want to put him down though. He was so happy to finally have a dog, and the best part for him was that it was like having a child with Alex, something they both shared together. Leo handed Alex the dog tag to read it. The front said the dog's name and the back said if found please call the Twist family at 555-555-5555.

Alex liked the sound of the Twist family. It then dawned on him, he looked up, "You want to take my last name?" Leo smiled.

"There you go, using your brain." Alex rolled his eyes as they walked, holding hands to the car. They drove back to the hotel and walked up to their floor. Leo's smile never faded, he was the happiest he had been in a long time. He was doing it, he was starting a family with the love of his life. Leo finally felt his dreams coming true, everything he ever dreamed about was falling into place.

* * *

They made it back to the hotel and to their floor. They went into their room and for the first time since they got the puppy, with the exception of letting him use the bathroom, Leo put him down. Alex put the dog bed on the floor next to a potty pad and started to take the tags off the toys they got for him. The puppy, being very excited, was barking and playing with Leo. Alex watched him as Leo sat on the floor with him playing with the toys.

A knock came from the door and Alex let Leo's parents in. They all sat around the dog playing with him. "Leo, I am going to see Janet and discuss tomorrow." Leo stood up and walked over to him. "You two better come up with a good plan, Alex. I just got the start of my family, and I am not about to lose it." He grabbed Alex by the shirt and kissed him. "Hurry back though, I will miss you." Alex nodded and headed out the door.

Twenty-Three

For Love

That night Alex did not sleep. He was afraid of never coming back to Leo. He spent the night wondering about what would happen to Leo if he failed. Leo was restless that night in his sleep. He rolled back and forth all night. Eventually, Alex put his arms over and pulled him close. Even in his sleep, Leo felt as though nothing could ever hurt him. He nuzzled in Alex's chest.

Alex could not bear the thoughts anymore, and he didn't want to say goodbye to Leo this time. He wanted to make sure that the memories he had of him were happy ones, not a saddening goodbye. He carefully got out of bed and dressed. He knelt down next to the bed and kissed Leo's head. He wrote him a note and grabbed his guns before walking to the door. A tear rolled down his cheek as he turned back to look at Leo sleeping with the puppy.

"I love you." He whispered and walked out the door. He

walked to Janet's room and before he could even knock on the door she opened it up.

"Are you ready to do this?" Janet asked. Alex nodded and the two walked to the elevator.

"How did you know I wouldn't wait?"

"When you stopped by last night, I could tell your anxiety was skyrocketing. Also, did you forget who trained you, I knew damn well you were not going to let a sad memory be the last thing Leo has of you." Alex chuckled and got into Janet's car. He turned on his phone and stared at the picture of him and Leo from the day they got engaged. Tears fell down his face and covered his phone.

"Alex, can you handle this?" Janet asked, putting her hand over his. Alex locked his phone and put it into his pocket. "We do not know what we are getting into, you can go back and be with Leo. I can handle this." Janet suggested to Alex hoping he would say to turn back around.

"I will be fine, and this J will regret ever messing with the royal family. Now drive." Alex demanded and Janet picked up the speed.

Janet reached into her pocket and handed Alex back his badge. "If you're sure, then I will reinstate Agent Twist for one more mission." Alex took his badge and pinned it to his shirt. "Now let's get this bastard." Janet put the car at high speed.

* * *

Leo rolled over and Skittles hopped off the bed and started to roll around with his toys. He was partially awake and reached for Alex. He looked at the clock which read 2 am. He sat up quickly noticing that Alex was gone. He turned on the bedroom light to see if Alex was anywhere in the room and only found a note. He picked it up and started to read it.

Princy,

The past year being your personal guard has been the hardest mission I ever had to do. I never wanted things to end this way, but if something was to happen to me, I wanted the memories of us to be happy ones. I hope you can forgive me for not saying goodbye. Janet and I are doing this mission alone. We don't want the royal guard to get in our way. We do not know what we are walking into. For all we know it could be a trap. If that is the case and I do not come back, remember that I love you, Leonardo. Over the past year, you have become my best friend and my lover. All I want is to make sure you feel safe again, no matter the cost. The time with you has been amazing and I would never trade that for the world. I love you, Leonardo, promise to never forget me if something should happen.

My heart is forever yours,
Your knight in shining armor

Leo felt his heart being ripped out of his chest, he grabbed Skittles and ran to his parents' room. He pounded on the door until it opened. His mother was standing there in her nightgown and a bathrobe. His face was covered in tears, and his mother pulled him into a hug.

"What is it, Leonardo?" Leo handed her the note and Skittles.

"I can't just sit by Mom, not this time. If anything happens to him because of me." Leo felt his heart racing as he rushed back to his room. He quickly dressed and grabbed the gun Alex gave him. He looked down at Alex's bag and saw he left behind his bulletproof vest. Leo grabbed it and slipped it under his shirt. He raced down to the parking garage. He hopped onto Alex's bike and held the wires in his hand.

"I have seen you do this a dozen times now." He started to brush the wires against each other until the bike started up. He revved the engine trying to get a feel for the bike and how it works. He took a deep breath and let out a whisper to himself. "Just like riding a horse."

* * *

Janet and Alex pulled up to the address Sebastian gave them. They both pulled out their guns and opened their doors. They walked through the house from the outside. They could tell it had at least four bedrooms and two floors to the house. Janet went to the front door and Alex went to the back. They both counted to three and kicked in the doors. Janet cleared the kitchen, and dining room, while Alex cleared the living room and laundry room. They met at the stairs and nodded to each other. They slowly walked up the stairs and checked each room. The last door was cracked open, and a lamp was shining through the crack.

Janet kicked the door open and Alex ran in looking for J. The room was empty. "Clear," Alex called back to Janet. He turned back around and saw Janet standing in the doorway. A gun was held to her head that became more clear and she walked in.

"Move a muscle and I put a bullet into her head." A deep voice spoke from around the corner. He pushed her into the room. "Drop your gun." Alex dropped his gun and kicked it at the man. He did not want to risk Janet's life. She was the closest thing he had to a mother. He raised his hands.

"Let her go," Alex demanded. He grabbed Janet by the arm and pushed her over the banister. Alex heard Janet scream and crash through a glass table. J walked into the room and Alex could see he was a muscular man and stood about six feet. J walked over to the small armchair and took a seat, keeping his gun pointed at Alex.

"What was the plan here, break in, capture me?" J asked, mocking him.

"Something like that," Alex mumbled under his breath. Alex put his hands down and tried to reach for the gun on his back. J shot at him and missed on purpose."

"I would not do that If I were you," J warned, crossing his legs. "Let's talk."

Alex did not move, he watched every move J made.

"So you have fallen in love with the Prince. How does that work? The CIA, a royal prince. I love a good tragedy. You two are worlds apart." J mocked Alex more. Alex could feel anger and frustration building inside him.

"Why do you want them dead?" Alex asked J who only laughed in return at first. He sat up and looked at Alex.

"It is because of the royal family I have none. Back then if you did not have money to pay them, to help them look good in the eyes of the people, you were nothing. My father and mother were walking me home one night, and the King's limo ran them over. They stopped the car and stepped out. I watched as the King shot my mother and father. He had to keep it a secret that he killed someone, even if it was an accident. I sat back and watched the King take power by charging more to those who already couldn't even come close to the pay he wanted." He spoke quickly.

"Why now, you could have ended it all back when you had my father killed."

"Your father." J laughed, "Your father was no more than a blubbering idiot. He gave me all the intel I needed to make a plan. Sure, he didn't realize it. Nothing, a little truth serum couldn't help." Alex's hand balled into a fist and he took a step closer to J.

"The first King's death was only the start. My goal was to kill each member one at a time and let them suffer the losses. I waited for my time to shine, and then you showed up to stop everything in its tracks. Somehow you are always one step ahead of me. But not this time." He pulled a kill switch from his pocket and waved it at Alex. "This time you die. It's just a matter of when you die."

"If you hit that switch we both die," Alex called out to him. J laughed.

"You think this will all stop with me being dead? There will always be another. Another person angered by the disrespect of the royal family. There will always be someone else looking to end the line." It hurt Alex to know that he was right. There will always be a threat out there to Leo. "At least this way it will be easier for them with you out of the way."

* * *

Leo felt his tears flying past as he sped to the address he heard muttered between Alex and Janet. He pulled up to the house and saw Janet's car. He stepped in through the front door and saw Janet on the ground. He dragged her out of the house before running up the stairs. Alex saw Leo from the corner of his eye. He didn't move but felt his heart fall to the floor. Leo ran into the room not thinking and J laughed.

"Prince, have you come to save your little American puppy dog?" Leo held the gun pointed at J.

"Leo, please put down the gun. Trust me." Alex begged Leo who put it down.

"Oh this is too good, I get to kill the happy couple together. Revenge has never tasted better. I think I will start with…" He pointed the gun at Leo. "The Prince. I never got to see a CIA agent cry. I imagine it must be a fun sight." Alex stood up and ran in front of Leo.

"No," Alex pushed him out of the room and slammed the door shut. "Drop the gun J, come peacefully, we can bring you in and you can live." Alex tried to reason with the man who everyone could tell had a few screws loose. Alex looked closer at the man's hand. He noticed the dead switch had no connector. There was nothing for it to go to.

"What's wrong pretty boy, are you having a hard time understanding me? "You're both gonna die one way or another." Alex closed his eyes and listened around, he could hear ticking.

Alex leaned down and picked up his gun, "You want to die. You planned on dying tonight before I even got here. Your true plan was to let the family suffer, never knowing when your next attack would be. Letting them never feel safe again then you could rest knowing they would step down, and be with your family. The bomb has been going before we got here, that dead switch in your hand is no more than the light switch to this room." Alex took a deep breath, "You rigged the whole building to blow." He looked at the clock sitting on the dresser that read 2:57. "You chose to die at the same time as your parents, 3 in the morning." Alex was buying his time, before he learned about the bomb, profiling him using what he learned from seeing Janet do it so many times.

Leo pushed the door open and ran back in. "You are partially right, Agent Twist." He spoke as he stood and fired at Alex. "I also want to see the Prince break apart."

"No," Leo yelled as he hugged Alex. The bullet hit Leo's back and he fell into Alex's arms. Alex pulled the gun from his back and shot J three times before picking up Leo and carrying him from the house. Janet regained consciousness and made a call from her car to the royal guards demanding backup. Alex managed to make it out the front door holding Leo as the house exploded. The two were sent flying from the explosion. Leo landed a few feet away from Alex.

Janet dropped her phone and ran over to them. Alex crawled his way over to Leo. His face was slightly burned and had cuts on his arms and face from the explosion. Alex picked up Leo's head and looked down at him.

"What happened?" Janet yelled to them.

"J shot him," Alex cried out. "J shot him." Alex cried, kissing Leo's head. Alex looked up to Janet, tears filled his eyes as he cried out all the pain he felt in his chest. "I failed again, Janet."

Janet ran over and hugged Alex. Alex buried his face in her shoulder and cried even harder. "I am so sorry, Alex," Janet whispered softly, rubbing his back.

He felt a third hand on his shoulder. He looked up and Leo stood there smiling at him. Janet helped Alex to his feet and Leo hugged him. Leo took off his shirt and smiled at Alex.

"For once I am glad you did not wear it." Alex wiped away the tears and kissed Leo. "It is nice to finally get to be your hero, Agent Twist." Janet smiled at the two and hugged them both. Leo leaned towards Janet. "I did promise to protect him, didn't I? Janet smiled. She turned and got into the car and made a call to her boss.

"He is right, you know Leo, there will always be another J out there ready to take his place." Alex looked up at him.

"I am sure I will be fine, the royal guard will continue to deal with the threats, and I have my secret agent to protect me." Leo helped Alex to the car and laid him down in the back seat. He thought back to the first time he was injured protecting him. Leo got in the car behind Janet and put Alex's head on his lap. He brushed his hair out of his face and leaned down to kiss him.

"I am not dying Leo, just tired." Leo laughed and watched as Alex closed his eyes. ched as Alex closed his eyes.

Twenty-Four

I Do

It has been three days since mission The Crown's Agent has come to an end, and things at the palace have returned back to normal. Alex has been in bed resting, and getting back his strength. Although the explosion did not do much damage, he still ached from head to toe.

Leo walked into the room and put Skittles on the bed. The puppy walked up to Alex, and started to lick his nose. Alex opened his eyes and smiled. Leo was holding the pup over him so he wouldn't cause any more pain. Alex lifted his arm, pet Skittles's head, and kissed Leo.

"He has been scratching at the door the past few days. He really missed his Dad." Leo spoke, putting him back down on the ground so he could eat.

"Thanks to a certain Prince, he still has two dads." Alex enjoyed the sound of being called dad. It reminded him that although one mission was over, another one started.

Operation Family.

"Mom wants us to go get the suits today, do you think you're up for it, Alex?" Leo turned to him as he got dressed. "If not I am sure I can talk her out of it. We can always postpone." Leo was interrupted by Alex walking to him and kissing him.

"We are not postponing anything." Alex limped over to the bathroom and started the water in the tub. He stepped into it and sighed. The hot water and jets felt good on his aching body. Leo walked in and started to wash his back for him. Alex looked up and kissed him softly. "When did you get so brave?" Alex asked him, opening his eyes and looking into Leo's.

"Around the time we first kissed, and I knew I would need to fight for us." Alex smiled at his answer and kissed him once more. He helped Alex out of the tub and to get Alex dressed. Leo walked over to the mirror and took a long look at it.

A happy blond-haired man looked back at him. A man who has tasted freedom and had a hunger for more, a man who has found love, and will never let go. He was happy with the person looking back at him. No longer a dreamer, but living his dreams. He held his hand out to Alex who took it and looked in the mirror with him. He rested his head on Leo's shoulder and smiled.

"Well Princy, you ready to go look at all the options your mother has for us, and choices for the wedding?" Leo turned to Alex.

"I've been thinking about that, what if we just do something small? I don't need a big fancy wedding to know you love me. What if we do something in the backyard, we have our day for us and no one else. Alex smiled and looked at his prince.

"I would love that." He pulled him into a hug and kissed

him softly. "But what if we did a little of both? A small royal wedding. After all, I am marrying a prince."

Leo turned to him, "About that, the prince thing not the marrying, my father wants to crown you Prince as well during the wedding."

Alex smiled, "So I am a knight in shining armor turned Prince?" Alex laughed. "Prince Alex Twist." He joked and held his nose up high. Leo smacked his chest and kissed him.

"Let us go break the news to them about the royal wedding idea."

Leo and Alex walked out of the room followed by Skittles whose little legs had a hard time keeping up with them. Leo knelt down and picked him up. They made it to the dining room where the Queen and Janet were sitting playing cards. Janet put her hand down and hugged Alex.

"It is nice to see you up on your feet. I got you something for a wedding gift. She pulled out a gift card for a couples spa back in the small town. Leo took the card out of her hands and slipped it into his pocket.

"I will hold onto this." He sat down next to Alex and looked at them both. "I wanted to talk to you guys about the wedding." Leo watched as his mother's eyes started to sparkle. "We were thinking of something small in the backyard. We will still welcome the press, but just us at the ceremony."

"That sounds very lovely." Sarah nodded, "I have a lot of work to do then. I need you both to go down to the suit shop and pick out your suits." She looked at Janet. "Can I ask you for some assistance?" Janet smiled and nodded.

"I would be happy to help, but first I have one more gift for Alex." She stood up and walked him to the garage. He pulled back a tarp and sitting there was a new bike. His eyes lit up like the Fourth of July. The bike had an orange finish on the wheels, the frame was black with embroidered skulls along it. It had two bags on the back. Janet tossed him the keys.

"And this one you don't need to hot wire." Alex caught the keys, ran up to her, and hugged her.

"But why?" He asked her.

"For a job well done. Everyone at the agency chipped in, considering it a retirement gift from all of us. Of course, I picked it out." Alex ran back to it and hopped on, Leo got on behind him. "Listen, Alex, this one goes a lot faster than your fathers did, be careful." Janet was cut off by Alex speeding out of the garage.

"WOOO," He yelled as he sped between cars and made their way to the suit shop.

* * *

Alex and Leo walked into the shop and were met by an older man. He had the old man bald on top with white hair on the sides.

"The Queen told me you two were on your way. Let's keep the outfits a secret until the big day." He pointed to one side of the store where another man who could have been his twin was standing. "Jim will help you."

Alex walked over and stood in front of the man. He started to take his measurements and looked around the store. He came back with four different suits. He pushed Alex into the dressing room and closed the door behind him. Alex started with the first suit on the pile.

He took a look in the mirror and snarled, purple is not a good color on him. The suit was purple with a lavender tie. He held up the rest of the suits and put them back over the door. He tried on the last suit, it was a sky-blue suit with a matching vest. He turned to see how the back looked on him. He noticed it had a tailcoat. He tied the blue and white diagonally striped tie around his neck in a balthus knot. He held his hair up and tilted his head. He opened the door and walked out.

"I think I found the one, Jim." He smiled while speaking. He was ready to marry Leo.

"We will have it delivered today," Jim spoke without looking up to Alex. He wrote his name on a sheet of paper and hung it on the hanger with a suit cover. "Just leave the suit in there and we will make sure it is pressed before it arrives." Alex smiled and thanked him before walking to the middle of the store. He sat there and waited for Leo to finish. He wanted to sneak a peek, but he knew Leo would get upset if he saw him in the suit early. He pulled out his phone and called ahead to make a reservation at the restaurant next door.

Shortly after, Leo came out smiling. Everything felt like a dream, but finally getting the suit for his wedding made it all feel real. He walked behind Alex and covered his eyes. He leaned down and whispered in his ear, "Guess who?"

Alex smiled and turned and pulled him onto his lap. "The sexiest man alive," Alex answered, kissing him.

"Babe, not here," Leo pushed Alex and they got up. The two walked out of the shop and Leo leaned against the bike. "So my knight now has his own trusty steed, where are you going to take me next?"

Alex took his hand and they went next door to eat. They both had some salad for lunch before walking out and hopping back on their bike.

* * *

Alex and Leo pulled into the garage and were greeted by Skittles once they entered the house. The two knelt down and enjoyed the puppy's kisses. The two walked to the backyard and went out. The King cut them off.

"Listen here boys, if either of you go out there, your mother will kill me. He looked at Alex. "And I would hate to think about what Janet would do." He turned the two away. "I am going to our room then," Leo called out and stuck his tongue out at his father. He took Skittles and ran up the stairs. Alex went to follow.

"Actually Alex, can I talk with you?" The King questioned and gestured towards the table. Alex took a seat and the King sat across from him. "After the wedding, I know you two are returning to America." Alex nodded. "You better keep him safe at any cost."

"You have my word, Your Majesty. Nothing will ever happen, and he will never want for anything. He will be loved from the moment he wakes to the moment until he falls asleep." Alex promised the King. "And you and the Queen are welcome whenever you wish to visit. I know Leo will miss you both."

The King smiled, "Of course, we will visit, and the same goes for you. You are always welcome here at the palace. You are this family's son as well as its hero. We all owe you our lives."

Alex stood up and joined Leo in the room. He grabbed his supplies for the night and kissed Leo. "Well, tomorrow is the big day," Alex spoke to him and kissed him.

"It will be a very long night." Leo proclaimed, "Without you being here with me." Alex smiled and looked at him.

"You will have Skittles to keep you company." Leo looked

away but smiled,

"The one night apart will be well worth the life of happiness I know is just around the corner." Alex pulled Leo close and kissed him softly. They said their goodbyes and Alex went to Janet's room.

* * *

The next morning Janet flipped the mattress to get Alex out of bed.

"Get up, you can't be late for your own wedding. People are already showing up. You are the talk of the country." Alex got up and looked at her. Her hair was pulled up in a braided up-do. She had on a red sleeveless dress. "Not a word ." Janet threatened. She wore the necklace he bought her.

Alex looked around the room and found his suit. He showered and dressed and did his hair before joining her at the door. Janet looked at him and straightened the suit out. She undid the messy knot from the tie and properly tied it. "Your father and mother would be so proud of you, Alex." She spoke softly pinning his lily corsage on him.

Leo on the other hand was up all night worried that he would somehow mess the day up. He finally managed to fall asleep petting Skittles. He rubbed his eyes and fought off sleep. He was so nervous that he couldn't hold onto the soap, towel, or his suit. He managed to get his pants and shirt on. He sat on the foot of the bed and was joined by his mother.

"What's wrong, Leo?" She asked. "Do you still want to do this?"

"More than anything, I love him. I'm just nervous that I am going to mess this all up." Leo spoke softly, slightly embarrassed. His mother stood him up and patted him on the shoulder. She hummed to him as she grabbed his tie off the bed. She draped it around his neck and buttoned his vest.

His father walked into the room and started to tie his tie. He smiled and patted Leo on the back. "Alex is very lucky to have your heart, my boy." He turned and left to prepare for the ceremony.

"Mom, what if…" Leo started to panic more.

"Hush, no wedding is perfect. You may be a prince but you don't live in a fairytale." Leo smiled.

"But what if I disappoint Alex," Leo asked, still panicking.

"Do you really think that could happen?" She laughed pinning the forget-me-not corsage on him. "Leo, he loves you. He accepts you for everything you are, he doesn't pick and choose what parts to love. I can tell by the way he looks at you. Leonardo, do not focus on any what-ifs today. Focus on what is. The man at the end of the aisle waiting to hold you in his arms, waiting to look you in the eyes and pronounce his love for you ." Leo smiled and felt relaxed finally. He took his mother's arm and she led him to the kitchen where they waited for their cue.

* * *

The bells started to chime at the palace, and Alex felt like his heart was about to beat right out of his chest. Janet walked next to him and looked at him. "Agent Johnson reporting for mission Happy Ending." She took Alex by the arm and pushed the doors open. She walked him down a red carpet to the King. There was a small pillow in front of him. Alex stood there staring at the King not sure what to do. Janet kicked his knee and fell onto the pillow. She stood there next to him and bowed to the King. Alex stood up and took his place and waited for Leo.

As the few minutes went by, it felt like a lifetime. His heart was ready to explode. He found his breath was quickening as well. The traditional "Here Comes the Bride" starts to play and the kitchen doors swing open and Leo and the Queen walk out of them. Alex smiled but his breath was taken away. Leo walked towards him and noticed his smile first. It made him smile even more. Leo's suit was ivory, from head to toe. As he watched his prince make his way down to him, he thought about the first time he met him. He never thought they would have ever become friends let alone make it this far.

Leo's eyes darted everywhere. He wanted to take in every moment. Cameras were flashing left and right and his mother guided him down the red carpet. He saw lilies and forget-me-nots scattered all over the floor and hung on the archway his mom and Janet spent the day working on. Under the archway was Alex waiting for him. His hair was half pulled up and half down, he even left some bangs out this time. It was a good look for him. Leo started to cry as they got closer to Alex. He still couldn't believe that this was finally happening.

His mom hugged him and handed his hands over to Alex who helped him up the stairs. "You look amazing, Leo," Alex spoke, holding back his tears. Leo blushed a bit.

"So do you, and I love the hair."

The King hugged his son and started to speak.

"Dearly beloved, we are gathered here today to witness these two in holy matrimony." Alex was lost in Leo's eyes, and Leo never took them away from Alex. The two stood there listening to the King talk for a bit. "It is my understanding that the two have written their own vows." The King turned to Alex.

"Leo, I promise to always be there for you. Through the darkest nights, I will be the light. You will never want for anything. I vow to love and protect you as your shining knight. I love you now and will forever. You are my prince, and my happily ever after."

"Alex, You have shown me what it means to really be alive, and I promise as long as I live I shall never forget you. I will never stop loving you. I live every day to make you smile. You complete me," Leo had to pause a moment to catch his breath. His mother reached up and handed him a tissue. "I promise to love you unconditionally for as long as I live and in death. I trust you with the key to my heart." He looked back to his father to signal that he was done.

"Do we have the rings?" The King asked the two. They both looked at each other and whistled at the same time. Skittles came running out of the kitchen holding a small pillow. He went up to Leo and sat down. The action was met by everyone in the audience. "Awww."

"Do you, Alexander Twist, take Leonardo Cambridge to be your husband? To have and hold in sickness and health till death do you part?"

"I do." Alex reached down and grabbed the ring sliding it on his finger.

"And do you, Leonardo Cambridge, take Alexander Twist to be your husband in sickness and health, richer or poorer till death do you part?"

"Hell yes." He yelled and slipped the other ring on Alex's finger.

"Then it is my pleasure to introduce you to Prince Leonardo

Twist, and…" the King turned around and took the crown off the podium, "Prince Alexander Twist. You may kiss."

Everyone in the audience stood and clapped as Leo swung his arms around Alex and they kissed. They could hear the flashing in front of them from all the cameras, Alex pulled away for a moment and looked at Leo.

"I love you, Prince Leonardo."

"I love you too, Princy," Leo responded.

They kissed again and danced to the song they chose. The two stared into each other's eyes sharing the happiest moment they both ever felt.

Twenty-Five

Happily Ever After

※

It had been two weeks since the wedding and Janet had returned to the West. The King and Queen have enjoyed their time with Leo, bringing both Alex, and Leo to shows, and enjoying time out of the palace. At the start of the third week, Leo sat in bed, the sun was starting to rise and he looked out the window. He leaned over and kissed Alex.

"Today is the day." He spoke as Alex stirred awake. "Today is the day we go back home and start our new life as a married couple," Leo whispered to Alex with a smile on his face.

"Come here, Mr Twist," Alex spoke, pulling Leo into him. The two lay in bed and looked at their hands. Their matching rings sparkled as the sun came in through the window. "Did your father make the call, the plane will be ready for us right?"

"Yes, we leave in four hours. It will just be us." Skittles jumped on the bed and laid between them. The two looked down at him, he had gotten bigger over the past two weeks.

"Yes, and you." Leo looked around and smiled, "I might miss this a little bit, but I get to start my life with my new family." He spoke, petting Skittles and kissing Alex.

A knock came on the door and the King and Queen opened it up, They both sat on the bed and Skittles licked them. Leo and Alex sat up and looked at them.

"Don't forget these," The King spoke, packing their crowns into one of the bags. "You are both princes now after all, even if you don't rule." He smiled, "I am going to miss you." He spoke, patting Leo on the head." He turned to Alex, "I will even miss you, thank you for giving me back my family." He spoke softly.

"We will come and visit often," Sarah spoke holding back tears, she hated saying goodbye more than anything. "And you are both welcome to come back here whenever you want." Sarah paused for a moment, "You will come back here right?"

"Yes, without a doubt," Leo spoke, sitting up and giving his mom a hug. Alex nodded.

"We will definitely come back, there are sights I still want to see."

The Queen and King left the room after packing the bags for Leo, and Alex. Skittles followed them out of the room. Once the door was shut Leo turned to Alex.

"Should we shower?" Leo asked.

"Or we could make love one more time in the palace," Alex suggested and watched Leo's face blush. Alex turned and rolled over onto Leo, and lifted his legs up.

"I guess we could do both," Leo spoke softly, kissing Alex.

* * *

Alex and Leo joined the Queen and King in the limo and headed to the airport. The Queen was holding back her tears and it was obvious to Leo and Alex. The King placed his arm around her. Skittles hopped onto her lap and tried to nuzzle her to keep her relaxed. The ride was pretty quiet until they pulled up to the airport. They drove right up the plane. Alex and Leo stepped out and Alex started to bring the luggage onto the plane.

"I will miss you both," Leo said, hugging his mother and father.

"We will come to visit very soon," Sarah spoke back. Alex stood at the plane door and Leo walked up to him. They watched as the Queen and King stepped into the limo and waved goodbye.

* * *

They landed around 6 am in Little Wood, Pennsylvania. They stepped down from the plane and Janet was there waiting for them. Skittles ran out of the plane and jumped into her arms. She opened the car door and drove them an hour to their hometown. They were driving through the town and Leo and Alex sat in the back of her car, their hands never parted. Skittles was hanging his head out the window.

"Wait, pull over Janet," Alex called to her. Alex had run into a lumber store. While he was in there Leo ran over the rundown restaurant and put the number for the realtor in his phone. He got back in the car just as Alex came back out holding a long receipt. Janet finished the drive home and helped them carry the bags into the house. She placed the bags in their room, she kept the house how they had it with the exception of taking down the decorations from the season before.

Leo and Alex plopped on the couch and Janet made some coffee. She joined the two of them and handed them both cups of coffee.

"So what's next for you two?" Janet asked, watching the two look at each other.

"Skittles need a dog house," Alex spoke softly and Leo smiled.

"And we have a restaurant to open, don't forget that," Leo added.

"And a certain prince has a photo that needs to be painted."

"Speaking of the restaurant, boys," She handed them the deed to the restaurant. "I pulled part of my savings as my last wedding gift for you two."

Alex took the deed and looked it over. He smiled and handed it to Leo. The two signed it, and they officially had their own restaurant.

"I did not dare go inside, that's all up to you two." She smiled and sipped her coffee.

"Thank you so much, Janet," Leo spoke and got up to hug her. She put her coffee down and hugged him back. She flipped him over her shoulder, then helped him up.

"That is for flipping me last Christmas." She laughed. " I have to go though, I am due at the office for a briefing soon." Alex nodded.

"Work awaits." He got up and hugged her. She kissed his head and smiled. She had what she always wanted: a family.

"Thank you for everything, Janet. For taking me in, for helping me find who I am meant to be. For everything." Alex felt himself getting worked up. Janet broke out of the hug.

"Okay. Okay, don't go all soft on me now." Janet joked as she headed for the door. She knelt down and pet Skittles one more time, and was off.

Leo and Alex took a seat on the couch together, Alex leaned into him and pulled the blanket off the couch to cover them both. Skittles hopped up and lay curled in Alex's legs. They watched television for most of the day until the doorbell rang. For the first time, Leo got up to answer the door. Alex sat up and grabbed his gun.

"Hello?" Leo spoke as he opened the door.

"Delivery for the Twist family." The man spoke while holding a clipboard. Leo signed the papers and told them to bring them to the backyard. They did as instructed and piled the lumber and stain on the back porch. Leo rejoined Alex on the couch. Alex snuggled back into him.

"It was nice to finally answer the door. But the best part?" He paused and kissed Alex's head. " Being called the Twist Family."

* * *

After a few hours of resting after the flight and drive, Alex stretched.

"You okay if I start working on his dog house?" Alex asked, leaning into a kiss with Leo.

"Yeah, that will give me time to start our painting." Leo stood up and went to his art studio.

He picked out the biggest canvas he had and set it on the easel. He watched out the window for a bit as Alex started working on the dog house. He smiled watching him out there doing what he loved. He smiled even more when he saw Alex stopping here and there and playing with Skittles. He sat down at the easel and started to paint. He remembered Alex's smile that day perfectly. He did not need to look at his phone at all.

The sun was starting to set and he looked out the window again. Alex had just finished the dog house. It was beautiful. It had a mahogany-colored roof with oak sides. A hole big enough for Skittles to grow into and some stairs. He built it so that it was off the ground as well. His painting however was going to need more time. He covered it with a tarp so Alex could not sneak a peek. He saw Alex finish putting away his tools and ran downstairs to greet him.

"That looks amazing," Leo said, kissing him. Alex wiped some paint off Leo's face.

"Still can't stop making a mess, Princy." The two smiled and ate some pizza Leo ordered.

"When do you want to start preparing the restaurant?" Leo asked.

"I was thinking we could go down tomorrow and take a look at what we are working with," Alex suggested.

"Sounds like a plan", Leo smiled and kissed his prince. The two made it up to their room, crawled into bed, and fell asleep for the first time as a married couple in their home.

* * *

Alex took the keys out of the bag and opened the doors to their new restaurant. They walked around the place and knew it needed some love. Alex walked around the dining room while Leo stood up at the hostess station. Leo caught up with him. They turned on the lights and saw that the floor was black and white marble. They both smiled. They already had an image in mind of what they wanted. They both enjoyed the 50's-theme diner they spent so much time in.

Leo turned on his phone and played a song. He held out his hand to Alex and bowed. "May I have this dance, Your Highness?" Alex took his hand and started to sing "Put Your Head on My Shoulder" by Paul Anka.

The two danced till the song came to an end. They made some phone calls to local distributors and antique shops. They took turns bringing out the old dining room furniture and cleaning the floors and walls. The distributors brought them the new furniture and set it up for them. All that was left was to clean the kitchen.

They looked around the dining hall and they had signs and photos of singers from the 50's. They even had some that were signed by Elvis and other singers and bands. The tables were red and white to match the 50's chairs and booths that were red and white striped. In the center of the room was a jukebox with over 500 songs on it. They could easily seat over 100 people. It was a modern 50's restaurant. While the theme was 50s, the food would be a modern take.

Leo turned to Alex, "Well what do you think?"

"I think it's perfect."

The two went back to their home, and Alex went to the kitchen to start cooking them dinner. Leo went back up to his studio and continued to paint. They met back up about an hour later and ate dinner before returning to bed and calling it a night.

"Alex, when should we do the grand opening?" Leo asked.

"I am thinking at the end of the month that way we can get the word out, and make sure that everything is ready," Alex suggested.

Leo pulled Alex close and kissed him.

"Have I ever told you how happy you make me?" Leo asked.

"Remind me." Alex teased.

Leo swung his leg over Alex and felt him start to poke. He leaned down and kissed Alex. "I think you know."

* * *

It had been a month since Leo finished up the painting of the two but had not shown it to Alex yet. It was the day of the grand opening of The Princes 50's. Since they were both princes they thought it would be a good title.

Leo was in the kitchen helping Alex prep the food for the night. Cutting hundreds of carrots, and potatoes. Alex was training the chefs on his menu, and keeping a close eye on Leo, who always managed to get hurt in the kitchen. Tonight was going to be everything, it would make or break them and they both knew it. The doors opened in 10 minutes, and they were ready. They both left the kitchen and changed into their suits for the grand opening. There was a line of people outside and it warmed Alex's heart.

Leo walked to the front door and greeted everyone as they came in, Leo went to close the door but was stopped by a red heel.

"Going to shut the door on me?" Janet spoke, squeezing her way into the restaurant. She hugged Leo and Alex. "It looks really nice, very cozy," Janet spoke admiring the scene.

"Table for one?" Leo asked, grabbing a menu for her.

"No, table for three. I have some guests joining me. They should be here any minute." As she spoke a limo pulled up and the King and Sarah stepped out. He took her hand and walked her to the door. "I made a few calls."

Leo ran out the door, hugged his parents, and walked them

into the restaurant.

"This is amazing Leo, Congratulations Alex," The Queen spoke.

"Not too bad, my boy." The King spoke approvingly. Leo showed them to their seats and took their order.

They served about three hundred people that night. The two were tired but could not be prouder of each other. They both pulled through and were sad but glad it was all over.

As the night slowed down and everyone left, Alex nodded. Janet had been flirting at the bar with someone and he offered them both one more glass of wine before cutting them off. The King walked over to the jukebox and played a song. He bowed to Sarah and took her hand and they began to dance. Janet joined them with her new stranger. Alex walked up to Leo and slid his hand around him pulling him to the dance floor.

Alex started to sing "I Can't Help Falling In Love".

"But I can't help falling in love with you." The King chimed in, singing to Sarah. They all danced till the music came to a stop.

The King and Queen walked over to Alex and Leo.

"Don't tell me you're heading back already?" Leo questioned.

"No, We are heading back in two days, and staying here in town, there is this cute bed and breakfast your father found." She smiled and looked at him. "He has been a little romantic since you guys left."

"Mom," Leo shouted. "I don't need to know."

The King took Sarah and headed out the door and into their limo. "We will see you boys tomorrow."

"Don't do anything I wouldn't do," Janet yelled to them. She walked over to Leo and Alex and hugged them. "I am staying there too, and I don't wanna miss my ride." She raced out after them and got in the limo.

Alex and Leo stood by the front door and smiled. They turned off the light and headed out. Alex got onto his bike and Leo hopped on after him. He held on tight and the two drove home.

Alex picked up Leo and carried him to the house.

He placed him on the couch.

"Stay here." He went outside grabbed a small shelf he made with their names engraved in it and hung it up in the foyer. He placed their crowns on it.

"I like it Alex, but one thing is missing." Leo pointed out and grabbed the painting he finished of them both and hung it up above the crowns.

"Now it's perfect."

Leo yawned and Alex pulled him close. "How about one more dance?"

"With you, Alex, always." Leo smiled and laid his head on his shoulder. They danced while Alex did the same to him.

"I love you, Alex,"

"I love you, Leonardo."

Alex picked up Leo and kissed him before carrying him up to their room. He laid him on the bed. He took off his own blazer before removing Leo's. They took turns stripping each other before getting under the blankets. Alex got on top of Leo and kissed him gently letting his hands travel up Leo's legs. Leo's hips began to thrust up into him wanting more. The two made love that night like they never had. Both enjoying the moment and knowing that there was more to come after.

"Alex," Leo spoke softly, holding him and running his hands through his hair.

"Yeah, Leo?" Alex looked up into his eyes.

"I am so glad you are my knight in shining armor."

"And I am so glad you are my sexy prince." The two kissed and fell fast asleep.

Twenty-Six

Epilogue

"Dad, Daddy." A little girl ran into Leo, and Alex's room and jumped on the bed. Skittles followed behind her and jumped up as well. Skittles was fully grown now, so he took up a lot of the bed. Leo opened his eyes and the little girl smiled and hugged him.

"Santa came." She shouted so excited for her first Christmas with them. She crawled up the bed and gave Leo a kiss on the cheek.

"Come on Dad, wake up." She ordered, pushing Alex.

"Liza, what time is it?" Alex asked.

"Dad, it's time to get up. Grandma Janet, Grandma Sarah, and Grandpa Richard will be here soon." Alex rubbed his eyes and sat up. He looked at a three-year-old girl with messy shoulder-length blonde hair and blue eyes. Leo got out of bed and took Liza's hand. They walked to her room where he helped her pick out her outfit for the day. Leo admired the bed Alex made her every time they went in there. Alex moved his art studio outside to a little shed Alex built him.

She chose a little red dress with a white flower on the shoulder. He started the tub for her and put in her favorite toys.

"When you're done, give me a shout, okay?" Leo told her as she stepped into the bathtub.

"Okay, Daddy." She smiled and waved as Leo left the room. Leo went back to Alex and smiled.

"Merry Christmas, Alex." Alex was getting up out of the bed.

"Merry Christmas, Princy." Alex joked. The two took turns showering before going to dress Liza. Alex did her hair with a simple French braid. The doorbell rang.

"I'll get it, Dad," Liza yelled and ran down to the front door. Leo was already there opening it. Janet walked into the house.

"Grandma Janet," Liza yelled and ran up to her. "I missed you!" She yelled.

"I missed you too, Princess," Janet replied. She put Liza down and hugged Leo and Alex.

"I will go make the coffee before Richard and Sarah get here, that way they have good coffee." She called back to them as she walked to the kitchen teasing Alex.

The doorbell rang again, and Liza began dancing around the room with excitement. Alex was in the kitchen with Janet shoving each other and fighting over who would make the coffee. So Leo answered the door. His mother came in and hugged him followed by his father.

"Grandma Sarah, Grandpa Richard. Look, I've been practicing with Daddy." She curtsied to them.

"Oh, very good Liza," Sarah spoke and picked her up. She gave her a hug. Liza saw a few boxes the King was carrying in the house.

"What's in there for me?" She asked, smiling.

He put the boxes under the tree and hugged his granddaughter.

"You have grown so much," Richard spoke softly to her.

"I am going to be a strong queen one day. I have to grow fast."

The King laughed and looked at her. "Don't grow too fast." He picked her up and spun her around the room.

Alex made breakfast for everyone. He had every burner working making eggs, sausage, and pancakes for his big family. He never thought he would be so lucky to have a life like this. They all ate and talked before they made their way to the foyer and around the big tree. Liza grabbed a box for everyone and handed them it.

"I made these with Daddy." Everyone opened it and it was an ornament she and Leo painted together. "Daddy and Dad have to share one because it has our family on it." Leo smiled and kissed Alex.

"We love it, Liza, thank you."

The King knelt down and handed Liza a box. "Be very careful opening this one."

Liza opened it and inside was a sparkling crown. "Every princess needs her crown." The King took it out of the box and put it on her head. He took the crown and placed it on her head. "I crown you, Liza Twist, princess of Britain.

"I love it, Grandpa, thank you." Liza turned to her fathers and ran over to them. She hugged them. "Look, Dad, I am a princess."

Everyone went around the room exchanging gifts and then sat in the living room by the fireplace and watched Christmas movies. Leo grabbed Alex and pulled him up to their room.

"I, Prince Leonardo Twist of London, promise to love you till my dying breath." He kissed him and put a necklace on him. Alex looked down and it was a locket. He opened up the locket and inside was a photo of them, and a small painting of his old dog. The back was engraved *may the memory of me live on forever inside you.* Alex teared up a bit and smiled before kissing Leo.

He reached into his pocket and pulled out a necklace for Leo as well. "I, Prince Alex Twist, of well… here. Promises to love you and always be your knight in shining armor." He put it around his neck. It was a lily that opened into a locket. He opened it and inside was the first photo they ever took together. He smiled and kissed Alex, pulling him close. The two went back downstairs and Leo pulled Alex close.

"Can you believe we have a family?" He paused and looked at Alex."I love you, Agent Twist."

"And I love you, Princy."

About the Author

Austin has followed his dream and published his first book. Austin enjoys writing romance novels of all kinds. Austins goals are to keep writing romance novels of all genres. Austin's goal is to write a m/m romance that takes place in medieval times. Stay tuned and keep your eyes out for Austin's next book.